Dedication

To Luke.

Come home soon.

The porch light is on and we are waiting for you.

The
Waiting

MARK A. REMPEL

Cover concept by Vince Brown.

Destiny Image Fiction

An Imprint of

Destiny Image₍ₑ₎ Publishers, Inc.
P.O. Box 310
Shippensburg, PA 17257-0310

ISBN 0-7684-2158-6

For Worldwide Distribution
Printed in the U.S.A.

This book and all other Destiny Image, Revival Press, MercyPlace,
Fresh Bread, Destiny Image Fiction, and Treasure House books are
available at Christian bookstores and distributors worldwide.

For a U.S. bookstore nearest you, call **1-800-722-6774**.
For more information on foreign distributors, call **717-532-3040**.
Or reach us on the Internet:
www.destinyimage.com

Acknowledgments

Any great work is not just the great achievement of one person, but many. It is with that in mind that I realize the words inside these pages bear the fingerprints of many. The passion of others has made this all possible.

I want to thank those who began this journey with me many years ago when it was just a simple idea. Individuals like Debbie Davenport, Jay and Beth Baier, Lou Palmer, Karl Feller, Kristen Stuyck, and Julie Gerdes who spent hours working with those first edits—they helped bring the story of John Michael to the next level. Mark Seger and a cast of others who took the story before it was ever a book and made it happen from the stage. Mike Davis, who loaned me his attic for several months—which allowed me to pour my heart and soul onto paper—and simply believed in this message from the start. My friends in Summerland (Paul and Sunia Gibbs, Jathan Gerdes, and Scott Andres) who believed enough to write original music that gave the story a breath of fresh life. Brad and Becky Davis and the team at Desert Springs who believed enough to see John Michael's story leap from paper into the lives of people. My earthly parents, Neil and Hilda Rempel, without whose unconditional love I could not have written this book.

Vince Brown, one of my closest friends, who has believed in this dream from the start. Words can never express how much your life has impacted mine. And Don Milam and team at Destiny Image. There was always something special about our relationship from the start. You have all been great examples to work with.

Finally, to my children Zion, Azsia, and Ezekiel. You allowed me to stay up many late nights to chase after a dream. I hope I can help you chase after your dreams someday since you have been so gracious to allow me to fulfill the journey of mine. And my wife, Brenda. Your optimism, stability, and faith has made this entire opportunity possible. Thanks for all the days you woke up believing when I woke up wondering.

Introduction

"Daddy," I hear a voice cry from down the hall. A few minutes pass by and I hear it again. The soft tone of my only daughter catches my attention and I rise to make my way to her room to put her to bed. She asks me to go through our nightly ritual. I scratch her back, rub her head, pray for her, and tuck her underneath the warm blankets. Her eyes start to close and before I know it she is fast asleep.

Fathering. The joy it brings goes beyond measure. No matter where we come from, all us have a deep need to be fathered. We were created that way. Unfortunately, we live in a world that has lost the true value of what a father should be. Many of you reading this introduction can identify with never having much of a relationship with your earthly dad. God knows that. That is why His arms are always open wide and there is a deep gaze in His eyes as He watches and waits for you to realize He is the greatest example of all that you need in a dad. That is why this parable was written. But, you will find more than a story inside these pages. For somewhere between the lines you find yourself wondering if that kind of dad could really love you unconditionally. As you read, I hope you come to understand how long, wide, and deep that love goes. Even if your journey in life has been filled with darkness, never forget He has left the porch light on for you. Go ahead and try the door. Yes, it is open. Go on inside, He's still up waiting for you…

Mark

THE JOURNEY OF THE PRODIGAL SON

In the Book of Luke, chapter 15, a story is told about a young man who was lost. He had run away from home and knew the only way back was to follow after the love his father promised would be waiting for him when he returned home. It is from that story that this one is written. A story about us all…

Jesus continued: "There was a man who had two sons. The younger one said to his father, 'Father, give me my share of the estate.' So he divided his property between them.

"Not long after that, the younger son got together all he had, set off for a distant country and there squandered his wealth in wild living. After he had spent everything, there was a severe famine in that whole country, and he began to be in need. So he went and hired himself out to a citizen of that country, who sent him to his fields to feed pigs. He longed to fill his stomach with the pods that the pigs were eating, but no one gave him anything.

"When he came to his senses, he said, 'How many of my father's hired men have food to spare, and here I am starving to death! I will set out and go back to my father and say to him: Father, I have sinned against heaven and against you. I am no longer worthy to be called your son; make me like one of your hired men.' So he got up and went to his father.

"But while he was still a long way off, his father saw him and was filled with compassion for him; he ran to his son, threw his arms around him and kissed him.

"The son said to him, 'Father, I have sinned against heaven and against you. I am no longer worthy to be called your son.'

"But the father said to his servants, 'Quick! Bring the best robe and put it on him. Put a ring on his finger and sandals on his feet. Bring the fattened calf and kill it. Let's have a feast and celebrate. For this son of mine was dead and is alive again; he was lost and is found.' So they began to celebrate.

"Meanwhile, the older son was in the field. When he came near the house, he heard music and dancing. So he called one of the servants and asked him what was going on. 'Your brother has come,' he replied, 'and your father has killed the fattened calf because he has him back safe and sound.'

"The older brother became angry and refused to go in. So his father went out and pleaded with him. But he answered his father, 'Look! All these years I've been slaving for you and never disobeyed your orders. Yet you never gave me even a young goat so I could celebrate with my friends. But when this son of yours who has squandered your property with prostitutes comes home, you kill the fattened calf for him!'

" 'My son,' the father said, 'you are always with me, and everything I have is yours. But we had to celebrate and be glad, because this brother of yours was dead and is alive again; he was lost and is found' " (Luke 15:11-32).

One

The Pit

Dark. It was totally dark except for one streak of early morning sunlight that had burned a hole through the musty green curtains. The room was damp and the scent of death consumed it. Bodies covered the floor. The deep, rhythmic breathing was the only signal of life. Life. There wasn't much of it here. Just empty hearts that had ached themselves to sleep. Lonely souls searching for answers. Harbored spirits docked from sailing any direction on the sea of life.

The stench would have choked any consciously awake person. Body odor and the scents of alcohol, smoke, and vomit filled the room. The smell was reminiscent of Al's Late Night Bar, the kind of establishment with the flickering neon light outside its doors. The sound of snores seemed to rattle the walls and shake the ceiling.

The sunny streak became a raging fire that poured through every crack in the curtain. There were still no signs of awakened life. An alarm clock next to one of the cots blared its high pitched sound: beep-beep-beep-beep-beep. The clock was quickly smashed to the ground. John Michael Davis took a deep breath and rubbed his eyes. They were burning and watering not from the sun, but, like many mornings before, from the stench. He covered his face with his pillow and focused his thoughts on memories of home. He was so far away from the sweet smell of morning air, a comfortable bed, and a soft pillow. He longed for the fresh scent of laundry detergent on his pillow case. The memories were far away and too painful to linger on. They faded quickly.

John Michael threw his pillow to the floor. It landed on someone sleeping near him. He dropped his feet off the cot, pulled the old wool blanket away from his body and started towards the bathroom. It was like walking through a mine field. He felt the bodies beneath his feet in the crowded room. A hand, an arm, even an occasional head was stepped on, but no one seemed to mind. They were too busy sleeping off the nightmares of last night, drifting away from life's responsibilities for one more day.

The bathroom was no better than the room he had just come from. It had been painted white sometime in 1972, but had aged to a dingy gray. Graffiti, gang signs, phone numbers, and crude pictures lined the walls. Two gray metal stalls housed toilets that seemed to be clogged on a nightly basis. An aged white pedestal sink stood next to a urinal stained from rusty water. John Michael reached for the handle of the small closet door next to a window secured by iron bars. The mop and bucket were in the same place they had been just 24 hours before. Although John Michael had prided himself on doing this quietly a few months ago, now it didn't matter. The bodies in the next room would never hear anyway. They were too far out of touch in their drunken stupor to even remember where they had gone to sleep. He turned the faucet on and let the water run through his fingers for a few minutes.

"Hot water. This place never has hot water," he said after cursing a few times. His mind wandered as he remembered the hot water that had run through his hands every morning back home. He laughed to himself. "It's funny what we take for granted when we live at home," he commented with cynicism. "Maybe we don't get everything we want, but our needs are taken care of."

He filled the bucket with cold water and set it on the floor. He slopped the mop back and forth, back and forth, back and forth. No matter how hard John Michael tried, the dingy tile never seemed to look clean. Even the fresh scent of soap had quickly vaporized into the familiar smell of bodies that lay in the other room. In and out went the mop. Now the water was no cleaner than the floor. He cursed again.

"I'm so tired of cleanin' this stupid floor," he said angrily as he kicked the side of the metal bucket. Water slopped out and left a puddle on the tiles.

There was bitterness in his voice. It was the same old routine morning after morning here at the rescue mission. He'd mop up all the filth that had landed on the floor just hours before. It seemed like a never-ending nightmare, one that John Michael couldn't seem to wake up from. In fact, the past two years of his life had been a deep, dark secret that only he knew about. The past seemed like an iron chain around his neck, pulling him deeper into a hole of depression he couldn't climb out of. John Michael wondered if he would ever be free. He longed to be free to laugh and cry again without regret or remorse casting their shadows across such innocent emotions. John Michael couldn't remember the last time he had felt any peace. Deep peace. The peace that allows the mind and body to rest at the end of the day. *That* night was on his mind again. The night he had left. How could he forget it? As the water washed down the drain, so did a few more pieces of his heart. The memories seemed to be the only pictures left in the scrapbook of his mind. Memories of a mother. Pictures of a loving father. The home he had grown up in. The bed he had slept in. The soft green grass he used to run through barefoot. The treehouse that had been built by his father in the backyard. The basketball hoop in the driveway. The leaves that decorated the lawn in the rural Kansas community every fall. His brothers. Much as he tried, he couldn't forget them, despite the differences they had encountered in the past few years. His anger flared. John Michael kicked the bucket across the room and left a trail of dirty water. The toilet at the end stopped it from rolling any further. He ran up and kicked it again.

"Why?" he screamed, pounding his fist on the cold wall.

His mind couldn't stop reeling. The images kept coming. The anger kept building. John Michael placed his hand over his stomach and doubled over from the pain of the past.

"Oh, God," he whispered, "that night. That awful night! I wish I wouldn't have left." There was desperation in his voice and confusion in his mind. He sat down in the puddle on the floor and started to cry. Every memory brought more tears. He couldn't overlook the night his journey started. An evening he wouldn't forget.

Two

"Where Are You, Johnny?"

Bang! The newspaper hit the front door of the house and bounced across the porch into the bushes that lined the sidewalk. The boy on the bike kept riding, ignoring his bad aim and sore arm. This was no easy neighborhood for a paper boy. Not only were the old farmhouses huge in Willowbrook, a small, quaint Kansas farm community, but sidewalks seemed like long country roads. It took a pretty good arm not to lose a paper or break a window.

The door cracked open. Jonathan Davis reached out for the newspaper, but couldn't find it. With a deep sigh, he stepped out onto the porch and scoured it for evidence. His deep blue eyes investigated the area. He had done this before. Finally, the picture on the front page caught his eye. He reached under the nearby bush and picked it up.

The rolled up headline intrigued him to open the paper before he stepped back inside to sit down at the breakfast table. He read: "Cars Collide. Two Teenagers Die." A snapshot of a badly mangled car with an empty airbag over the steering wheel triggered a thought as he headed into the house. This was big news for a small town. Families would be alarmed and speed limits would be enforced.

"Thank God my boys are all here," Jonathan sighed as he shut the front door.

He walked by the stairwell and again shouted for his middle son.

"John Michael, you hurry down, please. You're going to make your brothers late for school."

There was no response. Just an echo from the top of the wooden stairwell. They had bought the house for the stairwell. Its beauty had reminded John Michael's mother of the one Scarlet O'Hara had come down in *Gone With the Wind*. Elizabeth loved that story. It was full of the sacrificial love she'd always dreamed of building in her own family.

Jonathan felt the same way. Although his bulky 6'3" figure resembled that of Rhett Butler's, he was a very different man from the actor who had captured the attention of so many women decades before. Jonathan was gentle and kind—strong, but loving and patient. It was his patience that had attracted Elizabeth to him in the first place. And he had integrity. Not every judge in this part of Kansas did.

Lewis, the oldest, walked into the kitchen grumbling about something John Michael had done. They were going to be late again. "Why don't we let him walk?"

"Because we love him. He wouldn't make you walk, would he, Lewis?" said his father gently, yet firmly.

Lewis was irritated. He mumbled something about John Michael using up all the hot water.

"He wouldn't have to make me walk. When have I ever been late? Not in high school and not in college."

Philip, the youngest of Jonathan's three sons, slammed the refrigerator door and set the milk jug on the table. His dark blue eyes and hair mirrored his father's. "Last week, three minutes," Philip reminded Lewis as he poured the milk over his cereal. "We waited three minutes in the parking lot at Deer Valley Community for you."

Lewis's face was red. He was already burning with anger and it wasn't past 8:00 in the morning.

"Really," laughed their father. "Philip, I thought it was five minutes."

"Joke all you want, but three minutes compared to his average fifteen gives me a twelve minute lead." That was Lewis's style. He always fought to be ahead of John Michael. It didn't matter if it was basketball or a video game score, he always felt one step behind his younger brother. John Michael was secure in every area Lewis wasn't. Lewis fought hard to be better. *After all,* Lewis thought, *older brothers are supposed to be one step ahead of their younger siblings.*

"John Michael, are you coming? Remember, we're all sharing a car today. The Honda's down."

Jonathan's tone was changing.

John Michael stared at himself in the bathroom mirror. His large frame and stocky build seemed to be shrinking. The dark rings under his eyes made his face look hollow and lost. He brushed his sandy blonde hair away from his face. "I hate you," he whispered to himself. I HATE YOU! He noticed a razor sitting on the edge of the sink. He grabbed it and raised it to his wrist. *Can I really live like this?* he wondered. The awkward moment came to an end when he heard his father's voice echo up the stairs and filter down the hallway.

"John Michael!"

"Get off my case. I'll be down in a second," he said back in an irritated growl, setting the razor down.

The two boys glanced at their father. This wasn't exactly what everyone was used to. John Michael had been going through a metamorphosis lately and it wasn't a good change. As the older brother, Lewis saw this as a perfect chance to dig in.

"What's his problem lately, anyway?"

"He hasn't been the same for a while," Philip responded. He was the one who would have noticed. He cared deeply for all of them. When things weren't normal around the house, he was the first to notice. "Haven't you noticed anything, Dad?"

"Yes, I have," said their father as he poured himself a cup of coffee.

They all had. It hadn't happened overnight, and they'd all noticed the transformation. Only time would tell why John Michael was changing. Attitudes, anger, screaming, fighting, late nights, quitting the basketball team, bloodshot eyes, smoky breath, skipping school, falling grades, sleeping in, and dressing down were just a few of the alterations John Michael had made to his life. Jonathan no longer knew how to handle John Michael; the boy grew more distant every day.

"Notice the change?" spouted Lewis. "You don't live in the room next to him, do you? I might as well live next door to hell!"

"Lewis!" his father scolded.

Lewis knew that was uncalled for, but the worse he could make his brother sound, the better he felt about himself. He wasn't about to stop.

"It's true. Ask Philip. He'll tell you how he's been treating us lately. Like..."

Jonathan stopped him. "Lewis, I'm not going to ask you again. I get the picture. Remember, we all live with him. Do either of you know what's been bothering him?"

The table was silent. Lewis's eyes darted towards his younger brother. Philip stared back. He was the one with the ability to look someone straight in the eyes. Lewis knew what the problem was. He was hoping Philip wouldn't say it.

"Ever since..." Philip stuttered, then stopped mid-sentence.

"Ever since..." he tried again.

"What, Son? You can say it." Jonathan made it a practice to allow his boys the freedom to express themselves openly. It was not an easy task for a father who strove to balance a firm hand and a soft heart.

"Ah, Dad, never mind. It's not important."

"Everything you say is important to me, Philip."

Lewis piped in. "Just say it, Philip. We can't read your mind."

Philip's stomach was in knots. This was a subject that remained tightly tucked away in the back of all their minds. It was a memory still very sensitive to each of them.

"Since," he took a deep breath, "Mom died." His spoon slipped into the cereal bowl and clanked when it hit the bottom. Time froze as the pain resurfaced once more. It had been more than a year, but the wounds in their hearts were still fresh.

The thud of John Michael coming down the stairs and stepping into the kitchen brought the three at the table back to the present. He was in a bad mood again.

"Let's go. We're going to be late," John Michael said in a cranky tone while grabbing a box of cereal off the table for the ride ahead.

"Thanks for telling us. We can tell time, you know." Lewis was not about to let this go by.

"Lay off. If you wouldn't spend so much time fixing your pretty little face, I could get ready earlier."

The war was on.

"My face isn't the problem, John Michael. If you would get your lazy..."

"Me? Lazy? C'mon, big brother, when was the last time you did anything around here for someone besides yourself? Huh?"

John Michael was burning up. Lewis had strategized this well. John Michael set down the cereal box on the counter and went straight for his older brother. Like a magnet to steel, he was on his way. With a fist in the air, John Michael started to swing.

"Lewis! Philip!" Jonathan stood like a referee between two opposing players in a boxing ring. "Out to the car. Now!" Silence. Tension. Their father's heart softened. "Please."

John Michael let go of his brother's denim shirt and turned away. Philip grabbed Lewis's arm, guiding him toward the front entryway. Within a moment they were out the door and in the car. The silence in the kitchen was deafening aside from John Michael's heavy breathing. The fuse inside had been lit and now he was ready to explode. Sweat poured from his brow. John Michael closed his eyes and ran his fingers through his hair to wipe the sweat away. His father put a hand on John Michael's shoulder in an attempt to defuse his son's anger. John Michael pulled away.

"You OK, Son?"

"I guess. Why wouldn't I be?" he said with a sliver of sarcasm in his voice.

"Your look," said Jonathan gently looking deep into his son's eyes. They reminded him of Elizabeth's. John Michael looked away. "You just seem to be more distant than ever before, not to mention how much we've been at each other's throats lately. Is there anything I can do to help?"

"Yes, there is, Dad."

"What, Son?" said Jonathan gently.

"You can get out of my face! I'm fine."

John Michael turned to walk away. Jonathan grabbed his right arm and turned him around.

"This is fine?"

John Michael started breathing hard again, his lungs filling deep with air. The voices inside his head were screaming now. He couldn't take this anymore. If it wasn't Lewis, it was his father. Everyone seemed to add to what he was already going through. Lewis enjoyed his anger, Philip desired an explanation, and his father was begging for some understanding. John Michael's thoughts rambled. A feeling of isolation came over his soul. He felt like a prisoner in his own home. He was desperately trying to think and feel on his own without the opinions of those he lived with. Nobody could solve the problems lurking deep down inside of him. Only he knew the level of guilt and condemnation he was already struggling with. Feelings he wasn't ready to face. Feelings he thought were best left alone. Feelings he was desperately trying to run away from. Waking up at home every morning only reminded him of all those sensations. He grabbed his backpack off the floor and stomped out the front door. Something was happening inside of him. His emotions were beginning to unravel. John Michael desperately wished everyone would just let go.

Jonathan started after him, then stopped. John Michael needed some space. He turned toward the window and watched his son climb into the back seat of the car. Now the boys were waiting on their father. This was a ride he wasn't looking forward to. It would be silent, and he knew it. A tear fell from his cheek. He rubbed his hand across his face to wipe it away. It had been a morning he was not prepared for. He longed to help his son, but John Michael wouldn't let anyone get close right now. He'd done everything a loving father could do for his wayward boy. His only choice was to give him some room. He just wasn't sure yet how much space John Michael would take. His chest began to ache as his heart broke.

"I just don't understand," he whispered as he rested his head on the windowpane. "It's like I don't even know you anymore. Where's my Johnny? Where are you?"

Three

Missing You...

John Michael slopped the mop around again. "I'm right here, Dad. Stuck in this hell hole." The dirty water flowed across the mildewed tile floor. He started to mumble to himself again. "You didn't know me anymore, Dad."

"Shut up," screamed a shout from the next room.

John Michael didn't care. They wouldn't remember anything he was saying anyway. Each of them had so many problems of their own, they wouldn't remember John Michael's. Each of them had a story. Lives marred by their own failures and pain. Men searching for the truth and coming up short on answers. John Michael kept mumbling.

"Don't you get it, Dad? I had to get away. Away from you, from Philip, and from Lewis. Oh God, far away from Lewis. Away from that house, but most of all, from the memories of Mom."

For the first time in months, the scrapbook of his mind turned to his mother. He hadn't allowed himself to think much of her since he left home, but for now, it felt good to remember her. She was a beautiful woman. Her long dark hair sparkled in the sun, and her smile—any child would have been drawn to it, especially her own.

"Johnny, I don't think I said anything about eating yet," came a warm voice correcting a younger John Michael, who had taken a sandwich from the picnic basket and started to run away.

"But, Mom, I'm hungry," the boy said, stopping dead in his tracks.

"I'm sure you are, but just taking your lunch and eating it yourself is a little selfish, don't you think? Besides, won't you be lonely?"

He turned around with a pout. Elizabeth went to her son, who was standing on the edge of the blanket. Her loving arms wrapped around his shoulders and chest. Although John Michael looked away, he could still smell his mother's fragrant perfume. It was a familiar scent. The sweet smell triggered many thoughts in the little boy's mind. The most important one was the unconditional love he always felt from his mom. Whether he received an "A+" on a spelling test or was stealing a sandwich from the picnic lunch, his mother always loved him.

"Little Johnny," she whispered in his ear, "why are you so stubborn? Huh? I used to be stubborn when I was your age. I hope it's something you grow out of. Either way your mother loves you, you know."

Little Johnny was softening. Just the touch of her soft, warm hands made his heart tingle. She knew the language of love. Sometimes he would be stubborn just to get extra attention from the mother he loved so much.

"Will you remember that I love you?" she said whispering again tenderly into his ear.

Johnny shook his head up and down. She kissed his forehead and he melted. This little boy knew his mother cared for him. Johnny had no doubts. Elizabeth loved all her boys, even the stubborn one.

The pages continued turning like a photo album full of family pictures. Tight squeezes. A warm smile. Her soft hands. A soothing back rub. The smell of clean laundry. Fresh cookies with cold milk. Mashed potatoes and gravy. Band-Aids and kisses on the owies. Stories read at the foot of his bed. Strength through the thundering storms. A mother's kiss. A mother's touch. All that was missing from the memory now was...his mother.

John Michael could name the place he was standing when his mother stepped out of his life. He could even remember what he had been wearing that day. The football jersey was still tucked away in his dresser. It was like an archive waiting to be dropped off at the Smithsonian. The mere appearance of it at the bottom of his drawer was symbolic of how tightly he had tucked away the pain and grief of losing her. By holding onto his uniform, John Michael felt like he still had a piece of his mother's life. She had been at every game he'd played. Well, every one but the last, his championship game. He hoped that by preserving a memento he could bring her back.

He kicked the bucket again. John Michael wanted to stop remembering. It was too difficult. He rubbed his forehead with his hand. A tear trickled down his face. It rolled off his cheek and into the metal bucket, rippling the water inside.

"Mom, I really miss you."

Four

To Be a Kid Again

Although the sun had set over an hour ago, the judge of the Third District in Reno County, Kansas, was still hard at work. Sometimes it seemed that the needs of the judicial system would never end. Jonathan walked through the kitchen and set his briefcase on the table. He had just poured himself a cup of coffee and sat down to review tomorrow's case load when the phone rang. He set his steaming cup back on the counter as he stepped through the kitchen to retrieve the receiver that hung next to the pantry.

"Hello?" he answered. He listened intently to the other end of the line. "Absent? What? How many absences are we talking here? Yes, uh-huh. Failing his strongest subject? He's always been a great student. I know…yes, I'm aware that something has been different. Yes, I'm aware of that. Just a moment…can I call you back? I have another call on the line. Thanks."

Jonathan pressed the flash button on the receiver.

"Hello, Pete. Thanks for calling me back. I can't be in court as early as I had hoped; one of the cars is in the shop. It's overheating or something. We're down to one vehicle and that means I've got to take all three boys to school. Can we make our appointment for later in the day?"

The deal was almost done. A later appointment would get him and the boys out of this pinch.

John Michael ran into the kitchen and knocked over the hot cup of java that was cooling on the edge of the counter.

"Oh, man."

He grabbed a few paper towels to clean it up while trying to get his father's attention.

"Dad? Dad," he whispered. "I need to talk to you. Now."

Jonathan covered the base of the phone. He motioned to John Michael that he would be just a minute.

"Now, Dad," John Michael commanded.

Jonathan was irritated. He had taught his boys to wait to talk to him until he was off the line.

"Listen, Pete, I'll call you first thing in the morning. I've got a crisis here. Yes, talk to you tomorrow. Bye." He quickly hung up, suppressing his frustration with John Michael for being so rude. "Son, that is not how you get my attention when I'm on the phone. You know that..."

John Michael looked his father in the eye and stated what was on his mind. "I need to leave, Dad." Relief swept through his body. They were words he had tried to mention so many times before, now he was brave enough to say them.

Jonathan was frustrated again. *This is what I got off the phone for?*

"Excuse me? Where are you going? John Michael, you know we are down to one car. I've been working really hard to keep a schedule..."

"Dad, don't you get it? I'm not talking about the car, or your schedule. I don't care about your schedule. I'm leaving for awhile. Maybe forever."

Jonathan stared at him. He knew where this conversation was going. He had heard it before. Every boy dreams of leaving home and growing up. Jonathan had figured it was a passing phase, a way to deal with the emotional pain of losing his mother.

But, something felt different this time. *If I could keep him from leaving for just a little longer, there might be a chance for change,* he thought.

"Johnny, you're not leaving. Let's sit down and talk about this."

Jonathan walked into the living room and sat down on the couch. John Michael followed him, but instead of sitting, he paced nervously by the fireplace.

"I don't want to talk. I want to go. I'm 18, you know."

"Eighteen? You think that just because you're 18 you're suddenly more mature than you were at 17? Do you really think you're ready to take on what's beyond that front door? It's the real world out there, John Michael. It's unforgiving." Jonathan had cursed the legal age ever since he had become a part of the judicial system. One birthday doesn't make everything different. His son wasn't old enough to buy a bottle of alcohol, but the state said he was old enough to walk out of his home and family. It didn't make sense to Jonathan. Maturing takes years, not a few fleeting moments.

"Quit sheltering me. I'm old enough to make my own decisions! I can do what I want. It's the law, Dad."

"I understand the legal system, Son. You can do whatever you like. But as your father, I'm asking you not to. I've seen what's out there. I'm telling you, you're not ready." Things were starting to heat up. "Besides, Johnny, that's not the way we do things around here."

"Things have changed. I'm a legal adult, Dad."

Jonathan was now pacing in front of the fireplace next to his son. "There's a lot more to growing up than just deciding to leave. What about your education? And a job? You haven't worked a day in your life. What are you going to do about a car? How will you get around? What if you get sick? Who will take you to the doctor? That's growing up, Son. Are you ready for all of that? For goodness sake, Johnny, how are you going to live?

You haven't even graduated!" Jonathan knew he was starting to lecture.

John Michael was silent for a moment, then he advanced with a new plan of attack. "Dad, you just don't get where I'm coming from," he replied. "What do I have to do to get you to understand my world? My culture. My problems!"

That was the problem and Jonathan knew it. His son couldn't see beyond himself. He was facing so much right now and until he could see past it, there was no hope. Jonathan had noticed that the crowd his son had been hanging around with thought the same way. They'd already begun covering the pain by skipping school to drink or get high. They didn't seem to care much about the future. Their apathetic attitudes had left their dreams and visions for life frozen.

John Michael stopped walking and closed his eyes tight. He was thinking, contemplating, strategizing his next move. "I want my share of Mom's life insurance plan."

Immediately Jonathan knew John Michael was serious about leaving this time. It took him by surprise. The subject of the money had never come up before. Shortly after he and Elizabeth were married, Jonathan had set up a small life insurance plan in case something ever happened to one of them. It wasn't much, just a small fee every month. He never thought it would amount to anything. A few weeks after Elizabeth's death, the check came in the mail. He wanted to throw it away. Money could never bring her back. But, in an effort to give the boys something they could remember their mother by, he saved a portion of it for each of them to use for their college education. Jonathan couldn't even think of the funds being wasted like this.

"Out of the question. You're not thinking clearly, Son. That money was put away for your college education, not to waste on your whims. We just started using some of it to pay for Lewis's first year of community college, and I'm not about to yank your college money for you to just throw it to the wind. That money is special. Think about how your mother would have wanted it spent. We will use it when you finish high school."

There was a long pause. Jonathan was hoping he had finished the conversation. He thought he might have talked some sense into his son. John Michael turned and glared at his father.

"I'm ready."

"John Michael, read my lips. No! You're barely an adult."

John Michael raised his fist towards his father, flipping his middle finger in front of Jonathan's face.

"What is wrong with you, Johnny?! You don't even pick your clothes up off the floor in your room, or flush the toilet when you're done. When's the last time you put gas in the car? Johnny, I feel like I just took the training wheels off your bike!"

"You did take the training wheels off my bike, Dad. Ten years ago! I'm not some little boy anymore. Besides, I'm sick of living in stupid Kansas. This place sucks! I need to get away from you, from them, and most of all, from this!" He grabbed a picture of his mother that was sitting on the fireplace mantle and threw it on the floor as hard as he could. The glass that covered Elizabeth's warm smile cracked into hundreds of little pieces and scattered all over the wooden floor. The loud crash echoed through the entire house. Footsteps came thundering down the hall. Lewis and Philip ran into the living room.

"What happened?" hollered Philip.

Jonathan tried to take control. "Boys, let me finish with your brother."

John Michael wasn't about to let go of this fight. If he could get his brothers on his side, his father might soften. The end was in sight.

"No! They need to hear this. They need to know I want my fair share. It's our money, so let them vote." He turned and faced his brothers like a lawyer to his jury. "Don't you think I'm old enough to decide whether or not I can take my part of Mom's money and get out of this place? Well, don't you?"

Philip and Lewis stood in shock. It was understood that the finances would not be touched.

"You can't go, Johnny," said Philip with tears welling up in his eyes. These past few months had been hard on him. He loved John Michael.

Lewis assessed the situation and made his ruling. "I think he's old enough, Dad."

They all stared at him in shock. *Why would Lewis ever side with John Michael?*

"What?" shouted Jonathan at his oldest son.

"Why not? He's just ruining our lives here. If he's not happy, let him out. Really. It's not like he can't get his GED," he continued baiting John Michael, hoping for a bite.

Philip spoke, "You're just..."

"I'm what?"

"You're just jealous, Lewis. Jealous that Johnny is better at everything than you are. You've always been jealous."

The truth agitated Lewis. He had never liked the feeling of second place. Any opportunity he had to make his younger brother look bad he took, and he wasn't about to lose this one. He saw a possible win here. "He's always been Dad's favorite anyway."

"That's a lie," shouted John Michael, turning in Lewis's direction for another round. The glass cracked under his feet as he made his way towards his brother.

Before Jonathan could intervene, both boys were on the floor scrambling to be on top. John Michael held Lewis down and punched him in his mouth. Lewis's face dragged through the glass that covered the surface of the wooden planks. A pool of blood was starting to form under his cheek on the floor. It took both Jonathan and Philip to pull John Michael off of Lewis. John Michael took off out the front door. His father ran after him, heading down the quiet street in his bare feet. Jonathan knew he wasn't going to catch his son. His lungs took in the cold night air harshly. He stopped and bent over, staring at a crack in the sidewalk. Through his deep breaths he could barely scream.

"John Michael!" More deep breaths. More screams. "Please, come back! Come back home! Let's talk about this!"

Jonathan finally caught his breath and stood up. No one was in sight. He turned around and walked slowly back to the house. The cold pavement reminded him of what he would face inside. Philip met him on the porch.

"Where's he going, Dad?"

They both stared down the street into the distance.

"I don't know, Son. I don't know. Somewhere far away from his problems. Far away from here. I just hope he realizes that wherever he goes, his troubles go with him."

Lewis stepped onto the porch with them. He was holding his head with a towel that was stained with blood. A few drops fell from his cheek and onto his sleeve. Jonathan turned towards his oldest son and put his hands on Lewis's head. Gently, he took away the towel and surveyed the damage.

"Ouch!" screamed Lewis, backing away.

"You're going to be all right, Lewis. Let's get you to the car before you bleed too much. Philip, get me another towel, and grab my tennis shoes by the door."

"You got it, Dad," replied his youngest as he hurried inside.

Jonathan helped Lewis to the car. His strong, yet gentle arms cradled his oldest son's shoulders. Lewis had avoided his father's touch lately so Jonathan took advantage of the opportunity to affirm his son.

The trip to the emergency room was a quiet one. The hospital seemed empty as Jonathan pulled the car into the emergency room parking lot. The three of them walked through the sterile white corridor and made their way to the front desk. Lewis felt uncomfortable. Willowbrook was a small town. That meant everybody knew everybody and anything there was to know about everyone. He figured it wouldn't be long before the entire city knew his head had been bashed in by John Michael. Lewis cursed his brother under his breath.

"What are you boys doing out on a beautiful night like this?" asked a nurse dressed in white pants and yellow shirt behind a counter.

"Well, we've had an eventful evening," replied Jonathan.

"I should say so. What happened to you, Lewis? Let me get you in to see Dr. Manning right away. You're lucky she's not on call tonight."

Lewis shrugged as the nurse led them to a bed right off the lobby corridor. She pulled the green curtain shut. "In fact, we were just talking about your family the other night. And now, we get to see you. Dr. Manning will be so surprised."

Joan Manning had been a family friend for years. She was a perceptive woman, and had been a true friend to the boys since their mother had died. Joan knew hard times. She had worked hard to become one of the most successful African-American doctors in the state of Kansas. But despite the prestige and awards, she had a heart for people.

"Let me see that towel, if you don't mind," said the nurse pulling the red cloth from Lewis's head. "Boy, it looks like we've got a nasty one here. You'll probably need stitches. Why don't you press this gauze against it for a few minutes to make sure the bleeding has stopped. I'll let the doctor know you're here. I'll be back in a moment to clean you up before we do the stitches."

She left the room and headed out through the curtain. The three of them looked at one another without speaking. Each of them were dealing with issues of their own. This hospital held a great deal of memories. Elizabeth had been brought here. Two doors down Jonathan had been told she was dead. Four doors down, in a private waiting area, the boys had been told they wouldn't see their mother ever again. This place felt strange, almost cold and lifeless. Jonathan cleared his throat.

"Is there anything I can do for you, Lewis?"

Lewis shook his head, holding the gauze where his head had been cut open. It was still bleeding.

Philip looked awkwardly around the room.

"Dad, I'm going to get something to drink. Do you want anything?"

"No thanks. Just don't be gone too long."

Philip pushed away the curtain and headed down the hall. He wasn't going to get a drink, he was going to the waiting room. He had spent many hours there waiting, while his mother's life hung in the balance. He remembered watching his father walk in and out a number of times that night. As he made his way down the hall, he noticed his mother's emergency room. The green curtain inside was open now—then it had been shut. His feet stopped in place. They felt like lead. That was the last place he'd really seen his mother. At least as he remembered her. Her open casket didn't resemble the "mom" Philip had grown up with. He thought she had looked bloated, unhappy, and silent. He didn't remember his mother being very silent. He didn't want that to be his last memory of her. So, he chose to remember the body his father had asked him to see shortly after she had been pronounced dead. She died at 9:32 p.m. He glanced up at the clock like he had done when he came in to see his mother for the last time. It was 9:32 p.m. again. The same time. The same place. He turned his head and ran down the hall.

The waiting room wasn't far away. He pushed through a glass door and sat down inside a room a little smaller than his bedroom. There were three green vinyl chairs along with a coffee table that matched the '70s decor of the hospital. The television was on without the sound. Just like it had been that night. He remembered watching a sitcom without hearing it. Philip picked up a sports magazine and leafed through it. The evening his mother died he had thrown a magazine down on the table, angry that the world just kept going on while he was in the middle of the most tragic circumstance of his life. He remembered looking out the window and wishing everyone would just stop and feel what he was going through. *Did anybody care that my mother was never coming home?* He threw the magazine on the table the same way he had done back then. Philip tapped his fingers on the armrest. *Will these feelings ever go away?* He stood staring around the room with a final glance. He hoped he would never have to visit this room again. Philip stepped out and headed down the hall, this time in search of a soda machine.

Dr. Manning passed Philip in the hall on her way to see Lewis. She smiled and he smiled back. Reaching Lewis's room, she pulled away the green curtain and made her way inside. "Well, look who we have here!"

Lewis looked away. He was ready to let his father do all the talking.

"Hello, Joan. It's good to see you again," replied Jonathan. He stood and reached out his hand. Jonathan had appreciated the support she and her husband had given him over the past few months. Their understanding and love for him and the boys had been heartfelt. Joan had been there when Elizabeth was brought in. In fact, it was Joan who told Jonathan that Elizabeth wasn't going to pull through. That night, she had held Jonathan like his mother would have as he sobbed in her arms. Neither of them would ever forget that moment. It made a night like this feel safer. Why? Because Jonathan knew she really cared. Tonight, she was caring again.

"All right, let's see what we've got." She pulled the gauze from Lewis's head and stared at the wound. "Mighty deep cut here. I would guess about 12 stitches should do the trick." She set the gauze down and put on a set of rubber gloves, then pulled out a stitching set from a wall cabinet and placed it on a nearby tray. It wasn't long before she had half of Lewis's stitches in. Except for a flinch or two, Lewis had remained quiet like his father.

"Almost done here, Lewis."

"Good," he said with an irritated tone.

"That was quite a cut there. Now, how did you say this happened again?"

"I didn't," said Lewis sarcastically.

"You didn't? I thought I heard you mumble something."

"Well, if I did, it was about that jerk brother of mine. He did this."

Jonathan cut in. "Lewis and John Michael got into an argument tonight. A picture broke and there was glass everywhere. The two of them landed on some of it, and Lewis's face was dragged along the floor. Somehow his head got cut in the whole thing."

"I should say so," Joan said kindly, sewing up Lewis's final stitch. "It sounds like it was some fight. I've known your family for years and never noticed such animosity between the three of you boys."

"We've never had any until recently!" Lewis piped back. "John Michael's been treating everybody like crap."

Philip returned with a can of cola in his hand. He stepped in through the curtain hearing half of Lewis's sentence.

"Crap? That's a lie. You're the one who's been treating everyone like crap."

"Guys," said their father, "let's give the doctor a fair look at what's been happening lately." He turned his attention to her and continued to speak. "John Michael has been acting strange recently. Something is going on inside of him that has been producing some real difficulties and challenges for us as a family."

"Really? John Michael always seemed like such a good kid," said Joan. She looked from Lewis to Philip. "You've always been good boys—all of you. I remember delivering each one of you. Now, Lewis, you were a handful."

Lewis smirked.

"When you came out you were ready to get on with your life. And, John Michael...I don't know if his mother ever told him this, but he was breach all the way up to the delivery. I didn't know if that kid would ever come out."

Jonathan smiled, remembering.

"And, Philip. You just plopped out without a care in the world." She continued working on Lewis's wound. "All three of you have been different from the get-go. But, you have all been good kids in this community. John Michael *is* a good kid," she affirmed.

"He is a good kid. A great kid, for that matter. But over the last few months," Jonathan's voice cracked, "it's been different."

Philip took a deep breath and spoke candidly. "It started when Mom died."

There was an awkward silence in the room. Joan looked Philip's way, then went back to finishing Lewis's head. "Losing a mother is a rough thing. Everybody handles pain differently, don't they?" She tried to rinse the blood out of Lewis's hair with a soft wash cloth. "I was in medical school when my father passed away. I stepped out of classes for several months. It really took me awhile to get back on top of things." She stopped and looked into Lewis's eyes with honesty. "You know, it's been 12 years, and I still struggle with it. It just takes a while. Time. It takes time."

Jonathan rested his head on the wall and stared at the green curtain. "Time, it takes a long time," he said.

"Well," said Lewis to Joan, "I think you should just let him go. Your father, I mean."

"You ever let go of anything that was important to you?" Joan replied continuing to wash the blood out of his matted hair.

"Ouch! Yeah, so what?" said Lewis, trying to hide his feelings.

"How did it feel?" Joan said.

Lewis didn't answer.

"What did you let go of, Lewis?"

Lewis looked her straight in the eye. He squinted and sighed. "My mother," he replied.

Joan Manning knew she had said enough. Enough to make Lewis think, enough to let him know she cared. She wondered who was being a mother to these boys. "There you go. All fixed up. After we take the stitches out, we'll have to see if there is any scar tissue. Why don't you see me again next week sometime? Maybe Tuesday."

Lewis stood and collected himself, holding his head with his hands.

"The pain shouldn't be too bad. I've written out a prescription for you for the next few days. And here." She handed both boys a dinosaur sticker, smiling and joking with them. "Lewis, you get a sticker for being such a good patient; and Philip, you get a sticker for being such a good brother. Now, let me talk to your dad for a few minutes."

Lewis rolled his eyes at her.

"I'm just joking, Lewis. Loosen up."

"Thanks, Dr. Manning," said Philip.

"Sure thing."

"I'll be out in a minute," said their father.

Lewis and Philip made their way through the green curtain and down the corridor. Joan started to clean up what she had used to repair Lewis's head.

"Jonathan, if you don't mind my asking, are you doing all right?"

There was a long pause, then a slow response. "I don't know."

"Between you and me, that was a pretty serious cut on Lewis's scalp. Must have been a pretty bad fight."

"It was," he responded, running his hand over chin and mouth. "I'm dealing with a pretty angry kid."

"Sounds like more than one."

"What do you mean?"

Joan Manning turned Jonathan's way after she took her rubber gloves off and threw them into the chrome metal wastebasket. "Lewis. He sounds just as angry as John Michael."

"Sometimes I just sit on my porch staring into the distance and wonder how it all got this way."

"Jonathan, you've got three wonderful sons all handling the loss of Elizabeth in their own way."

"It's so hard, you know, having to respond to each one of them differently. John Michael's out of control, Lewis only cares about himself, and Philip's in between trying to be the strength in all the weak areas. As a father, I'm really struggling with how to handle all of this. I mean, I'm not over Elizabeth either, Joan."

"Jonathan, you do all that you can and then rely on what's most important."

"What's that?"

"Love. You love each of them right where they are. I'm telling you, Jonathan, I see it every day." Joan finished writing down a few notes, pulled the green curtain away, and led Jonathan down the hall slowly. "Love is the cure for meeting people at their greatest point of need. I can prescribe all kinds of alternatives, but loving them has to come first. It's the only medicine that offers hope of healing the heart."

Jonathan looked away for a moment, then responded. "Love. Unconditional love. How come they don't teach you this stuff before you're ever a parent? Before you know it, you're left to find it out on your own."

"Life is a process, my friend. It's all a matter of learning. Unfortunately, sometimes we're forced into the lesson."

Jonathan and Joan faced one another. He rubbed his eyes and sighed.

"Now," she said gently, "my prescription for you is rest. You need to get some sleep."

"I'll try. After John Michael comes home."

Joan reached out and hugged him. Jonathan welcomed the embrace. There is nothing like the care of a friend when you're in need. Tonight, he was in need.

Jonathan and the boys made their way out of the emergency room and to the car. They were finally on their way back home. Lewis had a pretty nasty gash above his left ear. Philip had an open wound in his heart.

Jonathan drove through the streets of the quaint Kansas village. The ride was a quiet one except for an occasional sniffle and a stop at the 24-hour drug store. All that could be heard was the roar of the engine and rotation of the tires. Jonathan dropped the boys off in the driveway and parked the vehicle in the garage. He got out and leaned his tall slender body against the car door for a few moments. It had been a long night. The light from the porch illuminated his hands. The blood from Lewis's gash was still on them. He shook his head, wondering what was happening to his own flesh and blood.

While Philip helped clean up the glass and crimson stains on the hardwood floor, Jonathan walked Lewis up to his room. He sighed, hoping the night would soon end. John Michael was still missing. His father wondered if he would ever come home.

"Let him go, Dad. He's just trouble anyway," responded his oldest son as he climbed the stairs. Jonathan looked at him, hurt by the comment.

"Dad, take a close look at my head. This is only going to get worse. What's next? Is he going to murder one of us when he gets angry again?"

"Lewis, don't talk about John Michael like that. He's your brother. Part of our flesh and blood as a family. He's not going to murder anybody."

Lewis walked into his room. Jonathan walked behind him, stopping at the threshold of the door.

"As far as I'm concerned, he's not my flesh and blood anymore," Lewis said as he slammed the door in Jonathan's face. He fell on his bed and stuffed his head between two pillows. This entire night had seemed like a nightmare. Now, he lay on his bed with a head that hurt and a heart that ached. Then he did what he'd only do alone. Tears filled his eyes and he started to cry. Quiet, muted sobs at first, then thundering deep breaths.

Jonathan rested his hand on the frame of the door. He ran his fingers through his dark hair and sighed loudly. Now he had two sons he didn't understand. He started to blame himself again.

"What's happening to this family?" he whispered.

He felt a hand on his neck, then turned and faced his youngest son. Philip reached out and hugged his father. Warm tears fell on both of their shoulders. Jonathan knew the storm was coming. But, for a moment, Philip's touch was all he needed to make the fear go away.

"I don't know, Dad. It's John Michael. Something's happening to Johnny."

Something was happening to John Michael. He had spent the night marching across the small town trying to walk off his anger. He noticed his old elementary school in the distance and headed in that direction, across a few streets, then through the front lawn of the building and past the front parking lot. He stared at the jungle gym located in the backyard. The crisp night air cooled John Michael's hot face. He couldn't help remembering the hundreds of times he had slid down that slide, played on those monkey bars, and spun on the merry-go-round until he had made himself sick. His eyes focused on his favorite piece of childhood playground equipment—the swings. He grabbed the cold steel chains with his hands and sat down on one of them. He pushed off the ground and started his upward climb. Lower at first, then as high as he could possibly go. For a few moments, John Michael was a little boy again. He could hear the laughter in his mind, feel the childish excitement, and for a few fleeting seconds he forgot about all of the day's problems. He was tired of facing obstacles. At this point running away from them seemed the only answer, not to mention the easiest. The problem was that in a town as small as Willowbrook, there aren't a lot of places to run. An attempt to run away in his mind would have to do for now. He felt like "little Johnny" again.

What I would have given to go back for a simple swing in the park! But now swinging troubles away wasn't so easy. John Michael couldn't stop thinking about the events of that evening. He glanced down at his hands wrapped around the chain. His own blood had now dried on them. The bloody nose he had earlier had flowed like a river, dripping on his shirt and staining his pants. John Michael stopped pumping his feet and dragged them on the dusty ground to a halt. He wiped his eyes with his sleeve. He too was crying. John Michael didn't understand what was happening to himself either. Ever since his mother had died, something inside of him had died too. Words could never describe how he felt. All he knew was what he felt. And that feeling wasn't always good. The anger was building. The questions kept coming. *Why? Why? Why? Why my mother? Why me? Why now?* When would he come up with the answers? Only time would tell. And for now, time would only remain silent except for the cool breeze flowing through the jungle gym past the empty swings as they squeaked. Now more than ever John Michael wished he could be a child.

If only he could crawl up on his father's lap like he had done so many times as a kid. The problems seemed to melt away there. But not anymore. He was too old, not to mention too full of pride. He was at an age where he had to take on every problem by himself rather than asking for help from the person who would understand him the most. *My father has enough to deal with.* Rather than add to the load by dumping his own struggles on his father, John Michael decided he would take on these hardships and deal with the barriers his own way—even if that meant they piled up like dirty laundry. Growing up was not easy. Oh, to be a kid again.

Five

Letting Go

A light breeze flowed along the grass and up to the house. All was silent except for the faint squeaking of the porch swing. A sense of innocence seemed to be in the air, sweeping the small town with a sweet peace. Jonathan made his way out the front door and onto the porch, staring into the darkness. It had been weeks since the living room incident. Although Lewis's head had healed, the heart of John Michael had not. Tonight, Jonathan was waiting again for a son who hadn't come home yet. This hadn't been the first time, and he knew it wouldn't be the last. John Michael had been avoiding any time at home like a child avoiding a nap. Jonathan yawned. He was ready for bed. Ready to rest his mind for another night. All the stress of Elizabeth's death had finally felt far away. John Michael's situation was stirring up a whole new set of problems. He stood on the porch for a long time. His t-shirt and shorts felt much more comfortable than the suit and robe he had to wear every day in the courtroom. He stared at the starry sky. The darkness seemed to hide what he was going through. The moon was shining brightly, soothing his thoughts and putting an emotional Band-Aid on his pain. Jonathan whispered a question to himself.

"How does a parent let go?"

He sat down on the porch steps and locked his arms around his knees, resting his chin on top trying to answer the question. His mind started to run through the years. All the noses he had wiped, not to mention the diapers he had changed. The broken arm he had nurtured Lewis through in the third grade. The colds. The stomach flu. All the football games he had coached. The basketball games he had cheered from the bleachers. All the girls he had screened on the phone. Countless hours of algebra, English, and science homework. The bikes, the baseball gloves, and the toys. Who could forget a house full of toys? Piles of laundry neatly folded on the family room floor. For the first time in his life, he missed seeing those piles there.

Why do children have to grow up? he thought to himself. He wondered if it would have been easier if his boys had just stayed little forever. Then maybe he would never have to face letting go. Letting Elizabeth go had been hard enough. Now, more than a year later he was grieving again, only this time it was harder. How do you grieve for someone who is still alive?

A beer bottle dropped and rolled off the porch floor into the bushes next to the house. Jonathan jumped to his feet, squinting in the direction of the sound. The porch swing squeaked in the wind. Jonathan made his way toward it.

"Philip? Is that you?"

No sound.

"Lewis?"

Nothing again.

John Michael? Could it be John Michael? But he was out with friends again. Prodigals themselves, in many ways. All searching for something they couldn't find at home in a father. Most of John Michael's friends had never had a dad.

Divorce. Separation. Hibernation from responsibility. A fatherless generation. They were growing up without ever understanding their need for a dad. They had a reason to search. But why was John Michael?

"Johnny, is that you? John Michael?"

Jonathan recognized the shirt in the light of the moon. It had the name of one of those rock bands John Michael was now listening to.

Jonathan squinted again in the faint light, recognizing the boyish features he had come to know and love. It was John Michael, fast asleep. Standing beside the swing now, Jonathan reached out and let his hand rest on his son's head. He pushed away the hair from John Michael's forehead. He almost liked John Michael this way. Quiet, peaceful, at rest with himself. He wondered why some children only seem at peace with themselves when they are asleep.

He moved John Michael's legs and sat next to him. He stared at John Michael's face. His smile, he missed seeing that smile. Jonathan wondered if he would ever see it again. Jonathan gently reached his hand over John Michael's shoulders, then whispered to himself.

"Your breath used to smell like bubble gum and cotton candy; now it smells like someone running from his problems."

He removed another beer bottle tucked behind his son's body and set it on the porch floor.

"I remember when you were just a boy. I would tuck you in bed and read your favorite story. Do you remember? Then I would rub your feet until you fell asleep."

Jonathan pondered that thought. Oh, what he would give to have a moment like that again! John Michael used to giggle for a little while, but soon would be asleep as his father gently pressed his fingers on John Michael's little toes.

"Everything seemed so simple then. The biggest challenge we faced was airing up a bicycle tire or playing a game of basketball." He remembered how he used to lift John Michael up and put him on his shoulders so he could dunk the ball. Johnny had always wanted to be a professional basketball player. He used to look up to so many of the greats, but now he didn't have any heroes. He could dunk the ball on his own if he wanted to.

"And now this. Why, my son? Why?"

His mind drifted back to a late afternoon in October of 1984.

The leaves were falling from the tree he and the boys had planted in their front yard years earlier. Jonathan had told them that would be a lesson in growth for them. Over the years the tree had grown quite large. He remembered how John Michael kept falling off his new blue Schwinn bike. Jonathan held the training wheels in his hands.

"You can do it! C'mon, son. There you go. Right foot on the pedal. Push, Johnny. Push. You've almost got it. Watch out for the curb. Oh!" John Michael was on the ground again. Nothing too serious, just a skinned knee and a few tears. "Climb back on, big boy. You've almost got it." Jonathan helped him back on his bike.

"But Dad, I can't do it. I can't!"

"Sure you can. You can do anything you set your mind to."

John Michael climbed back on. His father held the back of his yellow banana seat and pushed him off. Foot to pedal, pedal to foot. The silver spokes and black tires were spinning against the pavement. Jonathan's hand let go.

"There you go! You're doing it, Johnny! You're doing it! That's it. That's it!" He jumped up and down like a little boy cheering on his best friend. "You're doing it! You're doing it! Now keep peddling. Keep peddling, Son!"

John Michael rode off into the distance. Past the cars. Past his childhood buddies. Past the houses, fields, and a few falling leaves. And past his father.

Jonathan stared at the young man now lying asleep on the swing next to him. He had come to one conclusion that evening. *Being a parent is all about letting go,* he pondered. *Right? Whether it's a bike or something more crucial like your son's will, life is about letting go.*

He whispered again. "I've got to let you go, my boy. I've got to let go, but I'm so scared. What if you never come back?

What if you get hurt? I wouldn't be able to live with myself." His eyes welled up with tears. The thought of losing one of his sons always choked him up. "I love you so much. We can't allow anything to change that," he sighed quietly. "Before you pedal away, can we figure out what it is we've lost? We've lost something, John Michael. Maybe we never had it. Maybe we buried it with your mom."

Another tear fell from a father's cheek that night. Although it couldn't be seen in the dark, this father's broken heart proved it was there. Jonathan knew that somewhere, somehow, all the tears he had shed for his son were being bottled up in a place where they would not be forgotten. Every parent needs to feel that at some point and time. You spend all those years wiping noses, cleaning up spilled milk, tucking them in bed, kissing their owies and crying over them when they lie drunk on your front porch. The tears Jonathan shed that night mattered. If not to John Michael, then for every mother and father who had shed the same. They proved that an unconditional love really does exist despite the circumstances.

John Michael's body started to stir. His eyes opened slowly. It took him a few seconds to figure out where he was. He moaned and groaned several times and then sat up and covered his face with his hands. A Mack truck. He felt like he had been hit by a Mack truck. His head started to pound. He heard someone breathing next to him. The outline of his father came into focus.

"Uh, Dad?" he said with an embarrassed look on his face. "What are you doing here?" He rubbed his eyes to make sure the illusion was true.

"I just wanted to see you asleep, at peace, one last time," his father said gently.

John Michael tried to sit up, but couldn't. His stomach was churning and yearning for relief.

"Last time? What do you mean?" John Michael now sat up, blinking his eyes again to make sure this was real.

"Here."

Another tear rolled down Jonathan's cheek. In the light of the moon John Michael watched his father take something out of his back pocket. It was an envelope. Jonathan handed it to his son.

"What's this?" John Michael was puzzled. His mind raced as he stared at it. *Walking papers? A parental contract? Could it be an old letter from Mom? Is this some kind of manipulative trick to keep me home?*

"Open it," his father said gently.

John Michael turned the envelope over apprehensively. He wasn't sure what this was going to add up to. What could a father give to a son whom he finds drunk on the front porch of their house? This had to be some sort of disciplinary trick. It would have been so easy for Jonathan to beg, plead, and play some kind of emotional game to keep his son safe at home. Instead, he took the road less traveled. Jonathan let John Michael go.

"Dad, what is it?"

"You won't find out until you open it."

"Can I wait until the morning?"

"I think you'll want to see it now."

John Michael slowly ripped the back flap open and pulled out the contents. Inside the crisp white envelope was a folded piece of paper with a short note and picture attached to it. The note read...

"I can't hold you back anymore. I love you too much. You are free, but always welcome to call this your home. I'll be waiting for you. Always. Love, Dad."

The picture was of John Michael heading off to his first day of school. Kindergarten. A brand new blue turtleneck. A pair of Sears jeans. A shiny new metal lunch box. And who could forget those brand new running shoes? They were white with a blue stripe down the side. John Michael was proud of them. Holding him tight outside the yellow school bus was his mother. Elizabeth's orange sweater accented her beautiful deep brown eyes. Her smile tried to hide the tears that were flowing down her cheeks. Even as a child they had struggled to let go of him.

A green cashier's check lay under the note. It was payable to John Michael. The amount was for $110,000. His eyes widened when he saw the numbers.

"Go ahead. Take it out and look at it. It's your check, Son. You can go now. I can't hold you back anymore." Jonathan's lip was trembling. He wanted so badly to break down. But not now, not in front of his son. This was a big moment for John Michael. He needed to be strong for his boy. Like a child on Christmas morning, John Michael's heart raced with excitement. The day had finally come. But how? Why on earth would his father hand him a check like this? After all he had done.

"Dad, what's this all about? This can't be what I think it is? Not tonight. Not now. Look at me? I'm half drunk, Dad. Why on earth would you give your intoxicated son a check for 110 grand? What's the catch here? Is this some kind of guilt trip?"

Jonathan couldn't contain himself anymore. He started to weep quietly, then louder. He covered his face with his hands. The warm tears sifted through his fingers and a pool of water started to form on the wood floorboards. His stomach tightened just like it had the night Elizabeth passed away. John Michael felt uncomfortable. He was glad he was not completely sober. The last time he had seen his father cry like this was at his mother's funeral, when Jonathan had sobbed so hard the soloist couldn't be heard. John Michael remembered biting his lip then, and tonight he bit it again. It wasn't out of anger, but out of knowing there was nothing he could do for his dad to console him. Not many young men see their father cry. From generation to generation, they were taught tears represent weakness. For Jonathan, they were revealing his strength. Jonathan was showing his son how strong his love really was for him. John Michael stood up and moved away from the swing.

"I knew you'd come through, Dad. I knew it."

Jonathan just shook his head. He cleared his throat and tried to say something to his son, but nothing came out. He knew that if he ever wanted John Michael back, he had to let go. The thought of John Michael leaving home was unacceptable to him, yet he had to allow it. How could one of his own sons reject the home they had built? Jonathan felt betrayed. Everything he had worked so hard for as a father was being forgotten. The treasure of family. A place in the community. The heritage of a father, maybe that's what hurt the most. How could his son walk away so quickly from the pride Jonathan felt the Davis family represented? This family meant something in this little village. John Michael's actions were risking it all.

Jonathan's mind jogged back to a moment when John Michael was just a boy. He had gotten in trouble for breaking one of his mother's valuable pieces of china given to her as a family heirloom. John Michael had been sent to his room to think about his behavior. Jonathan remembered walking into John Michael's bedroom only to find a young boy packing.

> "Where are you going, Son?"
> "I'm moving."
> "Moving?"
> John Michael bit his lip. "Yep. I'm going to David's house. His mom and dad won't be mad at me there."
> "Really?"
> "Yep. David never gets in trouble."
> "He doesn't, huh?"
> "Nope. Never. So I'm going there."
> John Michael threw a sports magazine, a basketball, his running shoes, and a football jersey into an old oversized suitcase he had found in the hall closet. Jonathan tried hard not to smile. According to John Michael, this was serious stuff.

Jonathan sat down on the bed where Johnny was trying to fig-ure out how to shut his suitcase. "When do you think you'll be com-ing home?"

"I don't know. Maybe five days."

"Why five days?" said Jonathan, latching the suitcase for his son.

"David's mom will probably run out of food. Then I'll have to come home."

"We'll be here, you know. We don't plan on moving anywhere before then."

"Fine," said John Michael pulling the suitcase off the bed and dragging it through the doorway and down the stairs.

Jonathan stood at the top of the stairwell, watching his son reach for the handle on the door.

"John Michael," came a sweet voice from the kitchen.

John Michael turned around. "What?"

"Don't forget your lunch. It's Saturday, you know, and I don't want you to get hungry when you go outside to play."

"I'm not playing, Mom."

"I know, but you might later. I made this for you."

Elizabeth opened the suitcase and tucked a brown lunch bag under his jersey. She smiled, kissed him and sent him out the door. Through the window they both watched their son walk away. They knew he would return; it was only a matter of time. Once the sand-wich ran out he would be back.

Tonight, Jonathan wasn't so sure John Michael would return like he always had before.

"I guess I'll go pack."

He ran into the house like an animal out of its cage. Up the stairs and to his room he went, pulling out the biggest duffel bag he could find.

Jonathan sat on the porch and tried to collect himself. *That's it? No words of remorse? Not even a thank you?* He reminded himself that he had no expectations going into this, and was to have none going out. This father couldn't compel his son to stay home even though he knew the pain it would cause him and his son to let him go. John Michael had to experience a sense of freedom. It was almost as if Jonathan knew John Michael needed to find his own life, even at the risk of losing it. As a father, he understood it was human nature to fight for independence. As a young man, he had fought for his. Now his son was facing the same decision. Jonathan knew John Michael had to leave.

Philip opened the front door and looked to see if his father was still on the porch. His feet felt cold against the painted wooden floor. Philip sat down next to his dad.

"You didn't do it, did you?"

There was a long pause. The silence answered Philip. "But Dad, how could you do it? He just turned 18. Dad, he just started his last year of high school. How can you just let him go?"

A long silence again. Jonathan cleared his throat and turned to look into the eyes of his youngest.

"Son, I know this is going to be hard for you to understand, but I've done all I can for your brother. I love him more than you will ever know."

"Love?" questioned Philip.

"Love. Let me try to explain. It's kind of like this." Jonathan searched his mind for an appropriate word picture. He remembered a situation all of them had experienced together when the boys were younger. "Remember that bird we trapped in the backyard?"

"I've got it! I've got it!" yelled Lewis from the back of the house.

John Michael, Philip, and their father cut across the front yard, stepped over a few bushes and made their way to a corner behind the house where two fences locked.

"Did you get it, Lewis?" screamed John Michael running up to where his older brother was standing.

Jonathan was breathing deep as he finally caught up with his sons.

"I'm going to have to get faster to keep up with you boys."

"Dad, he got it. He got it!"

"Can we keep it, Dad? Please!" said Lewis, holding the wire garbage can over the bird's body. It flapped its wings and flew up against the wire that was keeping it from flying. Philip tried to touch it through the wire but his little hands were too large to fit through the holes.

"You think we should?" said Jonathan.

"Yes!" agreed all three boys.

"You sure? If its flapping its wings and trying to fly inside our garbage can, what do you think it will do inside a cage?"

Lewis and John Michael glanced at one another. Deep down inside they knew the answer to their father's question. But, for now, it seemed fun to have a pet. Even if they hadn't brought it home from the pet store.

"So," said Jonathan to his son, "what would have happened if we had put that bird in a cage and kept it?"

Philip thought for a moment. He gave the best answer he could think of.

"I don't know, Dad. I guess it would have constantly tried to get out or something."

"You're right, Philip. And every day it would have flapped its wings, hoping that this would be the day it would find freedom. It would have hurt itself trying to get out of that wire mesh until it found an open door or we let it out." Jonathan was struggling; there were a few moments of silence again. "Your brother is like that bird. He's trapped here, Philip, and we have to let him go before he hurts himself too badly."

"You mean, we just let him walk out of our family? But Dad, how can somebody just decide they need to leave?"

"They just do, my boy. They just do. And it's not always possible to stop them. Sometimes we just have to love them. Unlike the bird, the cage he lives in is our home. John Michael's home. Although it's hard to let him go, we have to. It's our only chance of getting him back." Jonathan gently put his arm around his son.

"You don't know for sure that he'll be back, do you?"

Jonathan paused and then teared up again.

"Son, when you can't trust my plan, trust my heart."

Jonathan pulled Philip near to his chest. Although a hug wouldn't make it all go away, he knew it would help. Philip wasn't looking for all the right answers, he was looking for someone to hold him and let him know that somehow it was all going to be all right.

The front door suddenly squeaked open. The light from inside the house hurt their eyes. A voice spoke out the darkness.

"I hope you didn't give him any of my share of Mom's money. I wouldn't want it to be wasted."

The door suddenly opened even wider and cast another silhouette in the doorway.

"Don't worry, it won't," said John Michael to Lewis. "I wouldn't think of wasting your money. You're already wasting it all on your boring life anyway. Watch me, big brother. I'll be back with more than I ever left with."

"Dream on," replied Lewis.

John Michael ignored him. "Uh, Dad, do you have any extra toothpaste?"

Jonathan stood up and made his way into the house. John Michael followed him.

"Upstairs. It's all I have. You're welcome to it."

"Thanks, Dad," said John Michael as he hurried up the stairs.

Lewis yelled after him sarcastically, "Oh, and you might as well take our shampoo. And the shaving cream, too. And don't forget my razor. In fact, why don't you just take everything you can find!" His tone had changed to anger now.

"Lewis," said Jonathan firmly. "Stop. You're only making this harder on all of us. He can have whatever he wants. I'd be willing to give him everything it if would help in some way."

"That's the problem, Dad. You're giving him everything he wants."

"As I would for you, Son. I love you just the same."

Lewis mumbled something under his breath. Before Jonathan could respond, John Michael made his way down the stairs. Philip yawned. It was late, but John Michael wasn't about to stop. He set a large duffel bag and his backpack at the bottom of the steps. The duffel bag didn't seem that full to Jonathan. Then again, when had John Michael ever packed for himself? Johnny headed for the kitchen. They all followed.

"You find everything you need?"

"Yep," said John Michael, making a sandwich.

Philip pushed himself up on the counter. "You can't go, John Michael. You can't just pack up and leave. What about us? What about me? What about Mom?"

"Have to, little brother. You'll understand someday." He put the peanut butter and jelly in a nearby cupboard while Jonathan, Philip, and Lewis stared. They were in shock. Could a member of their family really be leaving? Just like that?

With a sandwich in his hand, a backpack on his back, and a duffel bag strapped over his shoulder, John Michael headed for the door. It was all happening so fast.

"Love you, little brother. See you, Lewis. Thanks for believing in me, Dad. I'll call you when I get there."

"There? Where's there?" begged Philip.

"Don't know yet. But I'll get there." The front door opened...and slammed shut. The sound of it echoed through the otherwise still house. Time froze. The living room clock ticked loudly. The three of them stood by the door waiting to see if it would open again. Maybe he would have a change of heart. Philip started to scream uncontrollably.

"No, Dad. No. Please, no." He ran up the stairs like a little child with too many feelings and questions to know what to do with. He ran into his room as fast as he could. He ripped open the shades and searched the dark street for any signs of his brother walking away. There. He found him among the shadows of the streetlights. His brother, John Michael, walking down the street alone.

Jonathan couldn't contain himself anymore. He jumped for the door, grabbed hold of the handle and turned it as fast as he could. He bolted out of the house and to the end of the porch. He scanned the area for his son. He could faintly see him walking in the distance, duffel bag and all. Once again his face flushed red and his eyes filled with tears. Jonathan cupped his hands over his mouth yelling as loud as he could…

"John Michael! John Michael!"

The shadowed figure stopped. A dog started to bark and the porch light from next door came on.

"JOHN MICHAEL! I LOVE YOU! DON'T YOU EVER FORGET THAT! I LOVE YOU!"

Jonathan's hands reached through the cool night air towards his son, grabbing hold of nothing but a handful of the darkness. John Michael turned his head one last time to look back. Home. The porch light was on. He could see his father's silhouette standing there peering, looking anxiously for his middle son. The house looked so peaceful, so inviting. He wanted to run back to his father's arms, but not now. He needed to leave. He'd heard his father's words loud and clear. He turned around and continued walking.

Lewis stood inside the front door and stared. Philip stared from his window. Jonathan stared from the porch. All was quiet except for a few dogs barking and a chorus of crickets. The porch light next door went off. Jonathan kept his on just in case a very special boy he knew would need to find his way home.

Six

Tinted Windows

The smell of diesel fuel filled the morning air as another Greyhound bus made its way out of the terminal and onto the street. Another bus full of people traveling. Some of them visiting friends or relatives. Some of them vacationing in different parts of the country. Some of them running away from problems they didn't want to face. Bills. Marriages that didn't work out. Broken families. Torn relationships. Insecurities. Failures. Consequences. And home. Some of them just running from home. John Michael sat on the bench in front of the Willowbrook Greyhound Station. He didn't have enough cash on him to buy a plane ticket in nearby Wichita, so a bus was the next affordable mode of transportation. Maybe he wouldn't get a can of soda or a pack of peanuts, but at least he could get on the road.

He yawned, resting his head on the back of the bench. His bus was leaving soon; he decided to sleep on the ride. Last night seemed like a distant memory. He had spent most of the morning walking around the streets of Willowbrook. After calling a few airlines from an all-night donut shop, he made his way to the downtown bus station. He wondered if his father would come down looking for him. He hadn't seen any evidence of that so far.

Philip hung up the pay phone inside the lobby of the Greyhound ticket area. He had gotten up early this Saturday. This was very important to him. He had left a note on his father's bedroom door.

It seemed like no one at the Wichita Airport was willing to help him find his brother. It was too big, and there were too many people. He had his brother paged a few times, but had no luck finding him. The bus station was his only hope. He looked around the lobby. A bus just didn't seem like John Michael's style, but when you're running you'll take whatever you can get. He made his way to the revolving door and pushed forward to the street outside. He noticed a nearby bench and sat down. His body ached. The pain reminded him he had been walking all morning. He needed just a few minutes of rest. The man seated next to him turned the other way. The smoke from his cigarette nearly choked Philip. The man cleared his throat. It sounded like John Michael when he cleared his throat. When you miss your brother, everything seems to remind you of him. Another puff of smoke drifted in his direction. The man spit on the sidewalk in front of the bench. Philip turned and looked at the person, disgusted at the gross gesture. *It is John Michael*, a voice inside his head screamed..

"John Michael?"

John Michael turned his head. Even though it had only been a few hours, he looked so different already. Lost. Alone. Tougher. Harder. He wasn't the same brother Philip had watched walk out of the house not long ago.

John Michael threw his cigarette to his feet and stepped on it. He blew the last puff of smoke out.

"Philip, what are you doing here? How did you find me?" John Michael seemed irritated and shocked.

"I called the airport, and then a few of your friends. This was my last hope. I thought you might take a bus." Philip moved closer to him. Another bus left the terminal and headed down the street.

"I've got to hand it to you, little brother. You were right. Didn't have enough cash to do a plane. Anyway, I've got to go in five minutes." John Michael glanced at his watch and then pulled another cigarette out of his pocket. He lit it and a cloud of smoke swirled Philip's way.

"What's this? said Philip, grabbing the cigarette out of John Michael's mouth and tossing it to the ground. He was more firm with his older brother than he had been before. "Johnny, what's up? It's like I don't even know you anymore. What's going on with you? What happened to my big brother? I mean, you're the guy I've looked up to my whole life. And now, I don't even know how to look at you. John Michael, you really aren't going to leave, are you?"

There was a long pause. John Michael lit another smoke. "Why shouldn't I leave?"

"Why shouldn't you leave?" Philip stood and looked down at his older brother. "You have two brothers that love you, not to mention a father who really cares, and a mother who would step out of her grave if she knew what you were doing."

"Let's get this straight once and for all before I leave, Philip. That's one little brother who loves me and one older brother who couldn't care less, a father whom I just can't live with right now, and a mother who is in her grave. Forever! She's dead, Philip. Let's leave her there, OK?" He didn't like where this conversation was going. Why couldn't he just get on the bus?

It took Philip a moment to collect himself. "John Michael, I love you. Isn't that enough? Please, don't leave. I'll do anything. I'll clean your room, do the dishes when you're supposed to. I'll even do your algebra homework. I'll do that for you, too." Philip didn't stop there. He began pacing beside the bench, listing one idea after another.

John Michael stood up, grabbed Philip's shoulders, and looked him straight in the eyes. "Philip, I'm going."

That was it? Just like that? Philip looked away. He'd lost this one. The battle had been won by his older brother.

"But, Johnny, how will you make it? Where will you live? Who's going to pick up your shoes and wash your underwear? We've relied on each other ever since Mom died." The tears started flowing. Philip sat down on the bench overwhelmed at the thought of his brother leaving home. He knew there was nothing else he could say or do.

"It won't last forever, Philip. Think of it as time away at college or something. I'll be fine. Don't worry about me."

"But how can you just leave school? You're almost done, Johnny. It's your last year. Why now?"

"Why not?"

"But what happens when you run out of money? How will you get a job?"

"I won't need one, Philip. This check will cover me for awhile." John Michael pulled the check out of his pocket to show Philip.

"I guess Dad gave it to you, huh."

"I knew he would. I just didn't know when."

"That's a lot of money, you know?"

"I know. By the time I need to worry about cash something will come along, some kind of job, then I'll be standing on my own two feet."

Philip was taking it all in. He grabbed a handful of cash out of his coat pocket and handed it over to John Michael.

"Here," he said, struggling to make it through.

"What's this?"

"Some money I've been saving to buy myself some new basketball shoes."

John Michael took the money and started to count it.

"Seventy-five dollars? Philip, I don't need this. This is yours. Go buy your shoes."

He threw the money in his brother's lap and stood up. The dollar bills littered the ground by the bench. There was no way he was going to take charity from him. Philip collected the cash and stood up next to John Michael.

"You have to. I want some part of me to go with you. Save it. Put it somewhere you can get to it if you ever really need it. All right?"

"No way. I've already told you my check will take care of me."

John Michael pulled out his bus ticket and looked at his watch. Philip quickly stuffed the money into a small pocket in the front of John Michael's duffel bag and zipped it up. John Michael put the bus ticket back in his coat pocket.

"I've gotta go. I'll be fine. Look, you're not going to find my face on a milk carton," John Michael said, grinding his cigarette butt into the ground. "I've got my freedom, my space, my money, and best of all, I've got the rest of my life to just soak it all in. I know you don't understand, but I've got to do this. Don't worry, Philip. I've got everything I need."

"No, you don't, John Michael."

"What do you mean?"

Philip's eyes filled with tears. "You won't have me."

Philip embraced John Michael. They stood in front of the bus station and shared a moment neither of them would ever forget. The years together raced through their minds. The stones they skipped as boys. The bike they dropped on the hood of Dad's brand new car trying to get it off the hooks on the ceiling in the garage. Racing to the mailbox with brand new white socks on their feet. Jumping on their beds until they'd cave in. Raiding the refrigerator on Friday nights, sleeping in on Saturday mornings. Philip held on tight. The last time they had embraced like this, John Michael had told Philip their mother wasn't going to make it.

"It's Mom," said John Michael tearing up as he sat next to Philip in the small waiting room area.

Philip looked outside the small window and stared at the rain dancing on the window ledge. He was silent. The tone in John Michael's voice made it obvious what Philip would hear next.

"She...she didn't make it."

Both boys started weeping uncontrollably. John Michael grabbed Philip and held him close to his chest. The loud sobs soon turned to deep cries.

Lewis had chosen to stay in the hall with his head down. He glanced in the window occasionally only to see his two brothers melted together at the thought of never seeing their mother again. They stayed that way until Jonathan came in to take them to see Elizabeth's body one last time. As they walked down the corridor the three boys and their father locked arms. A nurse passed by but was cordial enough to go another direction after she noticed the looks on their faces.

John Michael and Philip let go of each other. Philip reached for his pocket. He pulled out a shiny brass key with a piece of string tied to it and placed it around John Michael's neck.

"It's from Dad. He told me to give it to you if I found you."

"What's it for?" he asked, as he held it in front of his eyes.

"Home. Whenever you decide to come home."

John Michael stared into the distance. His mind was a thousand miles away. For a split second he longed to be home. He blinked as his focus came back and quickly said, "I've got to go." He held up his boarding pass. There was an awkward silence and then he walked away. He turned and looked at Philip before heading into the station.

"I love you, little brother."

Philip sat down on the bench and watched him go. John Michael pushed on the glass and was soon swallowed by the revolving door. Philip was hoping to go home with his brother; now he would be going home alone.

As the bus left the parking lot he waved. He couldn't see his brother through the tinted windows though. It felt like no one was waving back, but he knew John Michael was. Maybe not with his hand, but Philip knew down deep inside, he was waving in his heart.

Seven

The Price of Freedom

John Michael rested his arm on top of the handle of the mop. He was staring into space. His mind was miles away, remembering Philip's face fading into the distance as the bus rolled away. He couldn't stop thinking about his brother's expression. He knew Philip was confused and disappointed, but he had to leave, even if it meant hurting him. John Michael placed his hands on the window reaching out for his baby brother one last time. But Philip couldn't see him. The darkened windows were reinforcing his reputation. Calm, cool and collected.

A man stumbled into the bathroom to use one of the toilets. His worn tennis shoes slid across the tile as he made his way to one of the stalls. John Michael ignored him and continued to mop. The toilet flushed and the man threw open the metal door and made his way across the freshly mopped surface. John Michael bit his lip as he watched the man scurry into a corner of the bathroom and lie down. He rested his head on one arm so his face wouldn't touch the cold floor. He fixed his eyes on John Michael and stared. He sighed. The smell of liquor on his breath wasn't new to him. He smelled it nightly, daily, and even hourly in some cases. The stranger lying on the bathroom floor continued to stare at John Michael. John Michael started to talk again.

"Stop looking at me like I'm such a bad guy."

The man didn't respond. John Michael started to mop again.

"I didn't ruin everybody's life. They were ruining my life. I had to do it, all right? I had to!"

He walked over to his new acquaintance.

"Just like you had to. Why? WHY? C'mon, you and I both know why, because we can't see past ourselves. That's why. My dad never let me go. I let go of him."

He started to mop again.

"Freedom. I wanted freedom. So did you. And freedom is what we got."

He turned around and cursed at the man.

"Would you stop staring at me? Everybody wants freedom, right? They just don't realize what it will cost them."

John Michael remembered back to a conversation his father had had with him several years ago. It was about mowing the grass. John Michael was begging for more allowance, but Jonathan insisted on not increasing the amount unless his son was willing to increase his workload around the house. John Michael agreed, and the lawn was his brand new stint. Up to that point he had split the duty with his brothers, but now it was all his. His first full-fledged job that put all the responsibility in his lap. John Michael was excited about his independence. Now, he could really make his father proud of him. He loved receiving his father's approval.

As the summer dragged on, Jonathan noticed that his sod was far from being cut on a regular basis. In fact, one afternoon Jonathan had been offered a weekly lawn service by one of his neighbors! He knew John Michael wasn't keeping up his end of the agreement. In an effort to help his son get priorities straight, he asked him out for dinner one late July evening to explain his thoughts.

"Johnny," his dad said, "you want to make more money, but you aren't willing to pay the price."

"Dad, I've mowed it a few times this summer. C'mon."

"How many times, Son? Honestly?" said Jonathan gently.

John Michael started getting restless. He stared into the distance. This would be an easy place to lie. He looked into the eyes of his father.

"I don't know. Maybe four."

"Two. I've counted. So has the neighborhood."

"If it looked so bad, why didn't you mow it then, Dad?"

"Whose job was it?" Jonathan said patiently.

John Michael studied the grain of the wooden table they were sitting at.

"Mine," he said softly.

This would have been a good place for a lecture on the expectations Jonathan had for his son, but that wasn't what John Michael needed. John Michael had been fully aware of what was expected of him.

"Johnny, if I covered your every mistake how would you ever learn what was right and what was wrong?"

"I don't know. Isn't that what a dad is for?"

"Oh, I wish that were true. I have to teach you that every decision you make has a price. This particular situation has a price tag. How much are you willing to pay for it?" Jonathan brought the conversation back to John Michael's world. "If you want more allowance, then you have to pay the price of doing more of the work."

"It looks like I failed this one, huh?"

Jonathan answered patiently again, "Yes, you did, but it's not fatal. You need to get back up on your feet and finish taking care of the responsibility you were given."

John Michael was quiet. He stared at the plate of food in front of him.

"So, are you gonna bust me?"

Jonathan thought for a moment.

"No," he replied. John Michael looked up at his father.

"Just blow the dust off the mower tomorrow and let's try again to keep that lawn from being the sore spot on our street. Deal?"

John Michael smiled. "Deal, Dad."

They shook on that one, but not on this. There was no deal today. Instead, he was paying the price. John Michael started talking to the man lying in the corner again.

" 'Count the cost,' Dad always said. 'Count the cost.' "

Eight

A New Life

John Michael stared out the bus windows at the twinkling skyline of the windy city. Big lights, big city. Or so it seemed. He had never been to Chicago, or any other metropolis for that matter. Except for Wichita, he had never really seen the streets of a major metropolitan area. Although he felt a bit of fear pounding inside his spirit, the excitement in his heart diverted it. His eyes were wide open, like a child opening gifts on Christmas morning. The buildings, from John Michael's perspective, seemed to stretch to the sky and beyond. It was more beautiful than anything he had ever dreamed. *The possibilities are endless*, he thought.

The bus circled the driveway and stopped. The passengers unloaded under a large canopy that sheltered them as they came into the station. John Michael collected his things and stepped off the stairs eventually walking away from the vehicle. It had been over 24 hours since he had left Willowbrook. He turned back to take one last glance at his only link to home. It was one of the greatest moments of his life —a cornerstone. *I am finally free!*

The streets were crowded and dark as he made his way towards the buildings that formed the skyline. He had never really been away from home, at least not on his own. There was a family trip to California, and he had gone on a business trip to Florida with his dad, but most of his life had been spent on the home front. Now home wasn't something he was thinking about. No more school. No more homework. No more authorities. This seemed like the life he had always fantasized about. It wasn't that he didn't like home, he just couldn't deal with being there right now. Too many issues. Too much pain. He started to think about his mother and quickly decided to meditate on something else.

John Michael's feet were getting tired. He had been walking for hours and was at a loss for direction and time. He looked up. The view was spectacular. All he could see were buildings. Big ones. Small ones. Old ones. New ones. A bus rolled by him and the smell of diesel fuel filled his lungs. He liked his new world. John Michael was finally living out his dream of independence. It felt good to be alone.

The check in his pocket meant freedom. He needed to get it cashed. All he had on him was a few dollars and some change. Enough to buy him a cheeseburger, fries, and a drink. He sat down on a bench off of Michigan Avenue and started to eat.

"Get off my bench!"

John Michael stopped chewing on his fries and looked around. He didn't see anyone.

"Get off my bench!"came the voice again.

He looked around nervously. The voice thundered back, this time louder and harsher than before.

"I said it once and I'm not going to again. If you don't get off my bench, I'll..."

John Michael jumped up. The fast food bag dropped to the ground. John Michael ran as quickly as he could down the one way street. He ran over 12 city blocks before he slowed down. He was carrying a duffel bag in one hand and his backpack in the other. He didn't know where he was, or what he was doing. All he knew was that someone had threatened him for sitting on a bench.

A man in a long black coat approached him. John Michael froze. The man proceeded to unbutton his jacket and open it. John Michael started to sweat; he was still a little shaken up from his experience at the bench. He envisioned a pistol being drawn, a shot fired, and his body dropping to the ground. Instead the stranger opened his jacket, pulled down the inside liner of his coat and showed him dozens of gold watches.

"The best Chicago has to offer. Rolex. Bulova. Seiko."

Before he heard another word, John Michael shook his head, pushed the man out of his way, and started running again.

As he rounded the corner and turned down an alley, he looked back. The individual in the jacket was out of sight. He turned back around and walked straight into two women. They were scantily dressed.

"Well, well, well. What do we have here?"

John Michael looked away. One of them reached out and stroked his face.

"Look at me when I'm talking to you, honey."

He continued to look in another direction. The smell of liquor was on her breath.

"Why don't you come home with us, sugar? You look like you've lost your mommy."

The two women started to laugh. One of them exhaled a puff of smoke in John Michael's face. He started to cough. They laughed again and he took off down the alley, through a parking lot, and then down a side street. His heart was pounding. His feet were racing. He began wondering about the price of freedom.

John Michael noticed another bench on the opposite side of the road. He tried to see if anyone was under it. Nope, nobody there. He waited until the light turned green and then crossed the street. His aching feet needed a rest. He sat down. His hands were shaking. He put his face in his hands and wiped away his sweat. He closed his eyes and rested.

"So where does a kid like you come from?"

It was happening again. John Michael looked up. A man stood next to him. He was not wearing a trenchcoat. In fact, he was dressed rather well. His outward appearance made John Michael feel a little more at home. His dark wavy hair, black pants, leather jacket and Doc Martin boots impressed John Michael. This guy had style. John Michael lifted his head more confidently now. This stranger had been the most friendly person he had met so far.

"Somebody cut your tongue out?"the man said more forcefully and less friendly. "I asked you where you were from. You gonna answer me?"

"Ah, away. Outside the Chicago area."

"I can see that. You don't look like a city kid."

"I don't?"

The man circled the bench.

"Look at you. Look at what you're wearing. And that fancy haircut. You aren't from these parts." He sat down next to John Michael.

John Michael felt it was safe to give a few answers. "I've never been here before."

"Dude, you're gonna get your butt kicked down here. A little rich boy like you. What's up? You runnin' away from home?"

"No way," said John Michael defensively. "I'm not. I'm old enough to decide whether I live at home or not, all right. Maybe this is my home."

"OK, man. Just an observation. I thought I'd ask."

The man reached out his hand. John Michael flinched at first, then shook the man's hand back.

"The name's Logan. I live a few blocks from here. You gotta name?"

"Ah, you can call me Michael. Yeah, Michael." He liked the name change.

"Michael, huh? Don't know any Michaels down here. You're the first. How long you been living here?"

"I don't know. What's with all the questions?"

"Dude, are you nervous or what? I'm not gonna pull out a piece and shoot you if that's what you think."

John Michael paused for a moment, then let out a long, deep breath. He was nervous, very nervous. His stomach was in knots. He hadn't let go of his grip on the bench since Logan had started the conversation with him.

"Sorry. I, uh, I've never been on this side of town. You said you live here?"

"Let's just say I frequent this part of town often. I saw you sitting here lookin' a little scared and I thought, now there's a man who needs someone to show him around."

John Michael pulled out a cigarette and lit it. He offered one to Logan.

"No, thanks. I smoke better stuff."

"Oh, really, what's that?"

"Hang with me for awhile and I'll show you."

John Michael thought he might. This man could be the ticket he had been hoping for. He was lost in such a big place. At least for now, at least for tonight he'd found someone who might be able to help. It was getting late, and John Michael needed a place to stay.

A few people passed by. Late night folks. They were drunk and staggered by the bench dodging into a nearby bar. Logan and John Michael stared at the skyline that surrounded them.

"Nice lookin' city, huh?" said Logan to John Michael.

"I've never seen anything like it."

"No matter how many times I stare at it, I always see something new."

"Really?"

"Like right over there." Logan pointed towards the John Hancock building. "See that building next to the tall one? The one with all the lights on top? I've never seen that before. Man, how do they build these things so fast?"

"The tallest building I've ever seen was in Wichita."

"Wichita? Where in the world is that?"

"Kansas. You've never heard of it?"

"Not really. I don't have a lot of business outside of Chicago. I stay pretty busy right here. So what's Kansas look like?"

"All I've ever seen are fields of wheat, cattle, and tumbleweed. Now, this—this is much better than a bunch of wheat."

"You're telling me. I couldn't handle it. I'd get bored too fast."

"Believe me, I know. Why do you think I left?"

Logan was starting to probe now.

"Why *did* you leave?"

John Michael stared at the lights on a nearby building. He was thinking about his father.

"Had to. I couldn't take it anymore."

"Take what? You look like you were well taken care of there."

"Let's just drop it, all right. I don't want to talk about it."

"Whatever you say. You need a place to stay tonight?"

A man with a cane made his way towards the bench. He was touching everything with his hands as if he couldn't see. The man knocked the cane into Logan's leg.

"Hey, watch where you're puttin' that thing."

The man looked down at them. He was wearing sunglasses and it was almost midnight.

"Oh excuse me. Would you happen to have some spare change for a blind man who could use a good meal?"

John Michael started to feel around in his pockets; he knew he had a few coins, and his father had always taught him to give to those in need.

"I think I have some. Just a minute." John Michael continued searching his pockets.

Logan gave the man a second glance.

"Wait a minute here. Don't I know you? You look really familiar. How long have you been blind?"

The man started to get nervous.

"A long time. A really long time."

"Since yesterday?"

"Could have been."

Logan was on to him. John Michael took it all in.

"I thought I saw a man that looked like you yesterday. Except he wasn't blind. As of 24 hours ago he only had one arm. He was begging for cash on the corner of 11th and Michigan."

The blind man looked stunned.

"My brother. That was my brother. I was born blind. He was born without an arm. Problems, every family's got 'em. I was the blind sheep of the family. Baa, baa. You know how it goes." Logan stood in the man's face.

"No, I don't. Why don't you tell me?"

Logan reached for the man's sunglasses and took them off. The man's eyes widened to the size of a couple of silver dollars.

"Wait a minute," shouted the blind man, "I can see. I can see! It's a miracle!" He started dancing around. "It's a miracle. I've gotta go tell my brother about the miracle. Maybe he got a new arm. Happens to starfish every day."

The man turned and ran as fast as he could. Logan chased him a few steps, then came back. All the action had brought John Michael to his feet. Logan put his arm around John Michael's shoulders.

"If you're gonna live down here, you gotta watch out for those guys. They'll take your money. All of it. That's if you got any. A little rich boy like you has to have some kind of cash."

They started to walk down the street together.

"Actually, I need money. I've got a pretty big check I need cashed. Do you think you could help me find a place to do that?"

"You're talkin' to the right man. I can take you to the bank where I do all my business."

As they continued to walk, John Michael continued to spill. The relationship was going right where Logan had desired. He was earning John Michael's trust. And that's what it was all about for Logan—earning this innocent boy's trust. If John Michael would trust him—then he would do anything for him. Anything.

They made their way down an empty Chicago street. Logan pulled out a set of keys and unlocked the back door of an old brownstone. Although the outside looked dreary, the inside of the building was totally different. It had been completely restored. It even smelled new. Logan made his way to one of the apartments located at the end of a long corridor. John Michael had always remembered his father's advice never to go inside a stranger's home, but tonight that advice seemed childish. Besides, John Michael felt like a man now. He could make his own decisions.

"My place is right up here," said Logan, leading him to a door numbered 231.

"Are you sure this is all right? I can sleep somewhere else."

"You ain't sleepin' no place else. You're with me. Besides, we're friends now, right? Somebody's gotta watch your back or these streets will be the end of you."

He opened the door. The loft apartment was tastefully decorated with trendy furniture. It reminded John Michael of an apartment he'd seen in an expensive magazine. Original paintings lined the walls, not to mention the large screen television and leather couch that sat in the corner of the room. The kitchen was small, but Logan wasn't much for cooking at home. In fact, it looked like it hadn't been touched since he moved in.

"You want something to eat? Everything's in the refrigerator. There's a case of beer and I think there's some bread to make a sandwich. Peanut butter is all I got."

"That's OK. I just need a place to stay for a few days."

"Hey, you can stay here as long as you'd like. You can sleep on the couch. If you need anything else, help yourself."

"Thanks, man."

"You're welcome. Tomorrow morning we can head down to my bank."

"Cool."

"It's down on Michigan. It's where I keep most of my cash."

"All right. Thanks, man. I appreciate all the help."

"Oh, you got it. That's what I'm here for, Michael." He turned around, pleased with how things were going with John Michael. His new prospect was starting to let his guard down. A door of opportunity was beginning to open for Logan. He knew John Michael wasn't dumb. But, he was simple. And that was Logan's specialty. He had built his life preying on the young and the naïve.

Nine

The View From Here

John Michael slept late the next morning. In fact, he didn't wake up until late afternoon. When he did, he noticed the apartment was empty. Logan was gone. John Michael figured he was at work. He sat down on the couch and stared out the glass pane. The view wasn't very exciting, just another brick building. There was no beautiful tree like the one he and his family had planted outside his bedroom window. John Michael walked over to the window, slid it up, and climbed out onto the fire escape. He took a deep breath and filled his lungs with the dirty city air. It was such a different world from what he was used to. Loud horns, people walking, people talking, occasionally even people screaming. He had traded white cotton ball clouds for puffy imitations of smog. It seemed like a bargain, at least for now. Tomorrow would be a new adventure, and yesterday would soon become a memory. Even so, in the pit of his stomach there was a feeling he couldn't shake. Home—deep down inside he missed home, but there was no backing out now. He had just spent the night in the apartment of a man he had only known for a few minutes. The next phase of his life would definitely be an adventure, and he knew it. What John Michael didn't expect was the kind of ride he was in for.

The sounds and sights of the city still intrigued him. The traffic never seemed to stop, and people were everywhere. He looked down through the iron bars he was standing on into the alley below. He noticed a man sleeping next to a garbage can. The man looked lifeless. John Michael wondered if he was dead. He vowed he'd never end up like that. A lady pushed her old shopping cart into the alley. She was wearing an old ripped tan coat. A red scarf covered her head, hiding her face. The cart was full of black garbage bags of trash that to her were filled with beautiful treasures. She started to sift through the dumpster the man was sleeping by. He woke up screaming, scaring her away. John Michael shook his head and turned to the skyline of Chicago. The enormous buildings seemed to touch the sky. He thought of all the people who worked in them. He glanced down at the man and then back at the buildings. He wondered how totally different people could be found within a few miles of one another living such different lives—the big corporate hot shots working in the skyscrapers and the beggar on the street. In Kansas, he'd always thought everyone lived equally. You work hard, raise your family, and then you die. He longed for something different, something better. Even if it meant sacrificing everything. He snapped out of his train of thought and made his way back into the red brick building.

Logan had scribbled something on the front page of an old newspaper and left it on the counter. "Went to take care of some things for you."

Why is this guy so willing to help, he wondered. He decided that maybe that's just the way people were here. Helpful—Logan seemed genuinely helpful.

His outfit had been glued to him for several days. John Michael knew he needed to change, so he opened his duffel bag and took out one of the two things he had packed to wear. He wasn't too worried about being a fashion statement. Once he had money from his check he could afford some new clothes—some nice clothes. He changed his t-shirt, but left on the same jeans. While he was putting on his hat he heard a key in the door. For a moment it made him nervous. Was leaving home really worth facing all of these fears? The handle turned and the door opened. Logan stepped inside. He had several packages in his hand.

"Man, I thought you were never going to wake up." He came in and set some decorative shopping bags on the couch.

"I didn't realize I was so tired," John Michael said, rubbing his eyes.

"Man, you were out."

"What time did you leave? I didn't even hear you."

"I don't know, around lunch time. Here. I brought you something to eat. Thought you might be hungry."

He placed a fast food bag on the counter. A hamburger and fries, John Michael's favorite. How did he know?

"Thanks, man. And thanks for letting me stay at your place. Really."

"A man with some manners. Where'd you say you were from?"

John Michael tried to change the subject. "I was outside for few minutes today. Is this a safe part of town?"

Logan started to unpack the bags and sat down on the couch. "Not really. You wouldn't want to be hanging out around here at night or anything. But, it helps me get the job done, if you know what I mean."

"What do you mean?"

"My work is in this neighborhood for now. So, I'll live here until it's done, then I'll move on. You're asking me more questions than I ask you. Here. I figured you wouldn't have much stuff so I picked up some clothes for you to wear."

Logan held up several outfits for John Michael to see. Top of the line. Name brand stuff that cost more than John Michael had ever been allowed to buy at home.

"You bought this stuff for me?"

"You got it. It'll help fill up that closet of yours."

"What closet?"

Logan handed John Michael a key.

"Few blocks over. Got a friend who said you could rent the place as long as you needed it."

John Michael couldn't believe this. Why was this guy being so good to him? It's not like he had anything to offer Logan.

"Are you serious?"

"Of course I am. We'll go see it later. Believe me, it's nothing much, but it will be a roof over your head until you get your check cashed."

Logan stared directly at him. He was hoping the gifts he had bought were the ticket to keeping John Michael around. Logan could see the potential in him.

John Michael started getting nervous. "Yes, my check."

"Listen, grab your food and let's head down to the bank. If you want, you can use my address if they need a permanent residence. I'll vouch for you. Then, we'll swing on over to the Java Club."

"Java Club?"

"It's where me and my friends hang out. It's kind of a coffee shop."

"Coffee shop?"

"Coffee shop. Dude, if this is your new home, then we'd better get you some new friends. And, that's where me and my friends hang out.

"Let's go. Grab your duffel. We'll drop you off at your new place later."

"We?"

"Myself and your new friends, Michael."

Logan and John Michael made their way on foot several blocks to the heart of Chicago's Loop. Their trip to the bank was a smooth one. Logan's eyes almost fell onto the bank teller's desk top when he saw the amount of his friend's check. Because of the amount, John Michael wouldn't be able to withdraw from it for a few weeks. So, Logan loaned John Michael a few hundred dollars to get by.

John Michael stayed close to Logan as he noticed the creatures the city seemed to bring out. Between an alley and a large brownstone building sat the Java Club. A neon sign that flickered on and off decorated the main window. John Michael noticed the old furniture and '60s-style light fixtures through the glass doors. It reminded him of a movie he had once seen. He expected to see a number of grumpy old men drinking coffee inside, and punchy waitresses taking their orders. Instead, he found what he had been longing for. A new life, a few new friends, and a chance to escape the reality of what he needed to face back home.

As he made his way through the glass door he squinted, trying to see through the smoke that was hanging in the air. Behind the counter sat a man with long hair pulled back in a ponytail. He had one ring in his nose and three in his ear. Pierced. Everyone seemed to be pierced. Young adults were hunched around several small tables. People just like him. Some had red hair, and some a shade of green. There was even one girl who had her hair dyed five different colors. Logan attracted everyone's attention as he made his way between the tables. He was everything that John Michael had dreamed of becoming—cool, calm, and convincingly collected. John Michael felt like he was in the spotlight following Logan. A few people looked him up and down. His conservative street clothes were drawing as much attention here as the colored hair would have done in Willowbrook.

"Logan, over here," came a voice from one side of the shop. Sitting closely together around a small wooden table were several individuals. Logan made his way to them.

"Hey, man, what's up? I thought you guys would be here." Logan said as he greeted each of them. The age difference between Logan and the group was obvious.

John Michael stared at the ground. He felt so uncomfortable. It was like walking into a family reunion only to find out it's not your family. He heard them whispering.

"Oh yeah. I want you guys to meet Michael. He's a new friend of mine."

They looked in his direction, immediately intimidating him.

"Uh, hi," said John Michael quietly.

"Let me introduce you to the family. This is Mort, he's my main man." An older looking man with a bald head and a ring piercing the base of his nose stared John Michael down. "This is my only woman, Esmerelda." A girl with orange hair and beautiful dark skin smiled and winked at Logan. She took a sip from her cup of coffee. Michael noticed the steel rod stuck through the middle of her tongue. "Shawnee, the other woman in my life." They all laughed and a scantily dressed Asian girl who reminded Michael of a beautiful China doll waved in his direction. "And this is Garret, but we call him Bob." Once again, they all laughed. Obviously, an inside joke. "He goes by a lot of different names. And that's Georgy and Stan. Everyone, meet Michael."

Between puffs of smoke and sips from coffee cups they greeted him. John Michael pulled up a chair and took out a cigarette. He liked being called Michael. For him, it felt even more like a fresh start in life.

"So where are you from?" asked Mort shifting his eyes in John Michael's direction.

"Uh, outside of Chicago."

"Really? Me, too. I used to live in Skokie," Shawnee said.

"Where is Skokie?"

Mort grunted and spoke up. "You don't know where Skokie is?"

John Michael started to blush. "No, not really. I live a little farther out."

Shawnee continued, "North side, 53rd Street. Now there's a convenience store where my house used to be."

There was a lull at the table. The conversation seemed to come to a halt with a visitor there. John Michael stared at the tiles on the floor.

"What brings someone like you down here, anyway? Are you here for the rave tonight?"asked Mort.

"I'm looking for a new place to live. Got tired of home and thought this place might work. I'd seen Chicago on a couple of television shows and thought it looked like a cool place to start a new life."

They all broke out in laughter, except for Shawnee. "What? I don't get it. What are you all laughing at?"

John Michael wondered what they were joking about, too. His face flushed red. He wasn't laughing.

"Hey, man, lighten up," said Mort. "We're just laughing because we can't believe you would want to live here. Most people you meet down here are tryin' to break out of this hole. It just sounds funny to hear someone say they want to live here."

"What I'm trying to figure out is how this kid ever trusted someone like Logan. He must not know you," Garret said, pointing to Logan. He was tall and thin, dressed in all black.

"Hey, hey there," said Logan back, "you can trust me. Right?"

Shawnee laughed innocently. John Michael didn't know how to respond.

"Trust," shot back Stan, a tall, lanky character with a snake tattoo that came up from below his neck and stopped with the tail on his cheek. "Who trusts anybody down here? Everyone's out for themselves. Take care of yourself and you'll be fine." He took out a long cigar from inside his coat and lit it.

Esmerelda stared at John Michael's hair. "I think we're going to need to make some changes, you know, if you want to fit in down here."

The guys started to laugh.

"Watch out, man," remarked Mort, "the girl is playing house again. Be careful or she'll change everything about you."

"I will not! I just want little Mikey to like it here."

John Michael looked away. He signaled the waitress for a cup of coffee. She signaled him back. It was not a friendly gesture however. A few moments later she dropped off a white ceramic cup and saucer with a steaming cup of hot java. John Michael sipped some down.

"So where are you all from?" he said innocently.

They stared back.

Mort spoke directly into John Michael's face. "Man, this boy likes to talk."

"I couldn't get him to say much last night. I bring him down here, and bam! he won't shut up," added Logan.

John Michael was starting to enjoy this. These new friends weren't so bad after all, were they? In fact, the thought of them being his new family gave him a sense of belonging he had been searching for. He was starting to feel good about himself again. He closed his eyes and held onto his forehead.

"You all right, new boy?" Stan asked a number of times.

John Michael was starting to sweat. "That's some strong coffee."

"I want some!" giggled Shawnee.

John Michael opened his eyes, but everything was still revolving. His legs and arms started to tingle. It wasn't that he felt bad, it just felt different.

"Man, I don't know what happened here, but I feel really weird."

"It looks to me like you're starting to feel really good, doesn't it?" said Esmerelda, winking at him.

"I think that's our sign to go," Stan said standing.

Logan helped John Michael out of his chair, between the tables, and out the door.

Although things looked normal to most in the coffee shop, a young African-American boy at a corner table knew different. Matt leaned down and picked up the hat that had dropped from John Michael's head. He bolted out the door and stared down the street. The group was already out of sight. All Matt could see were the bright headlights that passed by. He looked down at the hat in his hands and then placed it on his head.

"Michael," he said quietly. "I think it was Michael."

Ten

A New Friend

The knock on the door was continual despite the silence from the other side. John Michael awoke in a panic. Immediately his head started to pound. He sighed loudly and looked down to see if all parts of his body were connected. They were. In fact, he was still in the same jeans and t-shirt he'd been in the night before.

The night before. All he remembered was meeting a few of Logan's friends at the Java Club, and from there, the rest was blurry. He recalled drinking a sip of coffee and then everyone at the table started to laugh. The next thing he could remember was bright lights and dancing. He wondered if he had dreamed of dancing.

He quickly assessed the space he was lying in the middle of. A naked light bulb hung from the ceiling directly above him. The walls were green and the paint was starting to chip away. Much of it was already on the floor. To the left of him was a small room. An old Kelvinator and gas stove were in it. The refrigerator door was hanging open and looked like it hadn't been used in years. To the right he could faintly see a tile floor and what looked like the base of a toilet. A very dirty toilet. There was an old broken chair in the room he was lying in, and a mattress with a sheet on it in the corner. He picked himself up off the floor and noticed a note tacked onto the back of the door.

"Mike,

This is your new home.

—Logan"

The knocking began again. John Michael went to the bathroom and found the sink. He turned the faucet on. Red, rusty water poured out. He dunked his hand in it and rubbed some on his face. The reflection in the cracked mirror was someone he didn't know. Was this really the life he wanted? His first night in the big city and he didn't even know what had happened to him. A knock again. He made his way to the door.

"Who's there?"

Silence.

"Is anybody there?"

Silence again. Then an answer.

"It's Matt. I saw you last night at the Java Club."

John Michael slowly turned the knob and opened the door. Standing in front of him was a young man in his early twenties. His dark hair and skin reflected the dim hallway light. He was wearing blue jeans, a white t-shirt and black boots. John Michael had noticed the black boots last night. At least he remembered something. The young man extended his hand.

"Uh, Matt Goodin."

John Michael shook his hand. "John Michael. I mean, Michael. Yeah, Michael Davis." John Michael moved away from the doorframe as a sign to let Matt in. Matt made his way through the door and took a look at the place.

"Not much here," John Michael said.

"Yeah, I noticed. Here." Matt handed John Michael his hat. "You left it at the coffee shop last night."

"Last night? I don't even remember last night."

"Didn't think you did."

John Michael rubbed his face. "I feel like crap."

"I know the feelin'. You were really trippin' last night."

"Why do you say that?"

"Dude, you were a maniac! I thought you knew. Didn't you see Esmerelda pour that stuff in your coffee?"

"What stuff?"

"She poured some in your drink and from there you were gone. Dancing and kissing everyone. You were the hit of the rave."

John Michael sat down on the floor. He couldn't stand anymore. Matt sat down with him.

"I knew it must have been something. I don't remember much past that point."

"Dude, you were flyin'."

"What?"

"The rave. The party. Don't you remember? New kid syndrome. Seen it before."

It was all fuzzy in John Michael's mind. He closed his eyes. He could see the lights flashing, a few girls dancing, and kissing— he remembered kissing for some reason.

"What?"

"New kid. They're testing you."

"Looks like I've failed."

"Not in their eyes. Like I said, you were the hit of the party. I thought you were one of those kids they bring in from the suburbs."

"The suburbs?"

"You know. They throw a rave to bring them in to sell the drugs—ecstasy, cocaine, acid."

"What did I take?" asked John Michael.

"By the way you were kissing those girls—I'd say ecstasy."

"Really?"

"Listen, I know I should let you live your own life, but I overheard you sayin' something about being new around this place."

"Yeah, so what?"

"Watch out for those guys. They'll really mess you up. Really. Especially Logan. He's out for nothin' else but your money."

"What money?" replied John Michael defensively. He was wondering if everyone knew about his check.

"I don't know. Look at the way you're dressed. You got to come from some kind of money."

"So?"

"Just a warning. I've seen it all before. They bring you in, sell you drugs. The next thing, you're the seller."

"I don't know, man. Logan's been really good to me. He set me up, got me some clothes on my back, and a place to live."

"Yeah, some place."

"At least it's a roof."

"I just wanted to bring your hat back and check up on you."

"You did? I'm not a baby, you know."

"I know. I've just seen a lot of guys like you come, but only a few of them go. Some never got the chance to decide either way."

"What do you mean?"

"They're dead."

"Oh." John Michael hung his head.

"You seem like a pretty smart kid. I thought you should know. Think of me as an older brother."

"I already have one that I'm trying to get rid of."

"Well, as long as you're here you're stuck with me."

"Don't worry too much, I'm 18, you know."

"That's cool. Just be careful. Everybody needs someone to look after them down here."

"Who looks after you?"

"No one. I take care of myself."

"Then why should I let you take care of me?"

"Trust me."

"That's what Logan said."

"Yeah, I'm sure he did. But, I'm the real deal. You'll see. Listen, I've got to go. I've got things to do. You gonna be all right?"

"I think so." John Michael said as he looked at his arms and legs. "No damage done."

"Just watch out. If you need me, I'll be around."

"How will I find you?"

"Don't worry, I'll find you."

Matt got up and left. The door slammed and John Michael felt alone again. He stared at his new place. The light bulb dangled above his head. He curled up in a ball in the middle of the room and closed his eyes. Alone, he was all alone again.

Eleven

"Dad?"

In John Michael's eyes, life couldn't be any better. An endless supply of money, raves to go to every night of thc weck, beautiful women to be escorted home from them, and the high—John Michael never felt so problem-free in his life. Pills to pop. Needles to poke. A snort here and a snort there. Drinks that left him worry-free. John Michael was willing to try it all. He visited the best clubs Chicago had to offer...on the right and wrong side of town. He could dance the night away and sleep until dinner the next day without anybody telling him to get up. For a young sheltered Midwestern boy, this really was an entirely different lifestyle. It seemed exciting, inviting, and most of all, independent. He promised himself that he would get a job, but never seemed to find the time. Who needs to plan ahead anyway? So, he didn't. He lived night to night, party to party, drink to drink, and drug to drug.

The shoebox hidden in his closet never seemed to run dry of the green bills that were hidden there. Although it seemed like a silly place to store his money, it became a safe hideaway to store the cash he would withdraw daily from the bank. He was on a first-name basis with most of the tellers there. And his cash card had become John Michael's answer for just about everything. His drug habit had become an expensive one. The money ran like water through Logan's hands. In an effort to secure what he needed to support his habit, John Michael had even begun buying and selling from Logan. Logan told him to look at it as an investment. John Michael looked at it as a way to cope with being alive. The mountain of money he had received from his mother was starting to resemble a small mound. He was hooked. His dreams of buying a car, saving for a house, and making a life for himself were fading fast.

Like a spider closing in on his prey, Logan had naturally chased John Michael right into his web. And he did it with class. Logan wasn't like the drug pushers John Michael knew of growing up in his public school. Logan was a master at getting whatever he needed out of everyone he met. And Logan was waiting patiently to get from John Michael what had initially attracted him to this simple boy from Kansas.

The phone woke John Michael. He tried to focus his eyes on familiar surroundings. None found. *Logan's place*, he thought to himself. His mind tried to play back the memories from last night. He sighed. The taste of liquor was still on his tongue. *What did I do last night?* he thought again. Then he remembered. Snapshots of the rave flashed in his mind. He rolled over and took a deep breath, noticing a female lying next to him. It was all coming together now. He had crashed at Logan's. And, he had brought someone with him. His own apartment just hadn't seemed like a place a girl would like.

He fumbled for the phone. "Hello?"

It was Logan.

"Downstairs? Yeah, I locked the door. Your key? You gave it to me. Sure, I'll unlock it. I'll be out in a minute."

John Michael sat up and ran his fingers through his hair. He tapped on the woman's bare shoulder beside him. "Uh, hey. Hello? Whatever your name is, it's time to leave. You've got to get up now and leave."

She didn't respond. John Michael tapped her again trying to provoke some movement. Still, nothing.

"Hey, excuse me," he said again raising his voice a notch. "Excuse me!"

Her eyes opened. "What time is it?" she replied.

John Michael searched the room for a clock. She thrashed her arm out from under the blanket to look at her watch.

"Oh no," she whispered with concern. "I've got to get out of here."

John Michael felt awkward. This always seemed easier to deal with when he was drunk or high. Right now he was neither.

"I've got to go," she said again, throwing off the covers in a frantic search for her clothes.

"Uh, thanks. What's your name again?" he said to her awkwardly.

"It's Rachel. Don't you remember?"

John Michael paused. "Not much. I don't remember much."

"Well, I hope you didn't forget this was a paying gig."

John Michael remembered emptying his pockets on Logan's dresser. "Sure, Rachel, whatever. There's some money on the dresser."

She finished buckling her shoes and threw on a tan coat. "Is there enough there?"

John Michael sighed. She was starting to irritate him. "You tell me."

She stepped to the dresser to look at her reflection in the mirror. Without glancing back at John Michael, she grabbed a crumpled 100-dollar bill from the cash pile. "This is enough."

"Well," he said to her ungracefully, "I don't know what to say. Thanks? Maybe we can do this again sometime?"

"Whatever," she said, disappearing down the hall. Shortly after John Michael heard her unlock the door. The squeak from the hinges indicated her exit. Within a few minutes he heard Logan come in.

John Michael stepped out of bed and got dressed quickly. He threw on a white t-shirt and pair of jeans and walked barefoot down the hall into the main living area. Logan was sitting on a black leather chair thumbing through a magazine.

"I see you're taking full advantage of my friends," Logan said with sarcasm.

"Yeah. They're expensive."

"But, you got the money, right?"

John Michael sat down at the kitchen table. Laying a small mirror in front of him, he saw a reflection. Was that really him? The rings under his eyes were dark. He tried to rub them out before reaching for a sandwich bag piled high with white powder. He poured some on the glass and split it into piles with a razor blade. After forming a row on the mirror, he cleared his throat before inhaling it through his nose.

"Michael," Logan said with disgust, "it's 5:00 in the morning."

"That's the beauty. Now I'll really be able to sleep. Want some?"

"No, no thanks. But I will take the key from you. I can't even get in my own place."

"Oh, yeah. Sure. Just a minute." He leaned back, resting his head on the back of the kitchen chair. The expression on John Michael's face indicated the cocaine was starting to move through his system.

"Hey, there's something I've been meaning to ask you," said Logan as he put the magazine down.

"Just a sec," John Michael replied. After another snort, he was ready. Although his eyes were closed he was trying to listen. "What's up?"

"You trust me, right?"

"Sure. Whatever. I owe a lot to you getting me started and all."

"I thought you might. You know, with me opening up my place to you."

"OK, OK. What do you need?"

"I was...I was..." Logan said carefully, "I was wondering if I could borrow some cash."

John Michael didn't change his expression. He just sat there, eyes closed. "Sure. Whatever. I've got some extra bills on my dresser."

"Well," Logan said cautiously. "I was talking about a little more. Not even a few hundred. It's more in the thousands."

John Michael didn't think that seemed unreasonable.

"OK, how much?" he said, sniffing and wiping his nose uncontrollably. "How many thousands?"

"Twenty-five."

"Twenty-five thousand?" John Michael opened his eyes.

"Twenty-five is good."

John Michael was quiet for a few moments. His eyes rolled back and then he shut them again. "What's it for?"

Logan remained cool and collected. "I need to pay for a deal that I don't have enough paper on hand for. This guy has some stuff to sell but it's got to be in cash. Plus, I'm behind on a few bills."

John Michael shook his head a few times. "That's more than a few thousand."

Logan was quick to come back. "I know, dude. But, this deal could double my money. I'll cut you in on it. Half of what I make. That will pay most of what I owe, right?"

John Michael was too high to fully understand. He nodded his head in agreement.

"I think I could do that. Considering all you've done for me."

"C'mon," said Logan with in a patronizing tone, "I haven't done that much."

"Cut the crap. You've given me more than a place to live. Friends, a way to make some money, a job, and lots of women. That I like!"

Logan came and stood next to John Michael. Both faces were reflected in the mirror now. Logan ran his finger through a pile of coke and then licked the residue off his finger. "And this. I've introduced you to the good stuff."

"That you have," John Michael replied staring again at his reflection. The smile he tried to muster up looked painted. He could see the white powder at the base of his nose. "Don't worry about interest. Just pay it back, all right?"

"Cool. I should be able to as soon as I lift the deal from my friend. Then, it's money for us all the way." Logan paused; he didn't want to push too hard. "Cash OK?"

John Michael nodded. "Cash is good. I'll go down later and get it."

Logan laughed. "Oh, yeah. It's still 5:00 in the morning."

John Michael laid his head down on the table next to the mirror. He covered his face with his arm. "I'm going to stay a little longer."

"Stay as long as you like, Michael," Logan reassured him before heading into the bathroom and shutting the door. He took a cell phone out of his back pocket and dialed a few numbers. "Hey, it's Logan. Let's close the deal tomorrow, all right? Cash— oh baby, it's cash. Tomorrow. I'll call later."

John Michael slept for most of the day before heading back down to Sonny's Bar, one of his favorite places to grab a few beers. It wasn't located in the nicest area of the Chicago Loop, but it felt more familiar to him than any other drinking hangout.

The law of supply and demand was in effect. When John Michael needed some help to face reality, Logan was always there with something to keep him from facing reality. John Michael hated the taste of the alcohol, but he liked how it numbed the pain he was feeling deep down inside. Life didn't seem so overwhelming when you never looked at it with a clear conscience. He'd found a way to escape his life...for the time being.

In a drunken stupor, John Michael rested his head on the cool bar counter that sat at the outer part of the dance floor. The music was loud. There was smoke in the air. But John Michael's feeling that night wasn't good. He looked at the bartender.

"I think I'm ready for another one, Neil."

"Oh, I don't think so, Michael. You can't even keep your head up."

John Michael started to get angry. He was slurring his words together. "Sure I can." He cursed several times and demanded, "I want another one, now give it to me."

"I can't. It's against house rules. You're too drunk. Let me call you a cab."

"Cab? For what? So I can go back to that hell hole again?" At that moment, a man shuffled by the bar. John Michael turned, but the gentleman passed too fast. He stood to follow the figure through the smoke-filled room, but fell to the floor. Somebody tried to help him up.

"Get off me! I'm fine." He lifted himself off the dirty floor and started to push through the crowd. He cursed a few times and started to move towards the black hole the man had disappeared into. A cocktail table fell over as he tripped over his feet. A genuine draft bottle shattered and left John Michael in a pool of beer and glass.

"You son of a…" an angry customer said from his seat. He had lost his bottle in the shuffle and was mad enough to demand it back. "You owe me one!"

John Michael stood up and brushed the glass off his pants. People were starting to stare now, not that this was anything new for this kind of establishment. They were expecting a brawl. John Michael had no idea he was the star in this scene. All he could think about was the man. He started after him again.

"Hey! I said you owe me one."

John Michael moved across the dance floor. There were people everywhere. His eyes darted back and forth. He squinted trying to catch a glimpse of the figure he had seen through the flickering lights. He started to sway again. He felt like he was going to throw up. He stopped and focused on the shadow from the man he had seen before behind the crowded floor. John Michael watched the tall figure make his way out a back door exit into the moonlight. He darted across the room. He wasn't about to lose him again. He reached for the door handle along the back wall.

"C'mon, where are you!" he screamed. He felt a push bar and pressed it. He stepped out into the silent alley. The music and noise silenced when the door shut. John Michael stood there alone. He looked left, then right, then left again. He noticed the figure again under a street light about a block away. He tried to run after him.

"Wait! Hey, wait!" He tripped and fell. His hand landed on a broken piece of glass and was cut open. Blood trickled down his wrist. He picked himself up again. "Hey, wait! Would you stop!"

John Michael kept running. The man kept walking. He was within yelling distance for sure now. John Michael stopped, took a breath, and yelled as loud as he could, "DAD, WOULD YOU WAIT!"

The body stopped. John Michael started to walk towards it. "Dad? Is that you? Why didn't you wait? You saw me at the bar. Why did you ignore me? You don't love me anymore, do you? I knew it. I can't ever come home, can I? Can I, Dad?" He reached the man within a few moments. His hand was bleeding badly now. The adrenaline was starting to disappear and he felt the pain. He stopped directly in front of where the stranger was standing.

"Dad?"

The man just stared, and then spoke antagonistically. "Dad? You think I'm your dad?"

John Michael felt a hand on his shoulder. He turned around. It was the face from the bar. The one he owed a beer to.

"Where's my beer, kid? Huh?" Instantly, John Michael felt something hit him directly in the face. That's all he remembered, then his body fell to the ground.

He woke in a pool of blood. He had lost track of time. John Michael squinted his eyes and tried to figure out where he was. He stared at the sky between the brick buildings on both sides of him, then he felt it. The pain was overwhelming. He reached up to rub his face and noticed his hand was covered with blood. John Michael panicked. He tasted blood and spit it out on the ground. His other hand rubbed the right side of his face. His skin was tender there. He wiped away the blood and mucous that was running from his nose. He just lay there. The cold concrete made him shiver.

"I just want to die," he whispered. "Just die."

It would have been easier at that point. John Michael wanted to give up. Defeated, he just felt defeated. This feeling was worse than any football game he had ever lost.

"I hate you, Michael," he said to himself. "I hate you."

Another figure appeared in the dim light moving towards his body. John Michael wondered if it was the dude that had punched him out cold again. He closed his eyes pretending to be unconscious again. He figured if he was still out he couldn't get hit again. The footsteps came nearer until they stopped directly in front of his face. He could hear the man's breathing as he stooped down to look at him.

"Michael? Michael, is that you?"

The first thought that came to John Michael's mind was his father. Could this really be his dad? He felt a hand shake his shoulder before opening his eyes.

"Michael? You all right?"

John Michael squinted staring up at the darkened face. "Dad?"

"No, it's Matt. Man, what happened? Who messed up your face?"

John Michael tried to stand, but fell back to the ground. Matt took John Michael's arm and lifted him up.

"How did you find me?"

"Like I told you, I'm looking out for you. Man, your face looks bad. And, you're bleeding bad. Where you bleeding from?"

"I don't know. I think it's my hand." He noticed the open wound on his left palm. He got himself up and wiped as much blood away from his face as he could feel. He took off his shirt, wrapped his hand in it, and walked away leaning on Matt's shoulder.

"C'mon, let's get you back to your place. Before somebody tries to do it again."

"Thanks, man."

"Like I told you. Somebody's gotta look out for you."

Matt carried the burden of John Michael's body down the alley. It was a night John Michael would not forget, a moment that would be etched in his mind forever. With each step back to his apartment, he longed to be one step closer to home. Home. If only he really was going home.

Twelve

"I'll Be Waiting for You..."

The rural post office in Willowbrook was as good as any other post office in the country, maybe even better. Post office employees took their time caring for each letter and package that came through the small mail center. Jonathan noticed the mail carrier way before the post office employee noticed him. The mailman made his way up the winding street from one house to another. Unlike the paperboy, he carefully placed the letters to each address in mailboxes that hung empty next to the front doors of most of the homes. He was a sight for sore eyes for some, and an enemy for others. He brought the bills and the letters of love.

Jonathan glanced at his watch, then out the front window again. The mailman made his way up the sidewalk onto the porch. Jonathan breathed a sigh of relief. The mailman was on time once again, like clockwork on a Saturday morning. Jonathan backed away from the window so the mailman wouldn't see him anxiously waiting for the news that would be delivered. As soon as he heard the mail carrier step off the porch, he unlatched the front door and walked onto the porch. He waved at the postman, then dug in the mailbox for the letters.

Jonathan grabbed the stack out and made his way to the porch swing. He sat down and looked through the pile slowly. He knew how to do this. It had become a daily routine. In fact, Jonathan had made his way home many times between court hearings just to take a glance at what was in the little tin box. One afternoon he couldn't make it home because of a late trial case, so he phoned his next door neighbor, who checked the mail for him. What was he so earnestly looking for?

Jonathan plopped the pile of mail down next to him. The electric bill, a bank statement, a sweepstakes entry, and another credit card application. He picked the pile up again and scoured through it one more time. Nothing. He sighed loudly and looked away.

"C'mon, Johnny, the least you could do is write us a letter," he mumbled to himself like he had many times before. Bitterness was starting to settle in. It had been awhile since he had seen the silhouette of his boy walking down the dark street. He would give anything just to hear that he was all right. His heart ached just to know if his son was alive or dead.

Philip glanced out the window and noticed his dad mumbling something. He made his way out the front door and onto the porch.

"Dad, did you say something to me?"

"No, not really. I was just talking to your brother."

"Lewis is at the library studying, remember?"

"No, not Lewis. John Michael. I was just talking to John Michael."

Philip understood all too well. He had also talked to John Michael, even though he wasn't there. Grief was doing strange things to both of them.

"No letter today, huh?" Philip sat down next to his father on the porch swing, picked up the pack of letters, and sorted through them.

"Nope. Not today. Not yesterday. Not the day before," he said, frustrated. "Maybe tomorrow."

Philip slammed the mail back down. "Dad, he makes me so mad. The least he could do is send a postcard. A few cents could change our lives back home. Why doesn't he think of us?"

"Because, Philip, he can't think of anyone but himself right now."

"Dad, how can you say that? It's not fair. I mean, we've lived together our entire lives. How can you just forget about playing tag, smashing lightning bugs on the sidewalk, and eating chocolate chip cookie dough ice cream every Friday night! Doesn't he care about any of us at all?"

"Of course he cares, Son, but right now it's not enough. He's thinking too much about all that he is going through. You're different from him, Philip. You face your pain head on. John Michael stuffs it, then runs from it. He's running right now. And until he stops, we wait. I hate it, too."

Jonathan put his arm around Philip. He didn't expect him to understand. He was just getting over losing a mother, and now he faced losing a brother.

"Dad, I don't know how to let go. I mean, it's just that we've been through so much together." There was a long pause, then Philip spoke up again. "You were so busy that night at the hospital. There were so many doctors and nurses talking to you. It was John Michael that told me that Mom, uh, that Mom wasn't going to make it. He put his arm around me after he watched the expression on your face when you were talking to the doctor. He told me Mom was dead. How can you leave after you've been through all of that?" Philip sat quietly, then asked his dad an honest question. "Doesn't he love us anymore?"

Jonathan knew this wasn't going to be easy. As a father, how do you tell your own son the answers to the questions you're asking. "Love is a funny thing, Philip. It's easy to take for granted those you see all the time. It's easy to forget how special they make your life."

"Why is he trying so hard to forget us?"

"Because, Philip, he wants a new life. He got so used to the love we have here, that when he needed the support the most he just didn't know where to turn to find it. The love was here to help him make it through anything he was going through. It was staring him right in the face. I guess he didn't realize the love we still had at home here, even without your mother."

"But how can you miss something that's so obvious, Dad?"

"Sometimes the hardest thing to see is what is standing right in front of you. So, he went off to find a new love, a new life."

"Will it ever replace us, Dad?"

"Oh, for awhile it will. The new freedom he's found will feel like it is going to last forever, but at some point, he will come face to face with what he has lost."

"Us?"

"Yes, us."

"What if it's too late, Dad. What if he finds out too late?"

Jonathan stared into the distance, then back at his son. "Philip, never forget it's never too late. It's never too late for a son to come back to the arms of his father."

Lewis made his way up the sidewalk and onto the porch. He had walked home from the library. It had been a long morning. He had studied hard. College algebra was extremely difficult for him, along with a list of other subjects. His walk home had turned into a gripe session of how impossible his life seemed. The voices in his head had grown louder. He wondered if he would ever measure up, or move out of the shadow of his middle brother. His feet scuffled across the porch floor.

"What are you two doing out here?" asked Lewis.

"Mail call. We were hoping for a letter today from your brother."

"A letter? Are you crazy? He's obviously not going to send you a letter!"

"Like you care, Lewis."

"You're right, Philip. I don't care. In fact, I'm sick of hearing about John Michael. Look at you. You're both sitting here, waiting, like he's going to come walking down the street any minute. I'm telling both of you, he's gone for good."

"That's the way you'd like it, isn't it?"

"That's not true."

"Then why did you pack up all of John Michael's things and move into his room?"

Jonathan spoke up. "You did? Lewis, you didn't ask me about that."

"I needed more space, all right? His room is bigger than mine."

"But, Son, you don't just start packing up things that aren't..."

Lewis cut him off. "What's the big deal? He's not staying there anymore!"

"You can't replace him, Lewis," shouted Philip. "You're not John Michael. Why don't you stop trying to be like him and just be yourself."

"I am myself," he said and then cursed.

"Lewis!" Jonathan said sternly.

"No, Lewis, you're someone who lives here that I don't know. If you could be happy with yourself you would be out here waiting, too!"

Jonathan knew where the conversation was going. Anger was starting to boil over. He did what he could to calm things down.

"Guys, listen to yourselves! All of this fighting isn't going to bring your brother back any sooner. We need to prepare ourselves for when he comes home."

Lewis stood up. His face was red. There was sweat dripping from his brow. He looked at his father and squinted his eyes.

"Dad, face the truth. Your son is gone. For good. Now, let's get on with our lives and stop all this waiting. You're only wasting your time. He's never going to write you a letter so get used to it." He grabbed the mail from the porch swing and threw it to the ground. The letters scattered themselves across the porch. Lewis stepped on one of them. "He's not going to call you on the phone. He hates you. He hates me. Can we just get on with life? Our lives?" He grabbed his books and walked away.

Jonathan raced after him and caught his shoulder halfway down the sidewalk. He turned Lewis around.

"Son, I'll never stop waiting so you'd better get used to it. Not for you, not for Philip, and not for John Michael. I love all of you just the same."

Lewis jerked away and started to walk again. He couldn't handle what his father was saying. Jonathan knew Lewis was running. Every day he was running farther away in his heart.

"I'll be waiting for you, Lewis! As long as it takes, I'll keep waiting! I'LL BE WAITING FOR YOU, JOHN MICHAEL. I'M WAITING FOR YOU, TOO."

Lewis heard his father start to sob. He started to walk as fast as he could, shocked by his father's humility. There were no following footsteps, just loud cries of a father who longed to have all three sons home.

Thirteen

A Fatherless Generation

One party after another, John Michael had become a part of the system and he didn't even know it. He would spend his nights at the establishment of his choice, spend his money on the booze and ladies of the night, and Logan could get him any drug he wanted. Night after night, day after day, headache after headache, John Michael was in a routine. It was easier this way, dealing with life. He would meet his friends at the coffee shop, drink a few rounds of java, smoke a cigarette or two and then head out for a few drinks...or a lot of them. The bars were full of people that always seemed to have a reason to drown the reality of life with a drink or a drug. For John Michael, along with many others, it seemed to numb the pain they didn't want to face.

"Who's buying tonight?" asked Mort as he sat down at their usual table at the Java Club. Shawnee was already there waiting for them.

"Buying? Who's got cash?"

"I do," said John Michael as he headed to the table with a steaming coffee cup in his hand. He was already high. He felt like he could buy the whole world.

"When are you gonna run out of funds, boy?" asked Garret following behind him.

"Never."

Esmerelda walked inside the shop. Her high heels clicked all the way over to the table. "Has anybody seen Logan? I can't find him. He told me he would meet us here. You are buying, aren't you, Mikey?" She blew him a kiss. He smiled back. Everything felt good tonight.

"Of course I am."

They all sat down at the table. An ashtray was filling in the center. "I saw my mom today," said Shawnee in a timid voice.

"So?" said Mort insensitively.

"Mort, you sure know how to treat a woman, don't you? You insensitive pig," Esmerelda said, hitting him on the shoulder.

Shawnee looked down at the floor.

John Michael sensed she was uncomfortable. "Is that a good thing?" he said gently.

Shawnee looked up. "Not really. I haven't seen her in about six months. She got tired of me and my sister and left. She was too drunk every night to even get home, anyway. She decided to move in with her boyfriend so it would be easier on us. She pays our rent and we live alone."

John Michael couldn't believe what he was hearing, even being high. "You mean, she just left you? You're not even 18. How old is your sister?"

"Thirteen."

"No way. How could your mom do that?"

"What are you," said Esmerelda, "the people police? Where have you been? Michael, it has happened to everyone I know. It's no big deal. The way I look at it is if our parents can't look after us, then why should we have to look after them. Who cares what your parents do? They don't seem to care about us anyway."

"What kind of relationship do you have with your dad?" John Michael asked Esmerelda, lighting another cigarette.

"Never had a dad, and I never will. I never knew mine and I don't care to. He left when my mom became a witch."

Mort set his coffee down. "Ooo, spooky!"

"You got another scary story for us?" said Garret, taunting her.

"You've heard them all. Sorry, boys."

"A witch?" questioned John Michael. "Like the kind that flies on a broom?"

They all laughed. John Michael was trying to be serious.

"No. Where on earth were you born, Kansas? She's into witchcraft. She reads palms, tarot cards, and all that jazz. She believes she can see into the future," Esmerelda said, rolling her eyes.

"Do you believe in all of that?"

"I don't know what I believe. All I know is that some guy got her pregnant and I'm stuck in a life that I can't get out of. So, I do the best that I can."

John Michael was in shock. He stared at the grain of the wood table.

"What are all the questions for anyway?" Esmerlda asked back.

"I just wondered," John Michael responded.

Mort blew a cloud of smoke John Michael's way. "Yeah, well I suppose you have a perfect mom and dad, huh? Instead of 'Leave It to Beaver' we could call it, 'Leave It to Michael' starring our very own pal, Michael...." Mort struggled to remember John Michael's last name.

"It's Davis. And no, I don't have a perfect family."

Garret glanced in John Michael's direction. "Then what's your sob story? Do you have a mommy?"

John Michael felt like someone just stabbed him in the heart. He wasn't enjoying this conversation anymore. "She died a little while ago."

Mort started to mockingly sob. Garret joined in.

"That is so rude," shouted Shawnee, trying to protect John Michael.

John Michael kept talking to Shawnee while the rest of them laughed at the memory of his mother. "I lived with my dad. Then, I needed some space from him and the perfect little life he had built for me and my brothers."

"You have brothers?" asked Esmerelda. "Do they have money, too?"

"Yeah, you'll be running out of yours soon," shot back Garret.

John Michael was tired of their comments. They were starting to remind him of all that he had at home.

"Nice world we live in, isn't it?" commented Mort "Who's got a family anymore? For that matter, who needs 'em. I never even heard of a real father. Bunch of selfish jerks out there, anyway. They want things their way, and when they don't get it, you're out."

John Michael spoke up, "Hey, that's not my dad."

"Yeah, right. I'd like to meet him. Take me to him, long lost son. He's never going to accept you back. Look at you," Matt replied with cynicism.

John Michael looked at himself. His vision wasn't clear, but what he saw he didn't like. Guilt started to crash in on him. He exhaled his cigarette smoke. "Yeah, you're probably right."

"You know I'm right," Matt said with confidence. "Look around this place. Do you see someone who's had a decent father? They're a dying breed, my man. Like the dinosaur, only dry bones left. We live in a new world."

Logan caught Esmerelda's eye outside the glass door at the front of the shop. He signaled for all of them to come. They put out their cigarettes, set down their coffee cups, and headed for the door. All that remained was the conversation that was etched deep into their minds. Down deep in each one of their hearts was a longing. They longed to experience a real father. The kind of man who would give grace freely, and love without condition. Each of them yearned to be held in that kind of father's arms and to look deep into his eyes. Eyes filled with love. Eyes filled with compassion. Most of them had never seen that, except for John Michael. He couldn't forget his father's eyes.

Fourteen

The Bottom

The Chicago air felt muggy tonight. Dark clouds stretched across the sky setting the stage for a nasty storm to roll in. A few sprinkles of rain dropped from the sky onto the Chicago streets. A breeze blew through the open window into John Michael's empty apartment. He stared back at himself in the cracked mirror. John Michael was feeling different tonight and he couldn't quite figure out why.

He left his place and headed for the Java Club just like every other night since he had moved to Chicago. His eyes were bloodshot again. They seemed to be turning a permanent shade of red lately. He was getting high several times a day and drunk almost every night. It wasn't fun anymore, but he was caught in a trap that he couldn't escape. His world was crashing in, and he felt powerless to change it. Logan was seeing him less and less, and even his new friends were treating him like old trash. He wasn't buying them drinks anymore, but they had known that was coming—it was just a matter of time. Logan hadn't paid back any funds he had borrowed. John Michael didn't know it, but Logan had never planned to.

He hadn't slept in days. The buzz he would feel would keep him awake most nights. How could he sleep? He kept thinking about the money, his habit and his father. His mind never rested as he stared at the ceiling. But tonight, something was different.

It was starting to rain lightly when he reached the Java Club. He opened the door and walked into the shop. He looked around the cafe. That was odd, no one was there. John Michael felt something in his gut he hadn't felt before. He needed to find Logan. He was craving a fix. His hands started to shake and his forehead was starting to sweat.

"Can I help you, Michael?" asked a familiar waitress.

"Uh, Logan. Have you seen Logan? Or Shawnee? Have they been here?" He glanced at his watch.

"No, they haven't. Are you all right?"

"I'm fine." He answered as he wiped the sweat from his brow. "Really. I wonder why they're not here?"

"Did you check your apartment? Maybe they went there."

"My place? I was just there, but maybe. I could have missed seeing them on the way over here. I'll check. Thanks," he said as he ran out the door.

His shoes hit the wet pavement with a nervous pace. He was starting to shiver. *Where is Logan?* His shaky hands reached into his pocket for his keys as he ran past several brownstones and headed up the stairs to his apartment. A rat ran by his feet as he stepped down the hollow corridor that led to his place. He stopped dead in his tracks. The door was wide open. A cold breeze came through the window and was blowing the door open back and forth. He stepped in quietly. His legs were shaky and he had to squint his eyes to see. There wasn't much to throw around, but what little he had was everywhere. The old musty mattress was torn to shreds. His six pack of beer bottles from the refrigerator were smashed all over the floor. John Michael ran to the closet, panicked. He knew what he would find before he got there.

A piece of dry wall was gone and the shoebox that had once been full of cash now lay on the floor empty. *But, it was the perfect hiding place,* he thought. He banged his head on the wall and slid down to the floor next to the box. He cursed as loud as he could. It was all gone. Every dime. The only thing left was an empty cardboard container and an exhausted heart. What was he supposed to do now? His bank account was empty. The last time he had used his check card his transaction had been denied. He needed to talk to Logan. The security he had built his life on had now been stolen away. His soul ached as he started to cry. At first he made faint whimpers, then loud shrieks. He kept cursing over and over again, hoping it would somehow make him feel better. He knew the only thing that would give him any comfort was miles away, and he wasn't ready to face his father. Now he really could be called a complete failure. Who would want to love him now? He'd spent all of his mother's money on things that would have torn her heart apart. He banged his head against the closet wall. Life was all of the sudden becoming very realistic. He no longer had a place to hide or choices of his own to make. They were just made for him.

"Why? Why? Why didn't you see this coming?" he yelled at himself. Although there hadn't been much money left in the box, it was completely empty now. John Michael stood up and headed towards the door. He slammed it on his way out.

The air was misty now due to the light rain now falling on the city from the clouds above. He kept walking until his feet hurt. He finally sat down on a bench. He couldn't get control of what he was feeling. Anger. Frustration. No restraint. Guilt. Weakness. Failure. He slammed his hand on the bench. *So this is what I've made of my new life.* From the palace to the pigpen. There was a jingle in his pocket. Change? He stood up and pulled out several quarters, dimes, a few nickels and one penny. He counted it up. Across the street a neon sign blinked on and off "The House of Bottles." He headed to the liquor store. If he had enough to at least get something, it would take away the pain for one more night. He searched the store, but the only thing he could afford was a small bottle of scotch. It would have to do. He hated the stuff, but if it would ease his mind he would drink it all. John Michael dumped the last of his money onto the counter as a dime rolled onto the floor.

"Don't worry about it," said the attendant inhaling a cigar. "Have a good night."

John Michael didn't respond. He'd gotten what he came for, and now needed a place to forget the awful moments he was experiencing. A wooden bench at the end of an alley looked like a pretty good place. Quiet. Private. Painless. His shaking hands opened the bottle inside the paper bag and he began to drink it like water on a hot day. Down it went numbing his soul. He waited awhile staring at the buildings and clear night sky. John Michael felt his body start to tingle. The cheap scotch had tasted terrible, but it was helping to ease the pain. He finished off the bottle and tossed it under the bench. He was exhausted so he laid his head down on the cold bench planks. He put his feet up on the other side of the seat and closed his eyes. At least he would be comfortable for a little while.

Fifteen

The Search

Jonathan, Philip, and Lewis drove down the interstate and headed for the skyscrapers that formed the Chicago skyline dead ahead. It had been a long trip for all of them. Jonathan insisted that the boys come with him. He wanted them to be a part of what he was going through. John Michael had finally sent his first postcard. Oh, it didn't say much, but the postmark gave away the city he could be presently living in—Chicago. It was a big place. This would be like finding a needle in a haystack. That's why he brought the boys. Three could search a large area better than one.

The three of them headed into the Chicago Loop and parked the car. Philip had never been in a big city before. Its size and immensity overwhelmed him. He thought of his brother who could be lost somewhere in this intimidating place. Lewis at first had refused to come, but his dad pleaded, finally demanding Lewis's help. The postcard was marked with a South Chicago zip code. At least that would give them a place to start. Jonathan gave each of the boys a picture of John Michael and they headed down the street together. They stopped in a number of pizza places, quick store stops, and a few gas stations to see if anyone recognized his middle son. None did so far. Jonathan and the boys headed deeper into the heart of the south side of the city. A man came by and tried to sell them some marijuana. Jonathan declined. Three drunk women invited them to a bar for a drink, but once again, they refused the offer. It was getting dark now, and finding John Michael would be no easy task. Jonathan checked inside a few more places and asked a few more faces. Still no sign of his son.

"Dad," Lewis said as they walked down the sidewalk of a one-way street, "this isn't working. You can't just expect to drive into a city of millions of people and suddenly find your long lost son. That's in the movies, it's not reality."

Jonathan was patient with his son. He knew Lewis didn't understand. "Just let me have a little more time."

"Time? Dad, if it gets any later we may not have more time. Look around, the freaks are really starting to come out."

"Ah, let me check in here. Lewis, stay out here with your brother. I'll be back in a minute." Jonathan stepped into the Java Club. He looked around at the rough clientele and noticed a waitress talking to a few younger kids at a table.

"Excuse me, miss?"

She ignored him. The conversation she was having wasn't finished. Besides, he looked like a parent coming to drag his kid to juvenile hall.

"Miss, can I talk to you for a moment?" he politely requested.

She sighed and turned his way. "I guess. What do you need? Coffee?"

"No, just looking for someone." His gentle voice took her off guard. She softened up a little.

"You gotta name?"

"John Michael Davis." He reached into his pocket and pulled out his picture. She stared at it. Philip and Lewis watched from outside the large glass windows.

"What do you think?" asked Philip. "It looks like Dad might have found someone who knows something."

"Don't get your hopes up. He's probably ordering a cup of coffee to go."

"No, really. Look at the way that lady is staring at John Michael's picture."

"Yeah, I'd stare at that ugly face, too." Lewis responded.

Jonathan put the picture back in his pocket, thanked the lady, and shook her hand. She watched him leave.

"Boys, let's go. She's seen him. He hangs out here often. She hasn't seen him lately, though. She said he has looked troubled."

"Where is she sending us?"

"She gave me an address that she thinks is his apartment. It's only a couple of blocks away."

The three of them walked briskly down the one way, then down the alley John Michael had walked so many times before. Jonathan had promised himself that he wouldn't go after John Michael. He knew John Michael needed to experience his own frailties and frustrations of life. Jonathan could have made things better for his middle son, but that only would have postponed the inevitable. Jonathan knew John Michael needed to make this decision on his own. But there was something that drew Jonathan to the city. A feeling, a gut instinct, a father's discernment. Something didn't feel right in his heart. He knew John Michael was in trouble; he just didn't know how deep it really was. His pace was so fast the boys could hardly keep up with him.

Jonathan glanced at the piece of paper the waitress had written the address on. He looked closer at the slip. It said "Guest Check" at the top and had a few greasy stains on it. He matched the address on the paper with the address on the old worn brownstone building. Jonathan hoped he wouldn't find anything that even resembled his son inside the old red brick.

"Dad," said Philip, looking strangely at the building, "is this it?"

"I'm afraid so. Maybe the waitress was wrong, though. We can only hope so."

Lewis stared up at the building and shook his head. "Told you, Dad, this is a waste. If we find John Michael in there, I don't know if I want to bring him home. This is disgusting." And it was. The smell burned Jonathan's nose. He walked slowly towards the door and grabbed it. Locked.

"Just bang on it, Dad. Who are you worrying about waking up? They don't care around here."

Jonathan tried it again. A cockroach scurried between his legs.

"C'mon, somebody's got to be in there."

"I can't believe they would even lock a place like this," said Lewis.

Jonathan stepped away, crunching the roach under his heel. He was disappointed, and Philip was feeling sick.

"Let's check around the back of the building. Maybe there's a way in there."

The three of them walked down the dark alley and around the old brownstone. Jonathan surveyed the situation.

"Philip, do you think you can reach the bottom of that fire escape?"

"I don't know. I think so."

"Why don't you give it a try."

"All right," Philip said as he jumped for the bottom of the fire escape.

"C'mon, Dad. We're going to get in trouble for doing this. Can't we just go home?" remarked Lewis sarcastically.

"Home? Home is a day's drive away. Lewis, I'm not leaving until we at least know your brother is alive. We came so far."

Philip attempted to jump a few more times, then gave up. The fire escape was too high.

"I can't do it, Dad. What do you say we just keep looking around the neighborhood instead of breaking into this old castle?" Philip said, disappointed.

"You're right. In fact, why don't we split up for 15 minutes, then we'll meet at the coffee shop again. Philip, you take the one way street. Lewis, you take the alley to your left, I'll take the dark one over here. Now, if anyone finds anything, even information, yell for one another. Got it?"

"Got it, Dad."

Lewis was silent.

"Got that, Lewis? None of this maverick stuff. You call for us."

A loud crash of thunder was heard. All three men looked up at the sky. The stars had been traded for a layer of storm clouds.

"Aw, man, now it's going to rain on us. What a great trip!" said Lewis sarcastically.

"Look as thoroughly and quickly as you can. A little rain isn't going to hurt us. John Michael is somewhere in this neighborhood. I know it. Let's go." Jonathan could feel it. Call it father's intuition. A dad's gut feeling. Something he felt deep down in his heart. If he did nothing but find out that his son was alive, that would be enough. He knew he couldn't drag John Michael home, but seeing his father and brothers might create a desire for John Michael to return.

The three of them separated and stepped down their assigned streets. Jonathan headed down the dark alley with bravery. The dark didn't scare him; the prospect of not finding his son did. Philip headed down the one way street that lead to the Java Club. He relentlessly surveyed the street for a sign of his brother. He found nothing. Rain drops started to land on Lewis's forehead. He wiped them off and sighed. Lewis was frustrated and wasn't enjoying the mission his father had brought them all on. He continued down the alley. A cold wind blew between the buildings, chilling him to the bone. His foot caught an aluminum beer can on the ground. He smashed it sending it against the brick wall.

"That's for you, John Michael," he said after he kicked the can. Lewis picked up a piece of old wood and threw it at an old dumpster that was overflowing with garbage. "That is for all the hell you've caused our family," he continued. His hatred for John Michael was growing. He looked at the skyscrapers beyond the buildings he was standing between. A few more raindrops fell on his face again. "I hate you, John Michael. I hate you so much." His voice echoed through the alley. In Lewis's opinion, this entire mission needed to be aborted. In some ways, Lewis hoped John Michael was dead, then he'd finally be out of the picture altogether. He didn't need John Michael, and wished everyone else would just let him go. Discouraged, he walked out of the alley and noticed a nearby bench next to the shadowy street. He was done searching. Lewis decided he would rest for a few minutes, then head over to the coffee shop. He wandered over to the bench and sat down. He felt something under him and quickly stood up. He looked down at the bench. There was something under a pile of newspapers. He took a few steps back.

"Hello?" he said fearfully.

No response. He poked at the pile of newsprint. No movement. He pulled one of the papers off. His eyes widened. It was a body! Lewis was breathless for a moment. He tried to scream. Was this person dead? He looked down the street. Lewis wondered if he should run as fast as he could or stay and try to help the person on the bench. His father had taught him to help those in need, but he was scared. He grabbed the newspapers and uncovered the body. The man was wearing blue jeans and a t-shirt. A bag with a bottle in it rolled out from under the bench. He stepped closer to get a better view of the stranger. He moved to the side so the dim street light would give him some light. Lewis wanted to see the man's face. He'd never seen a dead person before. A drop of rain fell on the man's forehead. He started to rustle on the bench and turned around. He was alive!

The man opened his eyes slowly.

"Lewis?" he said.

Lewis stared pensively. He was in shock. John Michael was the last person he expected to see. On the trip to Chicago from Wichita, Jonathan and Philip had talked endlessly about how they hoped to find John Michael. With all of that money, his father had been dreaming that John Michael would have put it to good use and would come home with more than what he started with. Philip hoped his middle brother would be helping someone. He dreamed that someday John Michael would have an institution dedicated in his name because of his good deeds. That is what they hoped to find. A young man who had learned some painful lessons, but was on the right track of making right choices for his life. Lewis stared again. What he had found was so far from what any of them expected, even him.

John Michael reached up and rubbed his eyes. Lewis was the last person he expected to see. He must have been dreaming of home again. Lewis wouldn't travel such a great distance to find him. He wondered if Lewis was there to get rid of him once and for all, then decided his brother had come to reconcile.

"Lewis?" he said, trying to sit up and still wondering if this was a dream. The alcohol in his bloodstream was very apparent. He grabbed the side of the bench to anchor himself. "What are you doing here? Is that really you?"

Lewis shook his head. He was ready to let his brother have it. "Oh, it's me, all right. The question of the day is, is that really you?"

John Michael sat up and clutched his side. He took a deep breath. Consuming that much booze had left him in deep pain. He started to slur when he talked. "This must be a dream. Why else would my big brother come to visit me? Only in a bad dream, right?"

"Dream? You think this is a dream?" Lewis pushed his chest. "This isn't a dream, John Michael. This is real. Take a look at my face. What you're seeing is the real thing." Lewis liked nothing more than the position of power he was now feeling.

John Michael tried to get up, but he couldn't keep his balance. He crashed back down on the bench. He wiped the drool that had seeped from his mouth while he was passed out.

"Look at you. You're pathetic, just as I thought."

"What do you want? What do you want from me?"

Lewis stared at him again.

"I wanted to see if it was really true."

John Michael looked down at his feet. He felt like he was going to throw up.

"True? If what was true?"

"What I thought happened to you. Dad kept telling me this would never happen. He kept talking about how full of character you are. I told him he was wrong. I was right. Again," he said with a smug look on his face.

"You're wrong," John Michael said as he turned his head and vomited over the side of the bench. As it hit the ground it splashed up on one of John Michael's shoes.

A trail of it seeped from his mouth and ran down his chin.

Lewis started to circle the bench, continuing to dig. "Wrong? Take a look at yourself, John Michael. You're dirty. You smell like booze. God knows where you've been sleeping, not to mention with whom. And you just vomited all over one of your shoes. Now, you really think I am seeing things wrong? Huh? Answer me!" Lewis pushed on John Michael's chest.

All that could be heard were a few passing cars and a bus. Like a lawyer pleading his case, he kept on. "You call this character? I've picked up your slack long enough; now we'll see whose character rises to the top."

John Michael was getting angry. He tried as hard as he could to put all of his motor skills to work at the same time. He started to stand up, but his left leg gave way and he fell to the ground. His head hit the pavement and opened a wound that started to bleed.

Lewis stared at his brother for a few fleeting moments. He looked so pathetic. Drunk. Dirty. Bleeding. It was almost a comfort seeing him like this. Lewis had always dreamed of being better than John Michael—now he was.

"You make me sick," said Lewis disgustedly.

"For God's sake, Lewis, I'm bleeding." John Michael noticed the blood on his hands and started to panic. "It's everywhere! Oh God, it's everywhere." John Michael reached out one of his bloody hands to his brother. Lewis pushed him away with his foot.

"Your blood isn't mine anymore."

John Michael sat up on his hands and knees struggling to stand. He staggered in front of his brother, leaning into Lewis and grabbing onto his jacket with his bloody hands. Lewis pushed him away and tried to wipe the blood off his jacket.

"You know what your problem is, Lewis?" he slurred. "Maybe I left home, but you, you did something far worse than I ever could."

Lewis turned around. "And what could that be?" he asked pridefully.

John Michael stepped forward, almost falling again, and pointed a finger in Lewis's face. "You left a long time ago!"

Lewis knew his brother was right. Although he lived with his father, his heart was as far away as John Michael's. Lewis had always been the model elder son. He desperately desired to live up to the expectations of his father and be considered obedient and compliant. More than anything, though, he desired to please. The worst fear he had was disappointing his dad. But like many elder brothers, he envied his younger brother, who on the surface seemed less concerned about pleasing and lived for himself. Even when John Michael had left, Lewis was jealous. He was jealous that John Michael had the courage to leave in search of an answer to what he was going through. Lewis never would have done that, and he didn't. Day after day, night after night, he stayed at home. Imprisoned by his own bondages. Although he couldn't visibly see his chains, he knew they were there, tightly wrapped around his heart. That made finding John Michael even better. His younger brother's prison seemed so much worse.

"You're so drunk you don't even know what you're saying. I never left home."

"I may be drunk, but I'd rather be intoxicated and honest than sober and a liar!"

"Lying about what? Huh?"

"1967 Bethel Drive may be where we grew up together, but it's far from where your heart calls home. That left a long time ago."

There was an honest silence. Lewis glanced at the ground and tried to think of something to say back. He came up blank. He kicked a metal garbage can.

"At least I had the guts to get out. You just stay home and lie to yourself every day. You're just as angry and confused about Mom as I am. Admit it! You liar! You just fake it, don't you?"

Lewis started to back up. John Michael stepped forward.

"Look who's telling the truth now, Lewis. I may die out here," he said, wiping the crimson red blood from his brow, "but you, you'll die in here!" John Michael pointed to his heart as he fell to the ground.

"You just wait, John Michael, wait until I tell Dad."

John Michael spoke again. "Tell him what you want, you miserable, spineless human being. If I know you, you won't tell him anything. You'll just keep our little secret locked up inside, won't you? WON'T YOU?!"

Lewis knelt beside John Michael and grabbed his brother's neck. John Michael gagged for air and tried to pull Lewis's hands off.

"This is it," whispered Lewis. "Never again will I have to worry about you. All of us can finally be freed from your pathetic life."

John Michael stared into his brother's eyes. He saw hatred. Why so much hate? What through the years had John Michael ever done to breed so much hate between them? His vision started to get foggy, and quickly the lack of oxygen made his face turn red.

Lewis, too, stared into the eyes of his brother. His head was wild with voices.

"Get rid of him! No one will notice."

"This is your chance to be number one!"

"Your father will never know!"

"You will never have to hear about him again!"

"This is your only chance. Take it! TAKE IT! NOW!"

Lewis squeezed harder and harder. John Michael was turning blue. It wouldn't be long before his brother was dead. No more comparisons. His painful attempt to stay ahead of his brother would be over. Maybe then he could be himself. Lewis had always been obedient, dutiful, hardworking, and self-sacrificing. He was tired of not getting noticed. Obsessed about it, one could say. Obsessed enough to kill. Lewis tightened his grip. John Michael fought for oxygen.

"We're almost done, little brother. ALMOST DONE!"

Lewis turned his head. He could hear footsteps. They were getting closer. For a few seconds he thought about getting caught and spending the rest of his life in prison. Maybe then he would get the kind of attention he was longing for.

"Lewis, where are you?" yelled a familiar voice.

He looked up. His hands loosened from around John Michael's neck. His brother gasped and fought for the chance to breath again.

"Lewis? Where are you?"

Lewis dropped John Michael's head onto the pavement. He stood up and started to run past the bench, down the alley, and away from his brother's body. He hoped he'd held on long enough.

"Lewis!" he heard his father yell. "Lewis! Where are you?" Lewis saw his father coming towards him. He panicked. They couldn't come down here. What if they found John Michael? What if his father found out what he had done to his brother? In an effort to cover his tracks, he turned around and ran back towards his brother's body. He dragged John Michael over to the bench. Lewis covered him up with the newspapers that were still lying on the ground. He stepped back and noticed the blood and vomit. He remembered John Michael's blood was all over his jacket and his hands. Lewis tried to wipe it on the papers that covered his brother's body, but the stain wouldn't go away.

Philip and Jonathan seemed to appear quicker than Lewis had expected. As soon as he was done wiping his hands he heard his father's voice.

"Lewis," his dad said. Lewis stepped back to where Jonathan and Philip were standing. "Why did you run when I called?"

Lewis tried to think of something to say. "I," he stumbled, "I thought I saw something back here."

Jonathan tried to look behind him. Lewis kept moving in front of his father's sight. "Well, did you see anything?"

"Uh, no," said Lewis.

"You said you saw something, what did you notice?"

"It was nothing."

Philip and Jonathan glanced at one another.

"Lewis, why are so you so fidgety?"

"I'm not." He stopped moving around, but kept shuffling his feet.

"We haven't found anything. Philip said no one had any information either. How about you? Did you find anything?"

Lewis paused again. He looked at the bench out of the corner of his eye. John Michael was lying lifeless. "Yes, I did talk to someone, but nothing really came of it."

"How about this alley?"

Lewis's stomach dropped. Jonathan started to look around. He looked under a few pieces of wood, checked inside a nearby dumpster, and started searching the ends of the alley.

"Dad, I'm telling you there is nothing here."

Philip noticed the bench. "Then what's that on the bench?"

"Just a bum. Let's go. This place is starting to give me the creeps."

"Dad, you don't think that's John Michael, do you?"

Jonathan looked at Lewis. "I don't know. Lewis, did you check?"

Silence.

"Lewis, did you check?" asked Jonathan again.

"Yeah, I checked. Now let's just get out of here before we get shot."

Three loud pops echoed in the distance. There was a shooting going on. They looked at each other. Philip moved towards his father. Jonathan knew he needed to get his family away from this place, but his heart didn't want to leave one son behind. He felt so close. He knew in his heart John Michael was nearby.

"What did I tell you, Dad. Let's go. You heard the shots. Do you want lose your other two sons?"

Jonathan looked at the bench.

"Just a second. I just need to check this out. What if this were your brother and I came this close to finding him?"

A flash of lightning danced across the sky, followed by a crash of thunder. A few drops started to fall, then more. Within seconds they were pounding and splashing harshly on the alley pavement.

"NO!" screamed Lewis into the rain. The sound of his voice was drowned out by another crash of thunder.

Jonathan walked briskly to the bench. Philip ran to his side as Lewis followed cautiously behind. Jonathan reached for the wet newspapers that covered the man. He gave them a shake trying to rouse the sleeping body.

"Hello?"

The rain started to pound harder. A rush of water flowed down the rusty gutter pipes on each side of the alley. A car whizzed by, splashing dirty water on all of them. Their clothes were drenched. Water fell from Philip's hair and ran down his green nylon jacket. Another flash of lightning and booming sound struck close to where they were.

"Dad, let's go!" said Lewis in a panic.

Jonathan kept shaking the wet newspapers. Lewis stepped up behind his father and grabbed his shoulder, pulling him away.

"Dad, it's just a bum. We've got a 15-minute walk to the car. Let's get out of here." Lewis cursed. His father didn't hear Lewis do that often.

"Lewis! What has gotten into you? I'm trying not to startle the man."

Lewis pushed his father away and tore off the newspapers that covered John Michael's body. He left a page covering half of John Michael's face.

"There. It's not him. Now, can we go!" Lewis was beyond frustrated. His breath formed a vapor cloud in the rain, then disappeared in the air. "Dad, would you let him go!"

Jonathan looked down at the body now soaked by the pouring rain. He didn't recognize the ripped jeans and t-shirt. The dirty appearance looked very different from what he remembered John Michael wearing. Lewis started to walk away hoping his father and brother would do the same. Instead, Lewis's heart sank when he saw his father reach for the last newspaper.

Jonathan knelt beside the body. Philip put his hand on his father's shoulder. Both of them focused on the face that would soon be revealed.

Jonathan couldn't tell if the person was alive or dead. A crack of thunder startled them bringing Jonathan to his feet for a few seconds, then back down. He looked up at Philip, then back at Lewis. He started to pull the wet newspaper away from the person's face. Philip noticed an ad for a missing child on the paper. It was a picture of a small boy with the dates of his disappearance in bold writing. He remembered the promise John Michael made to him at the bus stop.

"I'll be fine. Look, you're not going to find my face on a milk carton..."

It wasn't a milk carton, but Philip wondered how long his brother would be missing. Jonathan pulled off the newsprint, but before he could focus he heard a loud horn followed by squealing tires. Jonathan turned to find Lewis on the ground, holding onto his leg and rolling around the wet cement. The car stopped for a moment, then sped away before they could get a good look at it.

"Lewis!" cried Jonathan, running to his side.

Philip stopped to look at the face on the bench. It didn't look like his older brother, but then he really couldn't see through the rain in the dark alley.

Jonathan knelt down at Lewis's side.

"Did he hit you? Lewis, talk to me. Did he hit you?"

Lewis started to breathe hard, then cry. "He swiped me, Dad. The back end of the car hit my side and leg."

Jonathan pulled Lewis's wet coat away and took a look at his side. No trace of a hit.

"Are you sure, Son?"

Lewis cursed. "Of course, I am. I feel it, Dad. He hit me."

"Where does it hurt, Lewis? Where?"

"It's my leg. I think it might be broken."

Jonathan called for Philip to help him pick up Lewis by the arms. They cradled his tall frame between their bodies with Lewis's arms around each of their shoulders.

"We've got to get him to the hospital. I think the car is this way."

Another bolt of lightning and clap of thunder persuaded them to walk quickly. They started down the alley. Jonathan paused for a moment and looked back. It started to rain harder than it had before. Their bodies were heavier with the added weight of water their clothes had soaked up.

"Philip, go cover that person up with the newspaper. I'll keep heading to the car with Lewis. We at least need to cover him back up. I won't be too far ahead."

Lewis let out a scream when Philip let go. He tried to watch Philip run back through the rain to the bench. Jonathan kept walking.

"Dad, it hurts. It hurts!"

Philip kept wiping his eyes as he walked to the bench. The rain was coming down so hard now that he could only see what was directly in front of his face. He grabbed the newspaper that Lewis had torn off and covered the body again. The newspaper started to rip because of the wet state it was in. Philip felt a chill run down his spine and started to hurry. He was thinking about how their trip was turning sour. Instead of searching for John Michael anymore, they would most likely be taking Lewis home. He reached for the last sheet of wet newsprint to cover the man's face when a bolt of lighting lit up the sky. Philip glanced at the man. For a split second, he thought he saw his brother. Philip wiped his eyes again. The flash only lasted a second, then it was gone. It was too dark and it was raining too hard to see. He thought that if it was his brother they would have noticed something familiar, but nothing resembled John Michael. Besides, he thought, John Michael would never live on the streets like this. With that, Philip covered the man's face, turned around, and ran down the alley to help his father.

Lewis turned one last time to look at the bench. His secret remained intact. He was grateful for the car that had gone by. Now, all he had to do was pretend that he was in pain. Philip ran alongside Lewis and put his arm under his shoulder. Lewis smirked inside. It had worked.

"Keep going, boys. We've got a ways to go still. How are you doing, Lewis?"

Lewis winced to let his father think he was in pain. His physical body wasn't hurting, but little did Lewis know, he'd almost killed his heart. That couldn't be carried on anyone's shoulders but his own.

Sixteen

Forgiveness

The sound of thunder cracked through the streets and alleys of downtown Chicago. The wind was blowing hard, but not hard enough to blow the wet newspapers off John Michael, who was still lying dazed on the bench. The drunken stupor was starting to wear off. His legs and arms started to move lethargically.

One eye opened, then two. It was dark under the soaking newspapers. John Michael was starting to wonder where he was and how he had gotten there. *Where am I?* A chilling wind blew up his legs and over his chest. His lips started to quiver. His clothes were drenched. He took in a deep breath as he began to wake up and felt something heavy resting on his feet.

"Oh, I'm sorry," said a voice he had never heard before. It was sweet, peaceful, and kind. It reminded him of his mother. He grabbed the newspaper that covered his head and pulled it away. What he saw reminded him of a vision of an angel he'd seen on television.

She was standing with an umbrella. A street light a block down reflected off her dark hair. She was wearing a pair of blue jeans and a short gray tank top. A black windbreaker kept her from the rain. Her deep brown eyes searched his. She looked innocent to John Michael. He tried to sit up, but couldn't. He felt like he was going to throw up.

"I didn't know you were there. I didn't see you. I guess I wasn't really looking," she said politely.

John Michael tried sitting up again. He rested his back on the bench and rubbed his head and face with his hands. "I must have passed out. I thought you were my father for a minute."

"Your father?"

"My father. I know this sounds crazy, but when I passed out I started dreaming that he was here. What a nightmare. I would never want my father to see me like this. He would kill me." He rubbed his face again. The thought occurred to him that his memory hadn't been a dream. "How long have you been sitting there?"

"Just a minute or so. Not long. I thought the bench felt funny. With the umbrella over my head, I just didn't notice anyone there. I was waiting for the bus to come by, then I heard you moan and felt you move. You scared me."

"Sorry."

"That's OK. I think I startled you, too!" She smiled at him.

"Don't worry about it. My fault for passing out here. Not the greatest place in the world, huh?" He reached out his wet hand. "My name is John Michael."

She reached back. "My name is Jasmine. It's nice to meet you."

"Yeah, you never know what you're going to find at your local bus bench, do you? You might even find a drunk man under a pile of wet newspapers." He looked at her closely again. Something about her seemed awfully familiar. "Have we ever met before?"

"I don't think so."

"Are you sure? I think I've seen you around here before."

"Well, you wouldn't have seen me around for awhile. The cops hauled me in a few months ago. I've been in juvenile detention."

"Detention? Aren't you a little old for detention?"

Jasmine looked away. She closed her umbrella since it had stopped raining. She looked at what she was wearing. "You think I look older? If you think that, then I'm sure everyone else will. I'm almost 18."

"How did you get out and back down here? No parent in their right mind would let their daughter leave to catch a bus here."

"A man named Logan helped me. He's kind of like my father. I do a bunch of tricks for him, and he takes care of me. You know what I mean?"

It was all making sense to John Michael now. He had seen her with Logan on occasion at the Java Shop. She was the prettiest and most gentle of the young ladies Logan would occasionally escort with him. John Michael always wondered how such a beautiful girl got caught up in such a dirty ring. One night stands. Hourly tricks. Laying all of your pride on a bed that would last a few hours at most. For a second, his heart felt a sadness for her that he hadn't sensed since he had left home. "Logan? A father? C'mon, I know the guy. Don't you have a real dad?"

Jasmine moved a few wet newspapers and sat down next to him. The comfort of having someone listen was a rare commodity on the streets. They were sheltering each other from their own personal storms.

"My dad left when I was a kid. Divorce. I haven't seen him in years. The only thing I know about my father is that he sent a check to my mom once a month. It was never enough, but at least it was something. That's my idea of a father. Logan pays my bills, so I call him 'Daddy.' Who has a real father anymore?"

John Michael watched a passing car, then answered quietly, "I do."

He paused for a moment. He couldn't believe that had come out of his mouth. He closed his eyes, remembering his father.

"What?" Jasmine asked.

"Well, I did. Before I left home."

Jasmine looked confused. "Let me get this straight. You had a real dad and you left him?"

John Michael shook his head.

"You're the first person I've ever met that had a real dad." She had a sparkle in her eye. She quickly turned to John Michael. "What was he like? Was he a good dad?"

John Michael stopped to think for a moment. *My father?* "Good? One word can't possibly explain my father."

Jasmine grabbed his knee. Her excitement was hard to contain. John Michael thought it was rather odd, but if she wanted to talk, he was willing to keep the conversation going. It was the first one he'd had in quite a while where he wasn't too drunk or high to remember it. The feeling seemed so right. She continued on.

"Tell me what he was like. Did he laugh a lot? Did he swing you around in his arms and tuck you into bed at night? Did he tickle you and make you laugh and wipe your tears when you would cry?"

"As a matter of fact he did."

"Really? I saw a dad like that in a movie once. That's as close as I ever got."

"He would make me laugh, and swing me around, and tickle me. He would always do that. When I was about four or five he tickled me so hard that I wet my pants." They both smiled.

"He was loving, joyful, full of peace, and gentle. He was kind and patient..." John Michael stopped.

"What?"

"I was just remembering how my dad was always patient even when I messed up. He never yelled or screamed or anything like that."

There was a lull in the conversation. John Michael could tell he had hit a soft spot down deep in Jasmine's soul. She looked away and said something he would never forget.

"I wish I could have a dad like that."

After much thought John Michael responded. "I'm glad I did."

"Then what are you doing here?" Jasmine had hit the most sensitive part of John Michael's heart. He had never let anyone in this far. He wondered if he could be honest with her and with himself.

"I don't know, running. I guess I'm running."

"Why are you running?"

"It seemed like the only answer. I was tired of people, but most of all my dad. I was tired of everyone telling me how to live my life."

"Why don't you go home and see him now?"

"I'm sure he's forgotten all about me now. Besides, how could I ever face him after all I've done?" John Michael looked down in shame. The choices he had made over the past few months ran through his mind. The money he'd spent. The drugs he'd taken. The one-night stands. It was too much for him. He bit his lip and grabbed the bench. His father would never forgive him. He felt trapped. Trapped into making the same mistake over and over...leaving. Why try when he felt so guilty of what he'd done? How could his father love him now?

"Tell me more. Tell me more about your father. Can we pretend that he's my dad, too? Just for a little while?"

John Michael pretended, too. He pretended that everything was all right.

"There was this one time I got in big trouble."

"What for?"

"I stole some gum from a grocery store. He found out on the way home when I took it out of my pocket. He made me go back to the clerk at the store and apologize for what I had done. When I got home, he sent me to my room."

"John Michael, I'll be up in a moment. I need to talk this over with your mother first."

John Michael dragged his small body up the stairs. He dreaded those meetings. It wasn't like he planned to steal. He opened his bedroom door and lay on the bed. His eyes started to tear up. He knew he had done wrong.

Jonathan made his way up the stairs shortly after John Michael had plopped himself down. John Michael heard his father's footsteps and clutched his pillow for support. The moment Jonathan stepped inside the room he looked deep into his son's eyes. His son had failed again. Jonathan sighed and sat down on the bed next to John Michael.

"John Michael, will you sit up and listen to me for a minute?"

Apprehensively, John Michael sat up. Like a prisoner waiting to be executed, John Michael awaited his punishment.

Jonathan reached out and touched his shoulder. "Son, I know you know how wrong this was, right?"

John Michael nodded his head. Jonathan placed his fingers under John Michael's quivering chin and lifted it up.

"And you know that I really believe in you, right?"

John Michael nodded again.

"Then you've got to remember when you're making decisions how much I believe in you. You see, Son, my love is stronger for you than anything you seem to be going through. And I'll always be there for you, even when you make wrong choices. We can make it, my boy. We can make it. I forgive you. Can you forgive yourself?" And with that, he wrapped his arms around John Michael and held him tight. Jonathan's arms made John Michael feel secure in his father's love. It was a moment John Michael had never forgotten. A moment he was glad to remind himself of today.

"He said, 'We can make it. I forgive you, you just need to forgive yourself.' "

John Michael caught himself mid-sentence. The same words his father had said years ago rang true today. "I forgive you, now you need to forgive yourself." Forgive yourself. Maybe he could go home if he would do that today.

"He sounds like a wonderful man," Jasmine said.

"He is."

"I wish I could meet him."

"Maybe you will someday."

A city bus traveled down the street towards the bench. Jasmine stood up and thanked John Michael for his time. John Michael tried to stand too, but sat back down. He still wasn't feeling better. His head felt dizzy and his stomach felt nauseous. Jasmine climbed up the steps, picked a seat, and waved to John Michael out the window. He waved back as the exhaust from the bus blew through his wet, moppy hair. Jasmine forced John Michael to think about his father like he never had before. But what about the dream? Would his father ever forgive him?

He remembered his father's words again. "You see, Son, my love for you is stronger than anything you are going through."

John Michael hoped that was still true as he stumbled away from the alley down the street. His father's love was stronger than anything he was going through.

Seventeen

The Toilet

John Michael firmly gripped the mop as he finished soaking up all the water that was running across the floor. *This is disgusting! I hate this job,* replied a voice inside his head. Although the room was disinfected, it wouldn't be long before it would lose the fresh clean scent. Within hours it would be a mess again. That's why John Michael cleaned it every day. It was his job to make sure the men at the mission had a clean restroom when they needed to hide from their problems for the night.

The man that was staring at John Michael had finally passed out. He drifted off somewhere in the midst of John Michael's last story. John Michael continued on anyway. When you need someone to listen, it doesn't matter if they respond or not. He was finally on his way to freedom. The more he talked, the more his heart seemed to mend. Admitting the things he was dealing with seemed to take a load off his mind. He found that confession was good for the soul. John Michael's mind was so full of emotional dirt that any shoveling he could do to lessen the load helped.

As he set the mop in the corner, a few men started waking up. John Michael's job for the morning was close to being done. He took out a scrub brush and some bleach. The toilets were next. He reached for the first stall door. He opened it and gagged.

It seemed there was always one more mess around the corner. He flushed the toilet with his foot and watched the dirty water go down. He poured in the bleach. John Michael was used to washing toilets. It was just a part of daily life now. Life. Who would have thought his life would end up this way.

John Michael threw the scrub brush into the water. He looked at the man and started to talk again. Cleaning the toilets didn't seem so bad when he spent the time talking.

"It takes me a long time to mop the floor. These toilets seem to take even longer. I wonder if they'll ever come clean."

John Michael continued to scrub the toilet. The ring around the top of the bowl wouldn't disappear. He flushed it again and watched the water go down.

"Man, it's going to take me a long time to flush all the crud down. It seems like I try and fail, then try and fail. What's the use? Huh? I thought this whole entire experience was going to be so cool. Being cool has worn off. I wouldn't be scrubbing toilets at home. Home. I can't go back there. No way. I've got too much pride to go there."

He was full of pride. Not the kind that puffs your ego up, but the kind that isn't willing to face the truth. John Michael wasn't ready to see his father. He wasn't willing to admit he was wrong or that he had failed. He wasn't ready to reveal who he'd become. He moved on to the next stall.

"I'm too prideful to go home, and too hurt to face the future. That's what brought me to this place. Some of the guys call it the 'pit' or the 'pig house.' No one ever thought I would end up here. Not even me. Now look where I stand."

He looked back at the sleeping man. "I said look, you dummy! You don't care, do you? Well, I never thought I'd end up here. Nobody ever does. But before you know it, one bad choice leads to another."

He poured the bleach into the toilet, wishing he could clean up his life.

Eighteen

The Snow and the Fire

Waiting. Jonathan was waiting for the snow to stop. It had come early this year. Late October wasn't the usual time for this kind of weather. The white flakes fell from the sky, forming a thick blanket that covered the already snowy ground. It had been snowing in Willowbrook since early that morning. The winds had picked up, making drifts that were several feet. It hadn't snowed in Kansas like this for several years. The town was quiet. The shops were closed. Even traffic had come to a halt. The only vehicles that could be heard were occasional snow plows and a few snowmobiles scurrying through a field nearby. Otherwise, the small town seemed asleep. Even the new McDonald's built right off the exit ramp of the highway had closed because of the weather. The entire population of Willowbrook was tightly shut in their homes waiting for the snow to stop.

Jonathan stared at the white fluff piling up on the porch in front of the living room window. He, too, was waiting. The sunset was starting to fade into the distance. He turned on the porch light. Jonathan crossed his arms and sighed. It was going to be another cold Midwestern night. He thought it might be a good idea to light a fire. He was stuck in for the night and wondered how long he would have to wait. This season of his life had taught him an awful lot about waiting. Every parent has to learn to wait. It had become a process for Jonathan. Early on he had realized that waiting would either make him stronger as a father, or weaker as a man. Waiting was never easy. Although it was good for him to learn, the advantages of being patient never seemed to outweigh the hardship that comes when you have to wait.

"Good things come to those who wait," he reminded himself as he stepped into the garage to grab a pile of firewood. There were so many things he had embraced by learning to wait. Faith, hope, courage, and a new outlook on what being a father is all about. He had done everything he knew to do during the years his boys were growing up. Elizabeth and he had trained them to love others, see the difference between right and wrong, and be secure in knowing they would always have a place to call home. Character had also been a main focus. Now, that might be the only thing that would bring John Michael home. Jonathan believed in character. His view of character was different from most. As far as Jonathan was concerned, character wasn't about brushing the pain of life under the carpet. He had been criticized in the Willowbrook community for allowing his son the freedom he had asked for. Even a few close friends wondered how such an impacting judge could raise a child, then just let him go. Jonathan ignored their condemnation. Nothing could ever separate him from the love he felt for his sons. Nothing. Even if that meant they made decisions he couldn't agree with. The others couldn't begin to understand how painful it was to let John Michael go. Waiting had helped him understand that every child has to come to a point when they make their own life decisions. Jonathan had learned that from the time they are born the process of letting go is underway.

He cradled a few logs in his arms and took them back into the house. He wished it was John Michael he was holding. His favorite age to cradle his boys was the first few months of their lives. They would lie so peacefully, at rest in his arms, totally dependent on their parent's love and care for them. Before long, they crawled out of his arms and into the world. Soon, they'd decide everything for themselves—first, which shoes to wear or what to eat, then where to live or whom to love.

After John Michael had left, Jonathan had felt so much guilt for letting him go. For months he blamed himself for John Michael's decisions. He'd tried to do the best he could as a parent. He had to let go of the guilt. For every wrong decision he'd made regarding John Michael's life, he had to remind himself of two or three things he had done right. It wasn't long before he was concentrating on the good rather than focusing on the bad. Mistakes? He knew he'd made many. Every father does. But the test of a real father, Jonathan decided, was not in how many mistakes he had made, but in how he had reacted to his children after he made the mistake. Humility always came at a high price that his ego had to pay.

Although he felt like his world had fallen apart, waiting had uncovered a hidden strength that had kept him together, despite the constant emotional weariness. Their recent disastrous trip into Chicago only proved even more to Jonathan that waiting for John Michael to come home was the only way to deal with the situation. Searching yet not finding John Michael made him feel even more empty. But at least they had found out that he was still alive.

The fire he had built burned brightly as he tossed on a few more logs. He hoped that somewhere, somehow his lost son felt the warmth of the roaring fire of love his father had for him. Jonathan knew at some point that warmth would bring his boy home.

John Michael sat in front of a fire he had built inside a barrel. He was in an alley between two abandoned apartment buildings. He was thinking about his father. The fire inside his heart had been stoked by the memories that were etched deep there. He placed his hands over the roaring blaze and felt the heat tingle through his fingers. His mission of freedom didn't seem that fun anymore. He was waiting for an opportunity to come to his senses. If he didn't it would only prove how wrong his leaving was. The last thing he wanted was to be wrong and allow Lewis to remind him of it daily. *I had to leave! I did!* His cold hands reminded him of the mistake he had made. The orange light danced in his eyes. John Michael was freezing. He wished he could jump inside the fire without getting burned—then he would feel warm everywhere. For now, he would have to settle with fingers. He realized the fire would never grow large enough to warm his cold heart.

Jonathan sat in front of the fireplace. John Michael stood in front of the blazing barrel. Both of them felt the sting of loneliness as they languished in their grief at not being with one another. Something was changing inside John Michael. An ember was starting to burn in his heart. Thinking about his father seemed to be the spark that was making his feelings ignite. An ember was also burning inside of Jonathan. It was an ember of hope as he patiently waited for John Michael to come home. Nothing could separate him from the love he felt for his son. Not even the miles between could change the fire consuming their hearts.

Nineteen

The Rush Street Mission

The Rush Street Mission's neon sign flickered on and off in the light of the moon shining brightly in the sky. The darkened Chicago streets would embrace the light of the sun soon. As John Michael walked by the mission, its neon sign reflected off his face. It had been days since Logan left him without a roof over his head. Now, stone cold and broke, he wandered the downtown streets of Chicago searching for any warm spot to sleep. Park benches. Alley corners. Abandoned buildings. Cardboard houses. John Michael had learned a lesson about shelter. It wasn't so much where he stayed as it was just having a place to stay. Sometimes he found shelter, sometimes he didn't. This particular night he hadn't. Aimlessly he walked past store windows and 24-hour restaurants. His stomach had been growling for days. A dumpster turned out to be a gold mine. He'd found some old cheeseburgers a Greek restaurant had thrown away. If he could get to the food before the rats, he had a meal. Maybe not a seven course dinner, but at least it would take away the hunger pains of an empty stomach.

An empty stomach. An empty spirit. An empty soul. John Michael had been completely emptied. Gone was the pride, the independence, the freedom to make it on his own. John Michael was crushed. Life had taken his spirit and left small fragments of who he was behind.

John Michael walked for several hours. The morning rays burst through the clouds that were hanging above the city. It was early morning. John Michael sighed. At least the night was over. He sat down on a nearby curb and rubbed his hands together. His lungs were aching as he coughed uncontrollably due to the cool night air he'd been breathing. A man in a suit passed by and dropped a quarter in his lap. John Michael tossed it back, but the man had already passed. He'd given out his charitable contribution for the day on the way to his executive office. A man dressed in a ripped flannel shirt, grimy jeans, torn tennis shoes, and an old hat ran into the road and snatched up the quarter.

John Michael stood up and started down the street. He didn't want another quarter thrown in his direction. He'd been humbled enough when the local police caught him raiding a dumpster behind Gino's pizzeria. As he crossed the street he noticed the Rush Street Mission. He had passed it hundreds of times, yet he had never stopped before. It was another pride issue. A sign in the window promised shelter and a hot meal. Shelter? Food? That about covered all of John Michael's needs at this point in his life. Reluctantly, he crossed Rush Street towards the mission. It looked like an old storefront that had been renovated in the 1970s. Cluttered between a donut shop and a neighborhood grocery store, it offered a roof over one's head without a lot of the extras. It definitely wasn't the Ritz Carlton, but at least it was something. John Michael stood staring at the sign one more time before walking to the entrance. As he stepped up to the door, his hand started to shake. He hadn't been nervous in months. Three knocks, then three more. He bit his lip and knocked one more time.

"C'mon," he whispered into the light wind. No answer. *Two more times, that's all I'm going to knock.* "This must not be right," he said to himself, disappointed, as he turned and began walking away. Before he reached the corner to go back across Rush Street, he heard the door open. He quickly turned around.

"Hello?" he said running back for the door. It was starting to shut. "Hello? Don't shut the door, I'm coming."

The door shut with a slam. John Michael cursed. He pounded his fist on the door in anger as he tried to catch his breath.

"Open the door!" he said between breaths. "C'mon! I can't live like this anymore. Would somebody open the door? For God's sake, aren't you people open 24 hours?"

He turned away and started down the steps towards the street.

"Twenty-three hours. We're closed one hour a day for a little rest and relaxation."

"What?" said John Michael turning back around.

"Rest and relaxation. You got a problem with that? Sheesh. You're not the only one who is having a hard time around here. Try cleaning the bathroom upstairs. Now that is a problem."

A man's head popped out the door, then back in. The door shut and a small mail slot opened up. All John Michael could see was the man's lips. He walked up the stairs and crouched down to the mail slot.

"Sorry. I have to do this for safety reasons."

John Michael looked at the lips puzzled. "What?"

"Is that the only word you know? It's no wonder you're having problems."

"I thought this was a mission."

"Read the sign again. Go ahead, read it."

John Michael looked up at the sign above the door again. The letters were cracked, but John Michael could still read them.

"The Rush Street Mission."

"Good. You can read."

"What?"

"There you go again."

"Am I at the right place?"

"Depends on what you want. All the jelly donuts are gone."

"I'm not here for a donut. I need a place to stay."

"The Drake Hotel isn't far. Just kidding."

"I don't have a place to sleep. I used to have an apartment around here, but I can't stay there anymore."

"Don't have any more money, huh?"

John Michael started to explain despite the awkwardness of talking to a mail slot with lips. "How did you know?"

"I've heard the story before."

"My story? I've never been here before."

"Let me guess. You left home, then ran out of money."

"I used to have a lot of money."

The lips smirked.

"Really! But I spent it all."

"Yeah, yeah. Drugs, alcohol, and sex, right? You and a whole city full of others."

"You don't understand."

"Listen, do you want me to get a violin out here? I've heard this sob story hundreds of times before. Must you share it again?"

"Mine is different."

"You and everybody else."

"I'm serious."

"And so am I."

"Do you have any room for me?"

"We're full. Try the animal shelter down the street."

"Full?"

"Full."

John Michael stood up. "Listen, I don't have to be here, you know. I have a home, and a father who loves me, and a warm bed waiting for me there."

Something dropped out the mail slot and landed with a thud on the ground.

"Here."

John Michael picked up a folded piece of thick paper. "What's this?"

The mail slot opened and the lips appeared again. "A map of the United States. Find your way home." With that, the flap slammed shut.

John Michael stared at the map in his hands. *A map?* He turned around and stepped away. "I can't go home. I'm not ready to go home. My father wouldn't accept me anyway." John Michael threw the map in the air as he stood in the middle of the crowd that was passing by. He cried out, "Where am I supposed to go now?"

A few faces glanced his way, then went on their way. The map unfolded and landed by his feet. He kicked it a few feet in front him. A pigeon noticed the map coming its way and flew into the air.

The door behind John Michael opened slightly. The man inside the mission surveyed John Michael's frame. His ripped shirt, jeans, and worn shoes revealed the truth. The door cracked open a little further, then further. John Michael heard the voice again.

"All right, we got room here. You can come in."

John Michael turned around, making his way to the door. A short, pudgy man was standing there. He had scraggly white hair and was wearing a brown robe with a sash tied around his waist. A pair of reading glasses had fallen to the tip of his nose.

"Let's go," said the man, "Get your things. I haven't got all day."

"You got it," said John Michael, scrambling for his ripped duffel bag. "I'm coming. Don't shut that door until I get in there." He jumped up the steps and ran inside the thick wooden door into a dark hallway. It smelled musty. It reminded John Michael of the apartment Logan had put him up in. The short, pudgy man reached out his hand.

"Hello. Douglas Weatherfrey. I'm the executive officer of the Rush Street Mission. That's a fancy term for "I run the joint." At least I think I do."

Douglas turned around and started down the hallway. John Michael grabbed his bag and followed him.

"Name?"

"Uh, John Michael Davis."

"Davis. Davis," Douglas said rubbing his chin. "Don't know any Davises. I know a Davidson, but no Davis. Have I seen you at the food pantry before?"

"No."

"Why not? Too egotistical to call yourself needy?"

"Ah, not really. I didn't know you had one."

"Sure, sure. Listen, kid, one thing we've got to make clear here. You're in need. Take a look at yourself."

John Michael looked down at his worn shoes, dirty jeans, and torn shirt. Yes, he was needy. What nobody could see was the hole in his stomach. It growled as Douglas led him up a flight of stairs and into a large open area. There was graffiti on a few of the walls. The dingy gray paint made it evident that the walls hadn't been painted or cleaned in months, maybe even years.

"We couldn't afford a decorator so we hired gangs to paint their symbols on the walls."

John Michael stared at him. Douglas hit him in the arm with his fist.

"Just kidding. Loosen up, kid. Sheesh. You need an enema or something?" Douglas laughed at himself as they started walking again. "The bathrooms are over there. That's where you clean up after yourself. We don't scrub down our residents. When you use the toilet, you're allowed no more than five squares of toilet paper. Five squares only. It's amazing how many squares you people waste. Besides, this building was built in 1946. The piping is old and small. Anything over five squares will clog 'em up.

Breakfast is at 7:00 a.m., lunch at noon, and dinner at five o'clock sharp."

"Sharp?"

"Sharp. During the day you work for me. It's our job to feed the hungry and shelter the homeless."

"Homeless? But I am homeless. That's why I'm here."

"What?"

"I'm here for a meal, not a job."

"I thought you were inquiring about our janitorial position. If you're here for a meal, you already missed it, buddy. Now, let me show you the door."

Douglas started down the stairs. John Michael stopped at the top.

"Wait. Please. I'll take the job."

Douglas turned around with a glare. "Oh, you're interested now? I see."

"Really. I am."

"What experience do you have?"

"Well, I, uh, don't have a high school education, but I plan on getting my GED."

"I need experience, not an education. When you're helping those in need, they don't normally need you to spell out words. What kind of experience do you have? Have you ever had a job?"

John Michael paused and hung his head. "No, I haven't."

"So, you've lived the easy life. Is that it?"

"Well, I mean, yes. But, this past year has been the hardest experience I've ever had. I'm sure I can do anything you need me to. I have to if I want to survive out there."

"Experience. I need experience." Douglas turned and started down the stairs again.

John Michael ran after him, falling to his knees and grabbing the back of Douglas's robe. "Please! I'll do anything. I'll wash dishes, sweep floors, or scrub toilets. Please, just give me a place to stay and some meals to eat. I'm begging you!"

Douglas glared at him. He rubbed his chin and paused for a minute.

"Well, you've found a soft spot in my heart today."

"Really?"

Douglas smiled. "Really, kid. But that spot may go away by tomorrow. You'd better show me how hard you can work or you may find yourself in line for food instead of servin' it. Got it?" he said, winking at John Michael.

"Uh, yeah. I got it."

"Here," Douglas continued grabbing a nearby mop left next to the stairwell. He placed it in John Michael's hand.

"What's this for?"

"To dance with! What do you think it's for? You can start by mopping the bathrooms. Oh, make sure you mop really hard around the toilets; the floor is a mess. Got it? I'll be down here." Douglas passed by John Michael and headed down the hall.

"Oh, and don't forget to use this," said Douglas as he turned around and threw a small item John Michael's way.

"What for?" he asked after catching it.

"It's to clean with after you mop. Now get started."

John Michael held a dirty, used toothbrush. The bristles were parted and smashed, indicating how used the brush was.

"You expect me to clean this place with a toothbrush?"

"Every day. I'll check on you later," Douglas answered as he went on his way.

John Michael crunched the bristles down in his hand. He headed back up the stairs, down a hallway, and through a door that led him to the men's restroom. It reeked of urine. He sloshed around in some water covered with wet toilet paper. One of the toilets had obviously gotten plugged up in the middle of the night. Instead of fixing it or leaving it, the residents continued to use it. John Michael leaned against the wall and stared at the mess he was about to clean. He couldn't remember ever having to clean a toilet or mop a floor. He wiped his face and decided it was time to get started. From a nearby storage closet, he grabbed a bucket and filled it with cold water and pine cleaner. He started to slop the mixture around the floor. Although a few pieces of wet toilet paper came up every now and then, the water was not going down. John Michael studied the problem. He was repulsed when he realized he would have to touch the mop to squeeze the excess water out. He stepped away from the bucket and mop for a moment.

Do I really want to do this? he thought. "Not really. My father would never make me mop this disgusting toilet water up. But," he sighed. "Do I really have a choice?" He saw a window through a doorway to another room. He could see the Chicago streets below. "I sure don't want to go back out there." He had lost all of his money, friends, and now his dignity. What could possibly be left? John Michael grabbed the mop and began mopping feverishly. His hands were starting to prune as he squeezed the water into the bucket. Three hours and four buckets later, proud of his accomplishment, he placed the mop and bucket into the side storage closet. John Michael had wondered if he could do it. He had proven he could. Douglas would be proud. John Michael hoped Douglas would keep him on board.

As he shut the door, John Michael turned his attention back to the bathroom area. He heard a stall door shut. Now someone could actually enjoy using the facilities with its fresh, clean scent. As he made his way down the hall he heard a sound that stopped him in the middle of the stairs. John Michael heard a toilet flush. He turned back, ran up the stairs and down the hall to make sure the plugged up toilet wasn't being used. In all of the effort to get the floor clean, he had forgotten to unclog the plumbing. "Surely," he told himself, "they won't use that toilet. They'll see the clog and use one that works."

By the time he was back to the bathroom his answer was clear. Water sloshed around his feet again. This time there were more wet toilet paper bits and pieces than before. John Michael hung his head in defeat.

"Aren't you done yet?" came a voice from behind.

John Michael turned around, startled by Douglas's presence there. "Well, I, just cleaned it up..."

"Cleaned it up? What have you been doing up here? Swimming? There's more water now than before. If you want a place to stay, you're going to have to show off your cleaning skills a bit more, if you know what I mean. Do I need to show you where the mop is again?"

John Michael wiped his forehead with the back of his hand. He was dripping with sweat. "No, I know where it is."

"Well, don't just stand here. Go get it!"

"Yes, sir." John Michael headed through the doorway and down the hall to the storage closet door. Opening it, he scanned the items placed there. Instead of grabbing the mop, his blistered hands reached for the plunger.

Twenty

"Thank You, Wherever You Are"

The smell of turkey filled the house with a scent that reminded everyone Thanksgiving had finally arrived. Jonathan pulled the bird out of the oven. It smelled delicious as the steam rose into the air. Jonathan had learned well from his late wife. He smiled at the turkey as he thought about how proud she would be. This was the first time he'd even attempted to cook a holiday dinner since her death. Glazed carrots, beans with bacon bits, fruit fluff, seven layer salad, and Elizabeth's famous stuffing would soon be on the linen table cloth. Philip was mashing the potatoes like his father had instructed, but there seemed to be more chunks than smooth spuds in the glass mixing bowl.

"Dad?"

"Yes, Son," said Jonathan as he placed the turkey on a china platter, then stirred the beans.

"Do you think he'll call today?"

Jonathan paused. "Maybe."

"It's been over a year, you know."

"I know. Three hundred eighty-nine days, to be exact."

Both of them continued with their preparations to ease the pain of the conversation. Neither wanted to face another Thanksgiving without John Michael.

"You know what I wish, Dad?"

"What?"

"That sometime during our day we will hear a knock on the door, run to open it, and find him standing there. I dreamed about that last night."

"Really?"

"Yeah. It was Thanksgiving in my dream, too. We were in the middle of eating our dinner when there was a knock. When I opened the door John Michael was there. And so was..." Philip stopped.

"Who else?" questioned Jonathan, checking on some rolls in the oven. He went back to stirring the beans.

"Well, it was weird. Standing next to him was Mom."

Jonathan dropped the spoon he'd been using into the pan of boiling beans.

"Ouch!"

"Isn't that weird, Dad?"

Jonathan held the thumb he had burned on the beans and answered, "I don't think so. In a way, I think it's rather real."

"Real?"

"Well, I'm not a dream reader, but I think it captures where your heart is, Philip. There is nothing more important to you than being able to spend such a special day with two people you really love and miss, your mother and John Michael."

Jonathan started to carve the turkey. The stuffing exploded out of the middle cavity.

"I really do miss them."

"So do I. Your mother, well, we can't change that. She won't appear at the door today, Son. The hardest one to face is your brother's absence. You and I both know he is out there, somewhere. He's spending this special day by himself. Alone. He may have a few friends with him, but what he will never have today is you, Lewis and I. We're the only family he has left. Until he comes to his senses and realizes he needs us in his life, he will spend days like today alone."

"Boy, I miss him."

"I do, too."

"Do you think Lewis does?" asked Philip while he placed the bowl of potatoes in the microwave.

"Somewhere deep in his heart, Philip, I really believe he does. Your two brothers have more in common than you think."

"They do? They look like opposites to me."

"I know. They try pretty hard to, but they're both searching. Searching to find out who they are. They just took different paths to come up with the answer."

"I never thought of that, Dad. When did you figure it out?"

"I have watched all of you grow up. As your father, I see a different perspective than you do. I can't expect them to see things the way I do. Until both of them realize that I love them for who they are, not what they do, they will continue to search." Jonathan paused. "I hope you understand how much I believe in, and love you, Philip."

"I'm starting to, Dad. I'm starting to."

"Listen, we'd better call Lewis down here before this bird gets cold. It might get up and run away."

While Philip ran to call his brother, Jonathan carried the turkey to the dining room table. He placed it at the center, then stepped back to look at the table before heading back to the kitchen. Two chairs would remain empty this year. Elizabeth's they couldn't fill, but John Michael's...Jonathan prayed he could.

"Thank you, John Michael," he whispered to himself. "Thank you for just being my son, wherever you are."

Twenty-one

A Broken Heart, A Broken Arm

Life at the mission had become almost routine for John Michael. Before the sun came up, he was on his feet with a mop in hand. After he cleaned the bathrooms, he assisted Douglas, along with a group of volunteers, in feeding the hungry and homeless. The only thing John Michael had ever known how to make in the kitchen was a sandwich or two; now he could cook up a meal to feed an army. His hands were scarred from the grill he cooked on three times a day. His feet were tired from the miles he seemed to walk up and down the stairs. During the Christmas season he broke his arm hanging a wreath for Douglas on the front of the mission building.

"It's still crooked. Up on the left," said Douglas, standing in front of the mission. "Nope, now that's too far."

John Michael rolled his eyes. He had become Douglas's personal assistant, or so it seemed. Any job that was undesirable to Douglas was handed down to him. From toilets to hanging Christmas wreaths, John Michael was the man   not always by choice, and certainly not always by desire. John Michael sighed and moved the wreath back to where it had hung originally. At least his needs were being met. A roof over his head, food in his stomach, and a job that seemed to help time pass faster than if he aimlessly wandered the city. Douglas paid him one dollar an hour on top of providing the basic needs he had. For the first time in his life, John Michael was learning to live on a budget. From a candy bar to a can of pop, if it didn't fit his budget, he couldn't afford it. Not an easy task for a young man who used to drop two to three hundred dollars a night on a few drinks and a lot of cocaine. He had been stripped of his self-worth and his self-respect. The freedom that had promised him an answer to the pain he had been running from was gone. It would no longer cover the wounds in his heart.

"There. I think that's straight. Does it look straight to you, John Michael?"

John Michael studied the wreath. "I can't tell. I'm on the ladder."

"Well, get down and help me here. I was never good at hanging pictures. Take a look at the ones hanging in the hallway leading to the office. You'll see..."

"You hung those? I was wondering if they were intentionally that way," said John Michael, stepping down the rungs toward the bottom of the ladder. As he reached the final rung, his foot slipped and he crashed to the ground. He had never felt pain like this before.

"My arm! My arm!" he screamed.

Douglas was in shock. "Oh my, oh my! I'll get Father Williams. Yes, Father Williams." He ran through the mission doors, disappearing from John Michael's vision.

John Michael tried to catch his breath, but his body throbbed in pain. His wrist was starting to swell. A group of onlookers was starting to form. Even the Salvation Army bell ringer stopped ringing and ran over to see the action. John Michael looked up at those staring. A man knelt beside him and spoke loudly in his ear.

"Sir, are you all right?"

More voices added comments and questions.

"Is he alone?"

"Did he fall from the top?"

"Somebody call an ambulance. He must have hit his head."

John Michael tried to speak, but nothing would come out. The pain was so intense that all he could do was lie there holding his wrist. He closed his eyes to concentrate on dealing with the anguish. The voices were sounding more faint and far away until he heard a familiar tone. He opened his eyes. Lewis, Philip, and his father were standing there.

"Dad, just leave him. He'll be fine," Lewis begged.

"Fine?" replied Philip. "Dad, look at his arm. It must be broken."

"Broken? He's faking."

John Michael stared into the eyes of his father. His silence said enough.

"Dad," cried Philip desperately, "should we call for an ambulance?"

"Not on your life. After all he's done he doesn't deserve an ambulance. What he deserves is this!" yelled Lewis, stepping on the arm John Michael had fallen on. The pain was sharp and intense, causing John Michael to cry out with a shrilling scream. The crowd stepped back to give him room to breathe.

"Dad," he cried out, "don't just leave me here. Oh, God, please don't leave me!"

"Dad?" an onlooker said puzzled. "Is his father nearby?"

The large audience looked at one another, waiting to see if someone claiming this young man would burst forth from the crowd, but no such man appeared. Douglas and a large man wearing black pants, a shirt and a clergy collar ran through the front door and pushed through the crowd.

"Move. Excuse me. We need to get by," said Douglas in a panic as he surveyed the crowd of onlookers that had assembled. He moved towards John Michael's body and knelt down beside him. "John Michael? John Michael?" he repeated. John Michael didn't respond. He was in too much pain.

"He asked for his father!" shouted a voice from the crowd.

"Father? He's thousands of miles from here!" Douglas snapped back. He slapped John Michael's cheeks, hoping for a response. Sirens could be heard echoing through the streets. An ambulance made its way down Rush Street and stopped in front of the crowd. The group of onlookers parted so the emergency medical technicians could get through. John Michael was lifted to a stretcher, then carried away. Douglas and Father Williams were told which hospital John Michael would be taken to. Father Williams took over Douglas's duties while he traveled to the nearby University Medical Center. Several bystanders asked Father Williams if there was anything they could do.

Father Williams gave them the best answer he could. "Just pray for the boy. Just pray."

A few of them promised they would. Father Williams took the ladder down and folded it. As he dragged it into the building, the wreath John Michael had straightened tilted to the left again.

The University Medical Center was a short drive from where John Michael had fallen. He had never ridden in an ambulance before. Though groggy, he tried to soak it all in. The paramedics tried to straighten his wrist until John Michael thrashed in pain. They checked his eyes for dilation. Both EMTs concluded he must have hit his head on the pavement. John Michael tried to explain himself, but kept slurring his words.

Douglas parked Father Williams' vehicle in the hospital's parking ramp next to a Mercedes Benz. He moved quickly to the electric door that led him inside.

"Emergency room?" he said to a passing nurse.

"Go down the hall, take the first right, then the second left," she replied.

Douglas tried to remember the directions as he briskly walked through the winding maze of white floors and walls.

Halfway there he noticed the signs that led the way and followed them.

The emergency room seemed quiet for this time of year. Douglas remembered beds being full when he was there last winter. A motherly nurse stepped up to help Douglas at the counter.

"Can I help you, sir?" she said warmly.

"Uh, yes. I'm from the Rush Street Mission and a man who works for me was just brought here in an ambulance. Can you tell me where I can find him?"

She pulled a registration list and began scrolling it with her index finger. "Hmm, I don't see anyone listed that has come in recently."

"But, he must have. He has dark hair, about 5'11" and is wearing a pair of worn out tennis shoes and a ripped nylon jacket."

She paused, then looked back at Douglas. "Is this a homeless man you're talking about?"

"Homeless? Well, I suppose he doesn't have a home, but he's been living at the mission. He's been working for us for several months now."

"Are you family?"

"Family? No. But for now, I'm the only family he's got."

"What's your relationship to him?"

Douglas thought about her question for a moment. What was his relationship to John Michael? John Michael had rarely mentioned his home, or his father. Maybe just a time or two was all Douglas could remember.

"I'm his employer."

"Employer? I'm going to need a family member."

Douglas' face was starting to turn a deep shade of red. He had never felt as attached to anyone he had worked with as John Michael. There was something about this young man that compelled him to care. Maybe it was the pain he saw when he looked into John Michael's eyes. Or, maybe it was just true compassion. Whatever it was, it was there. He had been called to take care of this young man, and he knew it. There wasn't a nurse on this earth that was going to keep him from getting to John Michael.

"Psst, Miss, come closer," he said leaning over the counter. She turned her ear towards Douglas. "I'm sure you're a nice lady and a terrific nurse, judging by your demeanor and all, but that boy doesn't have a father. Right now, I'm all he's got. Now, either you let me see him or I'm going to drop to the floor right here and make a scene until we work something out."

The nurse looked at him for a moment, then turned away. Douglas got on his knees and started to lie down on the floor.

"Uh, sir, just a minute. Let me find out where the homeless man is first."

"Thank you," said Douglas with a sigh.

The nurse disappeared into an adjoining room, then came back. "Last room on the right down the green hall." Douglas smiled, then headed for the green paint and tile that led to John Michael's room. Most of the rooms that Douglas passed were empty, but the light was on in the one at the end of the hall. Douglas pushed the sheer white curtain to the side and focused his attention on John Michael.

John Michael's eyes were closed. Douglas walked softly up to the side of his bed. A nurse stepped in and startled him.

"Oh, I'm sorry," she said quietly.

"No harm done," he replied.

"Are you family?"

"You could say that."

"That's interesting. We couldn't get a name out of him, so when the medics told us that he was found in front of the Rush Street Mission we just figured he was homeless."

"Homeless?"

"You know, a John Doe."

"Well, I'll take responsibility for him."

"Does that mean we can give you the bill?"

Douglas looked at her confusedly. "Uh, sure. I guess. Can you tell me what's wrong with him?"

"Broken wrist, and he must have hit his head on something. He's got one bad concussion."

"Does he have a cast on?"

"A temporary one. We'll put a more permanent one on in a week."

John Michael opened his eyes slightly. The room looked foggy to him. He could hear voices, but couldn't discover whose they were.

"Dad? Dad, is that you?"

The nurse stopped talking for a moment. "Did you just say something?"

"I don't know, I thought I heard some..."

"Dad?" John Michael repeated.

"I'll get his doctor," said the nurse as she rushed out of the room.

"Nope. I'm not your father. Too young, and too charming," said Douglas with a grin trying to lift John Michael's spirits.

"You're not my dad? I want my dad!"

"You do? A few weeks ago you didn't think you'd ever see him again."

"I didn't?" he asked, rubbing his head. "Then who are you and where am I?"

"Boy, you must have hit your head," Douglas said under his breath. "C'mon, look at this face. You don't recognize this cute face? It's Douglas, for pete's sake. You know, the guy who taught you everything about a mop."

"Douglas?" John Michael's mind started to comprehend. "Oh, Douglas. It's you." He looked around the room. "Where am I? What happened to my head and my arm? Why do I have this thing on my arm?"

"We tried to save the original, but couldn't. We had to settle for this lookalike." Douglas paused. "Just kidding. Don't you remember? 'A little to the left?' Bam, you hit the ground, and hit your head. The next thing I knew you were in an ambulance and here we are."

John Michael focused on the ceiling. It was all coming back to him in fragments and pieces. "The ladder," he said, panicking, "did you move the ladder?"

"Father Williams took care of it. Forget the ladder, I came down to take care of you."

"Really? Nobody else ever has."

"Well, I usually don't, but I feel like there's something different about you. Like someone's watching out for you and I've been sent to make sure you're all right."

John Michael immediately thought of his father. Could he really sense and feel the trouble he was in? "Did my father send you?"

"Did your father send me? Listen, I know that your time working at the mission has kept you from getting out and all, but do you really think that I was sent by your father to take care of you like some guardian angel or something? Remember, you came to me."

"Yeah, yeah. I was just wondering."

"You don't talk much about your father. How come?"

"There's not a lot to talk about."

"Then why did you ask for him when you woke up?"

John Michael's wrist was starting to throb. "I don't know. I just did."

"It sounds to me like you miss him, maybe even need him."

"Yeah, well, how would you know?" said John Michael as he stared out the small window next to his bed.

"Just a guess. I mean, you do good work and all, but don't you think it would be a good idea to go home so you don't have to do this every day? There's got to be something better waiting for you back there."

Douglas had struck a chord with John Michael. If a man who didn't even know him could sense the need he had for his father, maybe the whole world could.

"I can't go back," he explained.

"Why not?"

"Do you really want to know?"

"Sure. I'm not going anywhere. And evidentally neither are you."

"I think he's forgotten about me. All I caused him was grief. Why would you ever want a son like that back?"

"Because love is a funny thing," Douglas answered with a tear in his eye. "You will never know that until you test it. Maybe you need to give him a try."

"Forget it. Besides, if I go home with a broken arm, he would be so disappointed in me."

"You're lying to yourself. If he didn't love you, you wouldn't want to go back to him. Just admit it, you want to go back."

"No!"

"C'mon!"

"I said, no, all right? Now just drop it."

There was an awkward silence, then John Michael spoke up again. "So does this mean I've lost my job?"

"No, we'll just put you on full time kitchen duty."

"Who's going to mop?"

"You," Douglas said smiling. "Right after you're done cooking breakfast."

Twenty-two

"Hello...?"

A spring rain poured down hard on the streets of the windy city. Large drops rolled off the brick building that housed the sandwich shop John Michael sat in. He stared at the water trickling to the ground. It was spring, but it still felt like winter in his heart. He took another sip of hot chocolate. The liquid warmed his body and clothed his cold heart for the moment. He was thinking of home, and his father. He couldn't get his father off his mind. John Michael longed to hear his voice. He longed to get a hug. He longed to feel the safety he had felt as a boy. Now, as a man, he didn't feel safe at all. Only the security of his father could make him feel that way again.

Leaving the sandwich shop, he walked through an alley and down a one-way street. He'd seen it many times before. He had tucked its location away in his memory for a day like today. His cold, wet fingers grabbed for the silver door of the phone booth. He stepped inside. Rain tapped on the windows. He was breathing so hard that the windows started to fog. It had taken him a long time to get to this point. Now, more than a year after he had left, he was making his first call home.

He picked up the receiver and dialed the operator.

"Operator."

John Michael stumbled. "Uh, yes, I need to make a call."

"Person to person or collect."

"Collect."

"Your name?"

John Michael froze. He was afraid to give it. What if his dad refused to take the call? Or if he just simply hung up the phone? Was he ready to take the rejection? What if his dad reminded him of all the mistakes he'd made? What if Lewis answered? How humiliating. Then he really would have to face being a failure. What if, what if, what if... There were too many questions. John Michael hung up on the operator. He slid down the glass windows until he was sitting on the floor of the phone booth. He stared outside the folding glass doors. *Maybe it's just too soon*, he thought. *If not now, when? Will I ever talk to my father again?* He kicked the door with his foot. "Oh, God, I can't stand it!" he cried out. The rain silenced the sound. He would have to trust what he remembered about his father's heart. He took out the key that was still hanging around his neck and pulled it over his head. The brass key dangled in front of him on its tattered piece of twine. It was the only piece of home he had left. He held it tight as he remembered Philip's words at the bus stop.

> "It's from Dad. He told me to give it to you."
> "What's it for?"
> "He said to tell you to use it whenever you decide to come home."

John Michael blinked away a tear. He stood up in the phone booth and picked up the receiver again. He dialed the operator.

"Operator."

His stomach churned.

"My name is John Michael. Ah, John Michael Davis."

"Sir, do you wish to make a collect call?"

He was getting nervous again.

"I don't know. It's just a phone call. I'm calling from a phone booth."

She was getting frustrated.

"Is this person to person or collect?"

"Uh, collect."

"And the number you are trying to reach?"

"The number? I'm trying to reach my father." He spoke desperately.

"Well, I can't put you through until I have the number."

"My father, just put me through to my father. I need to talk to my dad!" He started to cry uncontrollably. John Michael was breaking down.

"Sir, can you give me the phone number to reach your father? I have to have his number in order to connect you to him. Or a name, can you give me your father's name?"

"A name and phone number? OK." He sniffed as he regained control of himself. He struggled to remember all the numbers, but was finally able to give her all the information she needed. It had been so long since he'd called.

"Thank you. Please stay on the line while I connect you."

He waited. His heart pounded.

"Sir, that line is busy."

John Michael's heart fell to the floor. He didn't know how many more times he could do this.

"Would you like me to try again?"

"Yes, I've got to get through. You don't understand. I haven't talked to him in so long. Do whatever you've got to do."

"I'll try again. Please hold."

Oh God, I am so scared!

He could hear the rain faintly over the sound of his heart pounding in his chest.

Jonathan had just hung up the phone. He had been talking with Elizabeth's father for a few minutes. Not about anything important, but he liked to keep in touch. He sat down in the living room and opened his briefcase. Tomorrow would be a trying day. Mondays always seem to be trying days in the judicial system. He sipped some coffee from a mug that sat steaming on the end table. The phone rang. *Probably Dad again. He must have forgotten something,* Jonathan thought to himself. He picked up the phone.

"Hello?"

"Hello, this is the operator calling. I have a collect call for a Jonathan from... Your name again, young man?"

John Michael couldn't breathe. This was it. He took a moment to decide if this was really the first step home he wanted to take. His voice was shaky as he answered, "John Michael. It's John Michael."

"Your name again, please?"

"John Michael. It's John Michael."

"Will you accept the charges?" she continued.

Jonathan dropped the phone. It took his breath away.

John Michael sat waiting on the other end inside the steamy booth. He was glad it was raining. He would be able to stay in the booth as long as he wanted. Who would want to run through the rain to find a phone booth? The silence seemed to last forever. It gave him plenty of time to fear the worst. He tapped his finger on the glass in front of him.

"Sir, your party's on the line. Go ahead."

It had caught him off guard. John Michael straightened up and cleared his throat. He couldn't think of anything to say.

"Johnny? Johnny, is that you?"

There was a long pause as John Michael gathered his thoughts.

"Dad?"

Jonathan knew that voice. He smiled. It was his son.

"Oh, Johnny, it is you."

Jonathan wanted to cry.

"Uh, listen, Dad," John Michael closed his eyes and squeezed the key.

"I called to say that, well, I..."

"Yes?"

"Well, that I've been thinking lately. Thinking about you, and that I..." He froze. "That I..."

"I'm here, Son."

John Michael wanted so badly to say it. Why was "love" such a hard word to say?

"Dad, I..." his voice started to quiver. He noticed a Father's Day display in the card shop window across from the phone booth. He rubbed off the fog to see it more clearly. "I just called because, uh, Father's Day is coming up and I wondered if there was something I could send you?" He breathed a sigh of relief.

Jonathan knew what John Michael wanted to say.

"Father's Day? I forgot all about it. Aren't you thinking about that a little early?" His response was gentle, kind, and compassionate.

"Uh, yeah, I guess I am."

"You know how it goes around here. Nobody usually remembers until the day before, then you boys rush out last minute to get something. I'm impressed, you're starting early." He was making small talk. It was taking everything inside of him not to beg him to come home, to ask him if he was all right, or to lecture him on how hard it's been not knowing if he was alive. Instead, he just kept listening to John Michael's every word and affirming him with every opportunity.

"Did you get my postcards?"

"Did I get them? Son, I carry them with me wherever I go. Sometimes in the middle of a boring trial I'll pull one out while I'm on the stand and just look at it."

"Really?"

"Yeah. My favorite one was the giant alligator in Lake Michigan. Didn't it say, 'Giant 'Gator Eats Chicago!'?" They both laughed.

"Yeah, it did. I thought you might laugh at that one."

"I did, Johnny. I did. You always had a way of making me smile. Father's Day, huh?"

"Yeah."

"Do you remember that Father's Day when you got up early to dig up a jar of worms for my present?"

John Michael started to relax. He even smiled. He remembered. "Yes. I had over fifty worms in that thing."

"I know. Then there was the Father's Day you and your brothers promised me a camping trip and halfway to the campground you realized you had forgotten the tent? Remember? We slept around the campfire until it started to rain, then we all crammed in the back seat of the car. Remember?"

"You remember that, Dad?"

"Of course, but I would have to say that the Father's Day I remember the most was the one right after your mother died. You and I went fishing. We never said a word that entire day, but we were together."

John Michael was quiet. He remembered that day. It had been raining, just like today. He and his dad kept throwing out and reeling in. They didn't talk, but it didn't matter. They were together. It was all John Michael needed that day and Jonathan knew it.

"I wish we would have caught a fish, Dad."

"So do I, Son."

There was an awkward pause. John Michael tightened up. Jonathan got up, walked into the kitchen, and leaned against the counter. He noticed Johnny's empty chair at the table.

John Michael stared out the window of the phone booth. The rain had stopped for just a second. The sun had poked its way through the clouds overhead. He noticed a boy walking with his father. They were stomping in all of the puddles and laughing. John Michael smiled. It was good to hear a father and son laughing.

"Listen, Johnny. I think I figured out what you could get me for Father's Day."

"You did?"

"Yeah, I did. It's right in front of me."

"What?"

"Well, you know that kitchen table we own."

"Yeah?" John Michael said puzzled. "What does that have to do with Father's Day?"

"Well, Son, there's an empty chair at it and I was thinking that the greatest gift I could get for Father's Day would be to see someone I love sitting in it. Won't you come home and sit with me?"

John Michael closed his eyes. A tear rolled down his cheek. It was raining inside the phone booth now.

"Uh, Dad, I gotta go."

"You do?"

"Yeah. I'll send something." He could think of nothing else to say but, "Bye, Dad."

The click startled Jonathan. That was it. That was all John Michael could say. Jonathan stared at the empty chair.

John Michael hung up the receiver and rested his head in his hands. The knock from outside the booth made him jump.

"Hurry up. I've been waiting!"

Back to reality. John Michael wiped his face, got up, and opened the door. He slowly walked away from the phone booth. It was starting to sprinkle again, but that didn't matter to John Michael. For the first time in months he found something to smile about.

Philip slipped into the kitchen and noticed his father in a trance. He was staring at a kitchen chair.

"Dad, are you all right?"

"I'm fine, Son. Just fine." He continued to stare.

"Who was that?" Philip looked at which chair his father was staring at. "Was it Johnny?" The thought of it took his breath away. "It was, wasn't it? Dad, tell me it was Johnny."

Jonathan looked at him and smiled. Philip started to scream.

"It was? Dad, it was Johnny? He really called!" He headed into the living room and started jumping up and down.

"He called! Johnny called! Johnny called!" Philip jumped so hard that the lamp on the end table fell to the floor and the ceramic bottom broke open. It didn't matter, he knew his brother was alive. They could replace a lamp, but not John Michael. He started to jump up and down again. "I knew he'd call! I knew it! Johnny called. He's alive! He's alive!"

Twenty-three

A Man With a Mission

The Rush Street Mission had been running at a steady pace through the early part of the summer. Spring was gone, the beds were full, food was on the table, and John Michael was still hard at work. Sweat dripped from his brow as he poured the scrambled eggs onto the hot griddle. The kitchen had warmed up in the early morning Chicago sun. The heat was supposed to set a record. His stomach growled as he stirred the eggs with a large metal spatula. Warm eggs didn't look very appetizing. It wasn't what he was hungry for. In fact, the eggs made him sick. They weren't the only thing that seemed to turn his stomach lately. Life itself seemed to make him sick. Not physically, but down deep in his soul. There was an ache that he couldn't get rid of himself. The desire to go home was stronger than ever, but the courage to do it still seemed buried. John Michael felt trapped. Like an animal in a cage, he couldn't find the way out. Although he had experienced similar feelings before he left home, the walls now seemed higher and stronger.

Working at the mission was wearing on him. He found himself jealous of his brothers, family, friends, and anyone he could think of who was living in the same circle as his father. He knew they were experiencing his dad's love the way he desired to. But he was still here with a mop and spatula in hand.

John Michael slopped some eggs on a plate and served them to a man who walked by the pickup window in the kitchen. Another plate, then another. The line seemed to be endless. More eggs, more plates, and more hollow eyes. As men and women took the dish from his hands, he saw an emptiness in their eyes that he recognized in his own. He saw a man like himself, afraid, but with a great desire to be forgiven. John Michael wanted to apologize to each person walking by. Not because he had wronged them in any way, but because he had robbed himself of his own life. Running away wasn't the answer, and he knew it now. True forgiveness was the answer, but it had been hidden for so long. He slopped the last of the eggs on a plate as one of the last men wandered by.

"Can I still get some eggs?"

"I guess. There's just a little left."

"It doesn't matter," the man went on. "I'll take anything. I just want to fill my stomach. I've been searching for some real food for so long, I'm grateful to find some."

John Michael handed him the plate, glancing at what the man was wearing. His clothing reminded John Michael of used rags. A torn shirt, cut off polyester pants, toes sticking out of an old pair of tennis shoes, and a grimy old fisherman's hat were all he seemed to have. The hat was hardly used for fishing. It was used as a deflector for the sun. John Michael felt like he was staring into a mirror. He looked down at what he was wearing. Not much difference.

"Thank you, sir. Thank you," echoed the man.

"You're welcome. Juice and rolls are on the table. Have as many as you want."

"Oh, I will. I sure will. Thank you, again." The man walked away.

"What a mess," said Douglas, stepping through the kitchen door. "Did you cook alone today? Martin didn't show up again?"

"No big deal. Martin is new at all of this. He reminds me a lot of myself when I first came on."

"You're telling me. I couldn't get you out of bed if the world depended on it. How many alarm clocks did we go through?"

"I don't know. I would guess quite a few," John Michael responded, taking off a plastic apron and setting it on the counter.

"Do you need some help cleanin' up this mess?"

"I'll get it. It will give me some time to think."

"Think? I've noticed you've been doing that a lot lately. You look like you're constantly in deep thought. What could be on your mind that much?"

John Michael tried to avoid the question. That would mean facing the answers himself. Douglas leaned against the avocado green refrigerator.

"Excuse me, can I get another cup of juice? The jugs out here are all empty," interrupted a man through the window that led to the eating area.

Douglas sighed and shot back a straightforward answer. "No. We've given out everything we have for this morning."

"Wait," said John Michael noticing who it was. "I'll get you some." He opened the refrigerator door pushing Douglas to the side. He filled the glass, then handed it back to the man dressed in rags. "I hope that's enough."

"It is. Thank you very much."

Douglas was confused by the situation. The man walked happily away. John Michael watched him go pensively. He was glad to have been able to help him.

"Anyway," asked Douglas, "you've been thinking about going home lately, haven't you?"

Douglas's question caught John Michael off guard. He slowly and silently put away the juice.

"Just what I thought. You miss your family, huh?"

John Michael tried to keep himself busy. He grabbed a few dirty pans and set them in the sink.

"I don't know. Kind of, I guess." He turned the faucet on and the hot water blew a puff of steam into his face. Douglas stepped over and turned the water off.

"John Michael, look at me."

John Michael turned toward Douglas.

"Look me in the eye. I've been feeling this for awhile now, ever since you fell outside the mission last Christmas. I have a few thoughts. This place is no home for you."

"I don't know about that."

"Look at yourself, son. You come from royalty, so to speak. What is a prince doing living like a pauper? Most of the folks that come through our doors have no family. From the pieces I've heard you share about yours, I think going back to them is the only thing that will make you happy."

John Michael turned on the water again.

"You don't know that for sure."

"No, but I do know there's a sparkle in your eye whenever your father is mentioned."

"Well, that's not very often, now is it?"

"No, but when it happens there's fireworks. And, I'm talking fireworks." Douglas turned the water off again. "Are you hearing me? Go home. That's where your heart is. For me? Home is right here. Rush Street. Taking care of Chicago's homeless. For you? It's being with your dad."

John Michael shook his head. "I don't know if I can go home and face him."

"Tell me something."

"What?"

"Tell me the most amazing thing about your dad. What is it? Go on."

John Michael dropped the frying pan in the sink. He stared at the last few stragglers that were finishing their breakfast. "Uh, the most amazing thing?" his voice cracked as he began to smile. "The most amazing thing about my dad was his ability to meet me no matter where I was."

"Then why would it be any different now? It sounds to me like he would be happy to be your father despite where you've been or what you've done."

"But what if you're wrong?"

"Life is about taking risks. You took one when you came here and you learned a few lessons, right? John Michael, now take the risk and go back."

"But..."

"No more excuses. You need to go. If he doesn't love you, you've always got a place here." Douglas touched his shoulder. It was the first genuine touch John Michael had felt since he'd left home.

"If you come back, don't expect a raise," Douglas said smiling.

"I won't," said John Michael, drying his hands on a towel.

Douglas grabbed the towel away from him. "Now get out of here. You go pack. I'll clean this mess up."

"You sure?"

"I'm sure."

John Michael stepped through the kitchen doors and past a few of the homeless men who were finishing their daily cup of coffee. He went up the stairs to the room he and the other homeless men shared every night. From under his cot he pulled out the duffel bag that had been with him from the start. It had a few more holes than before, but it would still hold the few items he owned. A pair of jeans, a few pair of underwear from the mission's lost and found pile, a couple of t-shirts, a pair of socks, and the toothbrush he had from the day he had left home. John Michael set the bag on his cot and sat down next to it. The sun poured through the window. He was thinking about the journey. He was finally going. The decision he had wrestled with in his heart had finally been made. John Michael was going home! He could only dream of the day he'd arrive....

> John Michael stepped onto the porch of the home he had grown up in and knocked on the door. He heard the doorknob turn. The door cracked open and from behind it came the father John Michael had been dreaming of.
> "John Michael!" shouted his dad.
> "Father!" screamed the son.
> John Michael stepped past the threshold of the door to embrace his father.
> "My son, I've missed you!"
> "And I've missed you!"
> "We've been waiting for you and want to take you out to eat at the best restaurant in the town. Your brothers have some gifts for you."
> "Gifts?"
> "Gifts. Only the best for you, my son. Only the best."

"Only the best..." John Michael whispered to himself as the sun shined in his eyes. He hoped it really would be the best. The reality was that he doubted how constant his father's love would truly be. How could his father really love him after all he had done? A voice from the inside clouded his thoughts.

"Put the duffel bag back under the cot and get back to work. Your father will never take you back. This place is the only home you've got. Don't lose it. If you do, you really will have nothing."

John Michael thought about Douglas and the mission. He stared at the rafters on the ceiling. This place really was the only home he had, at least at this point in his life. What if he lost this place, too? Then where would he go? Homeless. He really would be homeless then. Maybe he would be the one begging for more eggs and juice at breakfast. His brow began to sweat. John Michael started to put the duffel bag back under the cot.

> "Johnny," said a sweet voice.
> John Michael stopped dead in his tracks. That voice—it sounded so familiar.

"Johnny," it called again.

John Michael tried to place it. It couldn't be, could it? Not here, not now. How?

"John Michael."

Yes, it was. The voice, was from one he had loved and known, his mother. The voice was his mother's. John Michael froze. He was afraid to turn around.

"Johnny," the voice said again, this time continuing, "you need to go home."

He slowly stood.

"You need to go home," she repeated.

He slowly turned around. He closed his eyes tight. When he was fully facing the direction of the voice, he opened them slowly. There she stood, a vision of grace for his weary and beaten heart. Her long dark hair was shining as the sun broke through the strands of hair that fell from her shoulder. She was wearing the same outfit John Michael last remembered her in. He had helped her pick out the shoes a few weeks before when they were shopping for school clothes for him. He tried to speak but the words kept choking him up.

"But, Mom, I don't know if I can."

"You can. I've always said you could do anything you put your mind to, remember?"

"But, Dad... Mom, how do I know if he's still waiting for me?"

"Trust him, Johnny. Be confident in what you know about him. Oh, he's waiting for you, Johnny. He's been waiting. That's just who he is. He doesn't give up on one of his sons."

"I'm so afraid."

"You don't have to be. Take the courage you've always seen in your father and use it to go to him. You don't have to worry."

"But..."

"Shhh," she said softly, "it's all right, Johnny. Go. He's waiting for you."

Her deep brown eyes drew John Michael. He reached to embrace her, but she was gone. Her voice, her smell, and her words were no longer there.

"Mom!" he screamed. He could feel the warm sun splashing across his back. "Come back. Come back!"

John Michael sat back down on the cot. Maybe she was never there. But her words of encouragement were irreplaceable. He hadn't allowed himself to remember them since she had died. But today, maybe making the decision to go home allowed him to remember her without the pain and sadness.

"Go home," he had heard her say. "Your father is waiting for you."

John Michael unzipped his duffel bag and collected his things. For the first time since he had left home, there was courage in his heart, at least for now. John Michael's feet pounded down the hallway and out the door to the Chicago streets. He was on a mission, even though he didn't have a plan. Before he started the journey, there was one more person he needed to see. A friend who had helped him feel at home. A friend that seemed closer than a brother. His friend would be hard to find. He, too, didn't have a home.

Twenty-four

Shock to the Heart

John Michael walked briskly down Rush Street, through Michigan Avenue, then on down to the lower part of the Chicago Loop. It wasn't long before he was on the same streets he had come to know the first day Chicago had become his new home. As he walked by the familiar surroundings, he remembered that day. The freedom he had felt that evening had quickly evolved into a ball and chain he couldn't seem to rid himself of. The price he paid to be free was one he had never expected. If he had known how deeply he would pay for the choices he made he might never have left. Then again, he never would have learned. The year and a half had turned out to be an education he never could have paid for.

John Michael hadn't been to this part of the city since the evening he lay drunk on a bench next to an alley. It seemed like so long ago now. He had deliberately stayed away from this side of town. The memory of the money he'd spent and the mess he'd made of his life was painful enough. He needed new scenery in his life—besides, Douglas had given him a new start. John Michael was grateful for that. He wondered if he would see any of the gang he used to party with. The day his money ran out was the day his friends did too. Who would buy them drinks, not to mention share the drugs? John Michael had figured this was just the way to get their approval. So he laid his life down at the feet of his friends and they walked all over him. Despite the faces that seemed to disappear, one stood out in his memory. John Michael hoped he would find Matt. For all he knew, Matt could be living in another city by now. Or he could be dead, for that matter. He searched a few alleys, asked a few questions, then headed to where his friendship with Matt had begun, the Java Club. John Michael had hoped to avoid the coffee shop, not knowing who he would find there, but finding Matt was important to him.

John Michael pulled open the glass door and stepped inside. The smell of fresh brewed coffee filled the air, along with some fresh baked cookies that had just been wrapped in cellophane and set behind the counter. John Michael looked around the place nervously. Nobody seemed to recognize him. Even the waitress that had taken his order hundreds of times months before didn't bat an eye. She finally acknowledged him by saying she would be with him soon, but it wasn't service or a cup of coffee he was after. He was here for something much more important—a friend. John Michael surveyed the shop. He stared at the steam rising from a cup on one of the tables, then noticed a hat he hadn't seen in months. His hat! He looked at the cap again, then the face. He recognized that face. Was it? Could it be? Matt? John Michael headed to the table, pulled up a chair, and sat down. Matt was staring into the steaming cup of coffee in front of him. He stirred it with a spoon and noticed someone had sat down across from him.

"No way," Matt said.

"It's me. It's really me."

Matt pulled the hat off and rubbed his head.

"I can't believe this. Didn't think I'd ever see you again. You didn't even say good-bye."

"Matt, I couldn't."

"What do you mean, you couldn't?" Matt said with a smirk on his face. "Forget it. I understand. Besides, saw you servin' up food at that mission place you've been staying at. I just left you alone. I figured you were trying to get away from all of this, after Logan kicked you to the curb and all. I knew you wouldn't stay long after that."

"Yeah. I couldn't. I had nothing left, Matt. They took everything."

"Well, they didn't take your life. Yet. Logan's looking for you. He says you owe him some party money."

"What?"

"Party money. I don't know. It must be for drugs or something. I figured you went to the mission because you knew he'd stay away from there. Cops would be on him before he could turn his head."

"I went to the mission for me. I don't owe Logan a thing."

"Well, according to him you do. I also heard he was the one who ransacked your place."

"It doesn't surprise me. But that's the past. I came to talk to you about the future."

"The future?" said Matt as he opened a plastic creamer cup and poured it into his coffee. "This is my future. I'm living it. It wasn't too hard to track me down, was it? I got no place else to go."

"That's why I came to find you. Matt, I'm going home."

The table was silent. Matt looked down into his coffee cup again.

"Home? I thought that's what you were running away from?"

"It was," John Michael sighed, trying to explain. "But I realized that it wasn't really home I was running from, it was me."

"How can you go home? What's there for you anyway?"

"My father."

Matt took a sip of the warm liquid and stared at John Michael. "Father? I thought he was the reason you left?

Remember? You were sitting right over there. 'I just had to get away from him.' "

John Michael looked over at the chair he had sat in many times before. "Things are different now. My dad is the only thing I got left."

"How can you say that after all you've been through? I don't get it."

"I don't either. I just know he is. He promised me that he would be waiting for me. If that's true, then maybe I can get my life together instead of feeling so screwed up." He pulled out a dull brass key that hung around his neck tucked inside his shirt. Matt stared at it.

"This key, it could change everything for me," he paused, "and you. Matt, come with me."

"What? Do you realize what you're asking? Look at us. There's too many differences. Don't you get it?"

John Michael tucked the key back inside his shirt. "That's the deal, I do get it. You need a father, Matt. A real dad. We all do." John Michael looked around the room. "They do!"

"You're not getting it, Michael. I'm black, you're white. I grew up on these streets, you grew up in some big house. Your dad's got the bucks, my daddy never gave me nothin'!"

"It doesn't matter. We're brothers, right? Remember what you said to me that morning you brought me my hat?" John Michael picked it up from the table and held it in his hand. " 'Just lookin' out for you. Think of me as an older brother.' Well, older brother, now I'm looking out for you."

"Well, you don't need to."

"I know I don't need to, but..."

"Look," Matt said firmly, cocking his head towards John Michael, "you don't understand, so don't try too. Michael, I was born on these streets. This is all I know. My mom was a prostitute. She died from a drug overdose when I was eight. She died right in my arms, Michael." Matt looked away. He slammed his fist down on the table. The cup and saucer rang as they clanked together. "And my father, he could be anywhere. Anyone! Don't you think I've wondered who he is? Don't you think I've stared at every man that's passed by and wondered if it was him? Any of them could be my father! And you expect me to run off to some guy that you don't even know for sure will take *you* back. I don't think so!"

John Michael sat in silence. He didn't know how to respond. He had an overwhelming desire to help Matt. He felt Matt needed help more than he needed it himself. Based on what he remembered about his dad, he knew Jonathan could give love, hope, and a reason to live. He spoke softly, "But Matt, I know this would work. I just know it."

"Listen, I've already run away from any possibility of ever having a father. I don't want to be disappointed again. I can't afford to be disappointed again." One tear broke free from the prison that it had been living in. Matt wasn't one to cry. He didn't even notice it had fallen on the table in front of him.

John Michael knew this was the reason he had to see him before he left. If nothing else, he was at least able to give Matt hope that there was a real father out there. He was waiting for the return of his children.

"You've got to meet my dad."

Matt paused, took another sip of his now cold coffee, and looked John Michael straight in the eye. "Tell me about your father."

John Michael's heart leaped. There were even a few butter-flies in his stomach. He opened his mouth, but nothing came out.

"Well?" said his friend.

"I'm just trying to find the right words." He stared out the window, then looked back at Matt. "My father. The most important thing about my dad has got to be how much I know he loves me. He calls his love for me unconditional. Yes, unconditional. It means he is always willing to take me just as I am. It doesn't matter what I've done or where I've come from, he has always been there, waiting for me."

Matt leaned forward. "How do you know that for sure? How do you know that he'll still be waiting for you when you get home?"

"I don't. But I know his character. The night I left, Matt, he'd already started waiting for me..."

Jonathan couldn't contain himself anymore. He jumped for the door, grabbed the handle, and turned it as fast as he could. He leaped through the door making his way to the end of the porch. He scanned the area for his son. He could faintly see him under a street light walking in the distance, duffel bag and all. Once again his face flushed red, his eyes filled with tears. He cupped his hands over his mouth and yelled as loud as he could.

"John Michael! John Michael!"

The shadowy figure stopped. A dog started to bark and the porch light from next door came on.

"JOHN MICHAEL! I LOVE YOU! I LOVE YOU! DON'T YOU EVER FORGET THAT. I LOVE YOU!"

Jonathan's hands reached through the cool night air but grabbed nothing but a handful of darkness. John Michael turned his back one last time. Home. The porch light was on now. He could see his father's silhouette standing on the porch peering, looking anxiously for his boy. The house looked so peaceful, so inviting. He wanted to run back to his father's arms. But not now. He needed to leave. A tear rolled down his cheek. He heard his father's words loud and clear. He turned around and continued walking.

Jonathan stared from the porch. All was quiet except for the dog barking and a chorus of crickets. The porch light next door went off. Jonathan kept his on, just in case a very special boy he knew would need to find his way home.

"The last words I heard from my dad were, 'I LOVE YOU.' I hope they'll be the first words I hear when I get home."

"What if it's not?"

"How will I know unless I take the risk and find out?"

"Risk?" Matt replied, signaling the waitress for another cup of coffee.

"Risk. What do you have to lose, Matt? All of this? Your life here? Why should you keep living like this when you can have something so much better? I guess that's what I came to terms with when I decided to try to go home. Why do I keep punishing myself for my wrong decisions when I can be at home where my father will help me make some right ones?"

The waitress came by and filled Matt's cup with fresh coffee. "You're telling me that's the kind of father you've always known."

"Yes."

"Then why did you run away from home?"

John Michael paused; now he was talking to himself. "I thought I could make it on my own. I thought I could deal with my own pain, not to mention my life, but I've realized I need my father. He's all I've ever needed."

Matt's eyes danced at the thought of the reality of his friend's words. "Your dad ain't black, is he?" He smiled at his own comment. John Michael smiled back.

"It doesn't matter, does it? With my father, it doesn't matter what color you are, or your background, or if you have money or not. He's always been fair . Your color won't matter to him—the condition of your heart will."

Matt sighed and took a deep breath. Another tear rolled down his cheek. This time Matt noticed it. "First tear I've ever cried since I came out of the womb."

"Then you'll come?"

"I, uh, don't..."

"You've got to, Matt. I don't want to go home alone. Come with me. You won't be disappointed."

Matt thought for a few moments. His thoughts were far away from the Java Club. They were embedded in the past, and in the hope of the future. He knew what he needed to do. "OK, I'll go home with you."

"YES!" shouted John Michael as he jumped out of his seat and bumped the table. Coffee spilled out of Matt's cup.

"But if I don't like it there, then I'm coming back here. Deal?"

"Deal. But I know you'll like it there. I know you'll love my dad."

"Love? Just give me some time, all right?"

John Michael collected his things and reached for his duffel bag. "Let's get out of here. If we don't do it now, we may not get a chance."

Matt paid the waitress for his coffee and the two of them headed out the glass doors and onto the street.

"You got any stuff to pack?"

Matt looked back surprised. "Pack? I'm already packed. This is all I got. Like I told you, I ain't got no place to lay my head. All I got is right here on me."

"Then let's go. I got a few bucks so I figured we could head down to the bus station and see how far we can get."

"That's cool. I got a little cash on me. We can pool it together. Let's go."

"Wait. I need a phone booth. I'm going to make one last call and tell my dad I, I mean we, are on our way."

"I think there is one down the street."

"What am I talking about? I know right where there's one. I used it awhile back."

The two of them crossed the street in front of the coffee shop. There was something different about their steps. They walked faster, with more direction in life than ever before. Instead of aimless steps they now had focus. Home, they were both going home.

The sun was starting to set on the Chicago skyline. Matt and John Michael made their way through a dark alley. The phone booth was just beyond the brick buildings that now surrounded them. A crate dropped behind them. Startled by the noise, the two young men turned around to see nothing but shadows.

"So, I hear someone's planning on going home," came a voice from the end of the alley. John Michael knew all too well who it was.

"Logan," John Michael said, turning around.

"Michael, we meet again."

"Unfortunately."

Logan stood there, Esmerelda by his side. Her hair was dyed pink today. John Michael recognized her now. She had been sitting two tables over from them at the Java Club. John Michael had noticed her hair from the back, but had not seen her face.

"My little friend here says that someone is making plans to go home. I just wanted to make sure you weren't going to leave the city without saying good-bye to your good and loyal friend, Logan."

"Come to think of it, Logan, I hadn't even thought of you."

Logan took his arm off Esmerelda's shoulder. "Isn't that funny? Well, you may be able to forget about me, but I haven't forgotten you. You wouldn't leave town without paying your bill, would you?"

John Michael stepped forward. He wasn't about to become a coward now. Not after all he'd been through. "Bill? I don't owe you anything, Logan. If anybody owes, it's you."

"Really?"

"Really. I know it was you who ransacked my place and took my cash. You've got all your getting!"

"Maybe it was. The problem here is that you didn't have enough to cover your debt. So, I'm left paying for the services you took advantage of, including your fine home."

"Services? And you call that dump a fine home?"

"I'm not talkin' about that, but this." Logan took a joint from his black suit coat and lit it in his mouth. "You owe me,

John Michael. You owe me good, and, you know it. Now, I've come to settle up."

"I already told you, I don't owe you a dime."

John Michael took one step closer to Logan and Matt stepped in front of him.

"Logan, lay off. Just let the boy go home."

"Home? Are you forgetting the universal law, my friend? You reap what you sow. He ain't going anywhere until I get what's coming to me."

"Listen," John Michael said, gritting his teeth. "Don't you get it? That's why you didn't see me for months. I'm trying to change who I was when you knew me."

Logan blew a puff of reefer smoke in John Michael's face. "Too late, bro. A man's got to live up to his mistakes."

Matt spoke up again. "Leave him alone, Logan. He's just a kid."

"Then he shouldn't be tryin' to act like a man." Logan startled to circle John Michael. "You come into this city all proud and rich. You wanted freedom and, boy, you got it. You made your choices, not me."

"C'mon, Logan. You know that's not true. You took advantage of him. I know it, you know it, she knows it,"—Matt glanced at Esmerelda—"and now John Michael does, so just leave it at that. What's a few dollars to you, anyway?"

"This much," said Logan with an evil look in his eye. He reached into his pocket and pulled out a revolver. It was hard to see in the dark. Esmerelda flinched and hid behind him. Matt stepped in front of John Michael.

"Put it away, Logan. It's not worth this. Believe me. I've seen it before."

"I want my money."

"Then I'll find a way to pay what he owes," Matt cried.

"No!" yelled John Michael.

"Let me handle this, Michael. How much is it, Logan? How much does he owe you?"

Logan pointed the gun in John Michael's face. "I don't want your money. There's a lesson here that I want this boy to learn. He will pay it or he's a dead man."

Esmerelda sensed Logan's seriousness this time. She grabbed his shoulder hoping to settle him down.

"Logan, let's just get out of here. Please."

Logan ignored her. His hand started to shake as he continued to hold the gun in John Michael's face.

"Michael, get back. Back away!" There was fear in Matt's voice. He had been in this situation before. "I said, back away! Listen to me!"

John Michael started to withdraw. Sweat started to pour down his face.

"Let's go, boy! I'm gonna teach you a lesson! Before you go see 'daddy' we're gonna settle this."

With every step John Michael took back, Logan took one forward. John Michael tried to step back again but realized he had run into one of the brick buildings in the alley. There was nowhere else to go, nowhere to hide. The gun was held inches from his head. Logan was in a trance. Vengeance poured from his eyes.

"Logan! No!" screamed Esmerelda. Her whimpering echoed through the alley.

"Logan," demanded Matt in a pleading, yet stern tone, "put the gun down. Let the kid go. Let him go home. He's not worth this to you."

Logan glanced at Matt. "Nothing's worth anything, anyway." He cocked the trigger. When Logan looked back to check on John Michael, Matt grabbed Logan's wrist and pulled it down. He pushed the gun towards the ground. John Michael stepped back. Esmerelda started to run away. Matt struggled for a tighter grip, trying relentlessly to get the gun away from Logan. The two men fell to the ground and rolled through the alley. The sounds of a painful struggle could be heard. John Michael stepped back in fear.

A shot rang out. Esmerelda stopped running and turned around. John Michael jumped. The men came to a halt. Everything in John Michael's life stopped at the moment. He could hear his heart beating. Soft at first, then so loud he covered his ears. Logan got up and brushed himself off. Matt's body lay lifeless, blood pouring from a hole above his heart.

"Oh, my God!" John Michael cried, running to his body. "Matt, Matt!"

Logan picked up the gun that lay next to Matt's body and pointed it at John Michael. His hand holding the gun was shaking. He stared at John Michael for a few moments and then ran away. The heels on his boots echoed through the quiet alley. John Michael sat next to Matt's body and held Matt's head in his lap.

"Matt. Hold on. Hold on!" He started to scream at the top of his lungs. "Help! Somebody help! Can anyone hear me?" John Michael placed his hand over the hole in Matt's chest. He began to cry uncontrollably. He was shocked and afraid. "No, Matt! We were going home! Somebody help, we've got to get him home! He was going home!"

He heard sirens in the distance. A man from a nearby building ran out the back door and down the alley. He was wearing a chef's uniform.

"Oh, man, what happened here?" he said bending down to Matt's body.

John Michael looked up, his eyes full of tears. "He's been shot. My friend's been shot!"

The man tried to settle John Michael down. "Settle down, buddy, the cops are on their way. Did you see who did this?"

"The cops?" John Michael started to panic. What if they blamed him for shooting Matt? He stood up, letting Matt's body land on the pavement. His hands were covered with the blood pouring from Matt's wound.

"Hey," the man screamed, "don't go anywhere. I ain't gonna get blamed for this. Stay right where you are! You're the one who shot him, aren't you? Come back!"

John Michael started to run. He ran by a few tires, a wooden crate, and an abandoned car. The sirens entered the alley. The Chicago police car stopped by Matt's body. Two officers jumped out with guns in their hands. They pointed them at the man in the chef uniform.

"He ran that way. The man who shot him ran that way!"

Immediately one cop ran after John Michael while the other stayed at the scene. John Michael could hear the footsteps following him. He ran around the alley corner and into the street, Matt's blood still on his hands. He collided with a woman crossing the street, placed his hands on her arm, and fell to his knees. She screamed when she noticed the blood and the look on John Michael's face.

"Please," he pleaded, "you have to help me. I need to go home. I want to go home!"

Heels could be heard hitting the pavement as the policemen neared John Michael's frail, limp body. Exhausted, he had given up running. Overwhelmed, he dreamed about being home. If only he was home.

Twenty-five

A 1952 Smith Corona

The heavy door slammed shut, locking the iron gate securely. John Michael stood behind the cold steel and looked between the spaces of the bars. The cement walls were damp and smelled like the moldy basement of an old house. John Michael turned away from the bars and stared at the small room. His new home. It wasn't a luxury hotel, but it had all the necessities. A toilet sat in the corner of the room with a sink next to it. He noticed that there was no mirror. Then again, to look in his own eyes day after day might be more of a punishment than even the cell block. Across from the toilet lay an old, rusty metal cot with a bare mattress. Not even a pillow, or sheet. He had had those luxuries back at the mission. The cement floor was cold. He closed his eyes and rubbed his face with his hands. He felt naked. Even though he was dressed in a gray jumpsuit with a prisoner number painted on it, inside he felt vulnerable and afraid. He wondered when this nightmare would be over.

He was told that this was where he would be held temporarily until his questioning was over. No bail. No lawyer. He would have to wait until the court appointed him one. At this point, he was the only suspect the police had. A long sigh came from his lips. He had been stripped of everything—his clothing, his money, his dignity, his ego and...his freedom. Only one thing remained that could never be stolen...his thoughts.

John Michael went to the cot and sat down. He pulled his legs up on the mattress and tucked his knees under his chin. Just like his father would always do when he sat on the porch. His thoughts rambled. This was so far from where he ever thought he would be. He was so close to going home. Why now? Why this? His decisions had taken him places he had never thought he'd go, and cost him far too much. Now he would have to stay, right inside these prison walls.

"I'm alone," he said to himself. The prison didn't even come close to comparing with the emotional bars he had hid behind ever since he'd left home. Prison didn't scare him—the condition of his heart did. He began to realize that freedom didn't come by changing the outside, but by changing what was going on inside.

"Say it, say it!" he said, scolding himself and cursing. "Just say it!" He couldn't mouth the words. The truth was too hard to swallow. It seemed impossible to utter. Why was it so easy to tell Matt? He found that telling himself the truth was the hardest confrontation of all. "Say it!" he yelled. His voice echoed down the hall past the empty cell blocks. There were just a few inmates. They didn't care what he was yelling; they probably yelled a time or two themselves. "SAY IT!" There was silence, then John Michael said the words that began his journey back home.

"I'm so sorry, Dad. I, I want to come home. I want to come home!" After he said those words, tears poured from his eyes, from a fountain deep in his soul. He cried so hard the metal bed started to shake.

"Dad, I'm coming home."

John Michael never physically left that cell block that day, but in an incredible way he went home in his heart. It happened, with no one watching. There was no fanfare or parade. The news media didn't show up, and the newspaper never reported a thing, but a celebration was going on. It was inside of John Michael's cell. The prison bars couldn't hold it in. John Michael was celebrating. He had come full circle. A smile ripped across his face like an earthquake opens a dry piece of land. He couldn't stop thinking about his father and Philip and Lewis. He knew it would be uncomfortable to see Lewis. He placed his fingers around his neck remembering Lewis's grip. Even so, that afternoon he did what he had never thought possible—he forgave himself. For what? For believing his mother's death was his fault. He had always believed that if he would have gotten to the hospital sooner, he could have changed the outcome of his mother's death. He could run from his home, but he couldn't run from himself. He had left home because he couldn't face himself. John Michael believed he was doing his father a favor. How could his father love the son responsible for his wife's death?

The afternoon his mother was in the accident, John Michael was playing a state championship football game. Elizabeth was on her way to the game when a U-Haul trailer in front of her disconnected itself from the truck that was pulling it. The trailer stopped quickly, and so did her car, ramming into the back of the truck. She was alone that day. Jonathan was planning to drive separately after a court hearing that was running late. In fact, on his way to the game, Jonathan passed the accident. He immediately noticed Elizabeth's car. By the time he'd found a place on the highway to turn around, she had already been taken away to the hospital. He called the school from his cell phone, but couldn't talk to John Michael directly. He left a message with the school secretary.

"Johnny, your mom's been in a car accident. I don't know how bad. Stay put. I'll be by to get you."

The message reached John Michael during the third quarter of his game. He tucked the note into his gym bag and decided to play as much of the game as he could. After all, this was the last game of the season. How bad could the accident really be?

It was bad enough that his father never came to pick him up. Jonathan finally called a good friend who picked John Michael up an hour after the game ended.

Lewis, selfishly, was already at the hospital. He refused to pick up John Michael because he wanted to be there by himself. When John Michael arrived at the emergency waiting room, he found Jonathan embracing Lewis tightly. There were tears, and John Michael knew it was over. He would never see his mother again. Jonathan noticed John Michael standing next to him and reached out to take his second son into his arms. Within minutes, Philip was there. He had been waiting at the house for Lewis to pick him up for John Michael's game. Their next door neighbor had gotten a call from the school and had taken Philip to the hospital. Jonathan stepped away with the doctor one last time when Philip arrived. John Michael ran to him, tripping over a magazine rack. He took Philip by the shoulder, dragged him into a waiting room area, and looked him straight in the eye.

"It's Mom, Philip." He started to cry. "There's been an accident with a trailer or something. Mom tried to make it, but she couldn't. She's gone, Philip. Mom's gone. Our mom is gone!" They hugged for what seemed like an eternity.

John Michael felt so guilty when he left the hospital that day. From that point on he punished himself for his mother's death. In three years, he hadn't touched a football or even played another game on a field. All of that changed today, though. He was stuck in prison in his body, but he had been acquitted in his heart. He got up from the cot, where he had been sitting for hours, and splashed water on his face. The cold water felt good on his hot skin. His eyes were swollen and puffy.

"It's not your fault," he whispered to himself. "I forgive you." He looked up. "Mom, did you hear that?" The smile came again.

That night he celebrated with a beef and noodle dinner. It tasted awful. It was prison food, after all, but that night everything tasted better. He had an appetite again. There was a spring in his step, even though he couldn't spring very far. He even asked the guard for some paper and something to write a letter with. What they brought him he never expected. The only thing they could find was a 1952 Smith Corona typewriter. Since he couldn't have sharp objects like a pen or pencil, this ancient relic would have to do. It didn't matter though. Tonight he would type a letter that would change his life. There was no movie sound-track or anyone to cheer him on. It was just a boy typing a letter to his dad.

Twenty-six

The Letter

The little red light was blinking rapidly on the answering machine. The routine was the same. Jonathan would pick Philip up from school and head home. After parking the car, he would head into the house through the back door, check the machine, and head out to the porch to look through the mailbox, hoping for some message or postcard from John Michael. Tonight was no exception. Jonathan entered the kitchen and noticed the red light blinking in the dark. Before he switched on a light, he pushed the button to hear who had called. He listened attentively. The machine recorded two messages...

"Hi, I'm calling for a Mr. Jonathan Davis. This is First Bank wondering if you would be interested in our low interest credit card. We'll call back at another time to see if you are. Thank you."

Jonathan slammed his fist down on the counter in disappointment. The machine continued...

"Dad..."

Jonathan's heart jumped.

"Dad, it's, uh..."

Could it be?

"...Lewis. I just called to let you know I'd be home late tonight. I'm out with Andy one last time before I head to school next week. Go ahead and have dinner without me. I'll pick up something on the way home."

Lewis sounded more like John Michael than he ever dreamed. The two brothers really were alike. That was part of their problem. Neither wanted to admit it, so they tried to be as different as possible.

Jonathan reset the machine and turned on the light. Philip came in and headed down the hall.

"No message, huh?"

"Nope. Not tonight. Maybe tomorrow."

"Yeah, maybe tomorrow."

"We've got to keep hoping. He'll call again. I know he will. I can feel it. Something's happening. It's been too quiet. Something is happening in his heart."

Jonathan noticed Philip had already ran upstairs to set his backpack in his room. He was talking to himself. It wasn't the first time. There had been many nights Philip had encouraged himself to sleep. Not to mention the private moments he had found Philip looking out his window for hours, waiting for his brother to come walking down their street. Jonathan waited, too. Through the cold, Midwestern winters to the hot and humid summers, there wasn't a day he didn't spend time waiting on the porch just staring into the distance. Jonathan had always been a patient man, but waiting on Johnny had taught him about patience in a way he had never known.

Jonathan pulled out a Hamburger Helper box from the pantry and dumped the ingredients in a bowl. He needed some ground beef. He searched his freezer. Chicken. Fish. A frozen pizza. A half eaten gallon of ice cream. Green beans. No ground beef. That created a problem for Jonathan. He grabbed his keys off the counter.

"Philip, I have to run to the store to get some hamburger meat or we don't eat. Do you want to go?"

"No, I have to study for a test. First test of the school year."

"Are you sure? You could spend some time with your dear old dad."

Philip came to the top of the stairs.

"Sorry, Dad. I don't think you want to see me bring home an F, do you?"

"Not a good idea. I'll get the meat by myself."

Philip returned to his room. Jonathan headed towards the front door. He turned the door handle, opened the door and stepped out. The evening air felt different to Jonathan. He rested his head on the doorframe and stared at the sunset. Its pink and orange rays decorated the sky. For the first time in months, Jonathan felt almost peaceful. Although John Michael wasn't there, he really believed everything was going to work out right. He started to step off the porch towards the garage.

"The mail. I didn't check the mail," he said to himself. For a moment, he almost forgot the routine. John Michael hadn't sent anything for a long time; why would there be anything from him tonight? He relentlessly turned around. The keys jingled in his pocket. He stepped onto the porch and walked towards the black box posted next to the door. The mailbox top squeaked as he opened it. Junk mail. It all looked like junk mail. His stomach growled. He needed to get the ground beef. Jonathan grabbed the letters from the box and thumbed through them. There was a Visa bill, a letter from Ed McMahon, junk, junk, junk, his fishing magazine, and a letter from the Department of Motor Vehicles reminding him of the sticker that he needed to get for his car. He started to put the mail back in the box. A white letter at the bottom of the pile caught his attention. It was hidden under the magazine. The return address caught his eye: DEPARTMENT OF PRISONS.

That's funny, he thought. *I rarely get this kind of mail at home.*

Most legal documents or judicial information went to his office. Something felt different about this one. He looked at who it was addressed to: Mr. Jonathan Davis.

It was written in messy handwriting.

"Who has handwriting that messy?" he asked himself. He froze. *John Michael has messy handwriting*, he thought. He squinted as he looked closer. His heart started to pound. He dropped the rest of the mail on the ground and stared at the handwriting again. He started to whisper to himself.

"It's from John Michael. It's got to be."

He was puzzled by the return address, though. He backed up to the swing and sat down. The sun was just about gone now, but the glow left in the sky was just enough for him to read the address over and over again. He held the letter tightly in his hand. He'd been waiting for this day. Jonathan turned the envelope over and opened it. He grabbed the thin sheet of paper that was neatly tucked inside. He took out his reading glasses from his shirt pocket and put them on. In the faint light, he began to read the letter he had been waiting for.

Dear Dad,

It's awkward to sit down and write you a real letter. I never had to write anything serious with a postcard, you know. They're safe to use when you're running. As you can already see, I'm not the greatest typist. Excuse the letterhead, I'm sure you're wondering what I'm doing sending you a letter from prison. I'll explain sometime. For now, I've got other things I need to say, and if I don't take the time right now, I may never say them.

First, I need to ask you to forgive me. You read it right. Forgive me, Dad.

For everything. I've been really dumb. The choices I've made have not only hurt me, but I think they've hurt you even more. I'm sorry if I've screwed up your life, and Philip's and Lewis's, too. I guess that's what happens when you think only of yourself. I'm ready to start thinking about you.

Secondly, I need to let you know that I forgave myself. Can you believe it? I had never really forgiven myself for Mom's death.

I always thought that if I could have gotten to the hospital sooner, she wouldn't have died. I left home because I felt like a failure and I didn't want to be one anymore. What a lie. Now, I'm surrounded by my real failures. But, I'm finally able to forgive the person I had the biggest grudge against. That person was me. I guess I was able to do that because I remembered the love you had for me. And if you could love me, why couldn't I love myself? When you run away from the kind of father I had in you, it doesn't take long before you realize what you're missing. It just took me a mountain of time to get past my pride. It's not like anything is fixed yet between us, or that it's all better. You know me better than that. But at least we can start working on things.

All I ask is that you will take me back. If you are still angry, or can't forgive me, I understand. I'll stay away. I don't know when I'll be home, but when I do come I'll look for the porch light. If it's on, I'll know that everything is all right. If it's off, I'll know that things won't work out right now. More details later. I need you, Dad. Bye for now,
John Michael Davis

Jonathan set the letter in his lap. Although the darkness crept up the sidewalk and onto the porch, there was a bright light shining in his heart. In many ways, John Michael was home. The room he used to live in wouldn't be occupied by him, but something had happened tonight that was almost better than a physical reunion...forgiveness.

Jonathan had forgiven him, the night John Michael left home. It was John Michael who needed to forgive himself. Jonathan knew he wouldn't come home until that happened. He was caught between smiling and crying. If John Michael were there he would have gotten the biggest bear hug Jonathan could give. For now, John Michael would have to feel his father's love from hundreds of miles away.

"Ground beef," he said to himself. "I've got to get ground beef. We're celebrating tonight."

He folded the letter, put it in his shirt pocket, and opened the door. Philip heard the front door open. He yelled from his room where he had been studying on his bed.

"Are you already home, Dad?"

"No, I haven't left yet. I'm just putting the porch light on."

The porch light. Philip smiled to himself. He was glad he had a father who always remembered to put the porch light on.

Jonathan flicked the switch and went back out the door, skipping down the stairs and up the sidewalk like a child. He got in his car and backed out of the driveway and into the street. As he accelerated down the road, he began yelling out the window. "My son is coming home. Johnny is coming home!"

Words many parents long to hear. Words a father would never forget.

Twenty-seven

Seventy-Five Bucks

It had been a long week of questioning, but by the end, John Michael stood free. Logan's gun had been found inside a dumpster close to the alley where Matt had been shot. Logan had tossed it there, hoping it would be taken with the trash. And, it would have except for an old man who found it while scrounging inside for an early morning meal. Although his fingerprints were on it, the police were looking for more. Logan's prints were everywhere. A single bullet had been left in the gun. It matched the bullet that was found inside Matt's chest. That bullet should have been inside John Michael.

John Michael collected his things and traded his prison suit for his t-shirt, jeans, and nylon jacket. He had forgotten how worn and torn they were. He stuffed all his belongings back into his duffel bag. It had been a rough couple of months. Even so, he felt real peace. *Real* peace. Not the kind that changes you for a moment, a day, or even a few months or years. This was a lifetime peace. For the first time since his mother died he wasn't fighting himself anymore. In that letter to his father he let everything go. Although present circumstances were far from tranquil, John Michael didn't mind. He was enjoying the overwhelming sense of peace in his life. Although he looked like a vagabond, inside he was a new man ready to go home.

The only souvenirs he took from his time behind bars were a police escort back into the city and a bad cough. He coughed uncontrollably in the back seat of the squad car. When the driver asked him where he wanted to go, John Michael didn't even know.

"It doesn't matter. Anywhere, I guess." He thought for a moment. "Do you know where the Java Club is? Down in the Loop. That's where I want to go."

The drive seemed longer than John Michael had remembered. It seemed to take forever. John Michael looked intently out the window. It was fall again. The leaves were blowing around the streets like paper falling down in a ticker tape parade. Although there weren't thousands of fans lined on the sides of the streets, John Michael felt like his ride in the back of the squad car was a celebrated one. In many ways, he felt like he had come full circle. He took a deep breath. Free. He was almost free. Free from the past, free from the present. And soon, when he met his father he would see how free he was for the future. Would his father really love him despite all the mistakes? Only time would tell.

The squad car dropped him off where it all had started, the Java Club. An officer opened the back door and said a final good-bye. John Michael thanked the policeman and shut the door. The car drove away, leaving him totally alone. John Michael looked through the windows of the coffee shop he had once frequented. The lights were out. The tables were gone. All that was left was the shell of a building and a neon sign that was off. John Michael noticed a sign on the glass door: CLOSED — UNTIL FURTHER NOTICE.

John Michael put his hands in his pocket, turned, and walked away. The fall wind felt cold against his nylon jacket. John Michael spent the last part of his day walking around the downtown district of the city. The place that once had seemed so exciting to him now felt hollow. Even though it was full of people, for John Michael it was empty of the individuals he needed the most. He sat down on the bus stop bench he had stopped at when he first entered the city. This time there was nothing under the bench except a few smashed aluminum cans and a grocery bag of trash. He took out the key that hung around his neck. It felt good to wear it again. In prison it had sat in a tiny box in a locked drawer along with the rest of the items he owned. He squeezed it, then dangled it in front of his eyes. How was he ever going to get home? He stared down at his feet. Although he held a key in his hand, his feet would have to be the key to his long trip home. He grabbed his duffel bag. He unzipped the bag and looked through what was inside. A t-shirt, a dirty pair of socks, a belt, a gum wrapper, some pennies on the bottom, and a pair of old khakis. Before Matt's accident, he had packed just what he needed to get home. He was in such a hurry that he threw just a few things in his pack. It was just like the night he had left home. He started to check the pockets. John Michael hadn't worn these pants in months. He pulled out a twenty-dollar bill.

"Yes!" he exclaimed. Twenty dollars a few months ago wouldn't have seemed like much, but now it was a treasure. He zipped up the bag and started down the street. Twenty dollars. He headed to the bus station. Twenty dollars would at least get him closer to home. Walking around the city reminded him of what he had been fighting for when he arrived there. It was now what he hoped to forget. The past really is the best teacher. Step after step John Michael thought about what this time in his life had taught him. He wondered why he had taken so long to go home. He had waited. Something had changed in him by waiting. John Michael thought about all his father tried to share with him. Why did it take him so long to realize that? He wondered what it would be like if he had never left. Although this journey had cost him a great deal, he was starting to realize the importance of knowing the difference between right and wrong. His father was right. He wondered if his dad would be filled with the same compassion he had expressed to his son the night he left.

John Michael made his way across a busy street and then down a sidewalk that led to the bus station. He was flooded with the memories of his arrival in Chicago. The station had seemed so big then; now it seemed small. He heard a bus sound its diesel engine signaling its soon departure. He hoped he would be on the next one. Inside the station things seemed calm. It was empty except for a few benches and a corridor that led to the loading area. He walked to the ticket counter.

"Can I help you?" said a warm voice from behind the window.

"I need to buy a ticket," he said.

"What is your destination?"

John Michael thought for a moment, and then smiled at his answer. "Home."

The answer startled the middle-aged woman behind the counter. "That's nice," she said. "Now, where is home?" She looked at John Michael's appearance and immediately felt compassion for the young man. His torn jeans and jacket, worn out shoes, dirty shirt, unshaven face, shaved head and bloodshot eyes expressed words to her he would never be able to communicate any other way. The journey had obviously been a hard one.

"Kansas, it's Willowbrook, Kansas. That's near Wichita. Few hours away. I've only got a few bucks to get there, though."

"Really? How much?"

"Uh," he paused, "twenty bucks."

"Excuse me?"

"It's all I got."

"I'm sure it is, but I don't think I can help you, honey."

"Won't it get me anywhere?"

"How about the mall?" She was starting to get sarcastic. "Just kidding. Young man, I want to help you, but I can't just give you a ticket."

"Will twenty bucks get me anywhere?"

"Listen, sweetie, I can get you somewhere for ninety-five dollars, not twenty. The base ticket is ninety-five."

John Michael scanned the board above the agent. Ninety-five dollars? "Will ninety-five dollars get me to St. Louis?" At least that was halfway home. He could walk or hitchhike the rest of the way.

"Uh, no, it won't. That would be one hundred and twenty-five."

John Michael's face dropped. The hope drained from his eyes. The lady behind the ticket counter noticed that his countenance changed. She typed something into her computer again and then looked at John Michael.

"Listen, I like you. You seem like you really need to get home. We do have a bus that stops in Willowbrook via Wichita. I'll do it for ninety-five just between you and me. My part in helping get you home."

"But I only have twenty-dollars!"

"I'm sorry, hon, but ninety-five is the best I can do. Do you have any friends that would loan it to you?"

John Michael thought about his friends. Matt was dead. Logan was a running fugitive. He didn't know where to find the rest of his friends, unless he headed back to the streets again.

"No, I don't really have any friends."

"Can you call your mom or dad? What parent wouldn't wire their child the money to get home?"

"My father?"

Not now. Not after all this time. John Michael wanted to do this on his own. He wanted to save any compassion his father had for him for when he got home. Calling him for money felt way too risky.

"No," he said quietly, "I can't call home." He dropped his arms from the counter and turned around. He sat down on one of the vacant benches. He put his head down and started whispering to himself. "I was so close to making the right decision. Why does it have to be so hard?" He remembered his father telling him that right decisions were never easy to make, but always easy to live with. He pounded his fist on his knee. John Michael wasn't about to give up, not after all he had been through. He picked up his duffel bag and ran out of the terminal. He would find the money somehow.

John Michael left the bus station and headed towards the Java Club. Even though it was closed, he might be able to find someone he knew in that area. He felt like he'd been walking for hours when he realized that his watch was missing. He bent down and unzipped his duffel bag. John Michael hoped he'd be able to sell the watch to someone. It had been given to him by his father for his sixteenth birthday. It was handed down from his grandfather, who had bought it while he was fighting in Germany in World War II. Logan had offered to buy it several times, but John Michael kept it for sentimental value. Now it might be his ticket home.

He rummaged through the bag. He hadn't seen it since he was taken into custody. He had planned on giving it to Matt if the young man didn't go home with him. His hands couldn't feel anything in the bag. John Michael started to worry. Who would have taken it? He dumped the bag's contents in an alley next to an old hardware store that had closed. Nothing. He stared at the things on the ground and finally sat down next to them. It was getting dark again.

He would have to spend his first night out of prison on the streets. At least he knew of a few places to stay. He could go back to the mission if he needed. He had often wondered if Douglas thought he was home. Maybe Douglas would be willing to loan him the cash? John Michael sighed and took the duffel bag in his hands one last time. He turned it inside out. Still, nothing. He noticed a zipper along the inside and thought the police may have put the watch in there. He unzipped it and felt inside the pocket. John Michael pulled out a metal object. The watch!

Something fell to the ground when he took out the time-piece. He bent down to pick it up and found money: three twenties, a ten, and a five. John Michael picked up the cash, closed his eyes for a moment, and remembered.

"What's this?"

"Some money I've been saving to buy myself some new basketball shoes."

John Michael took the money and started to count it.

"Seventy-five dollars? Philip, I don't need this! This is yours. Go buy your shoes."

"You have to. I want some part of me to go with you. Save it. Put it somewhere you can get to it if you ever really need it. All right?"

"Philip, it must have been Philip. He must have slipped it into my bag when I wasn't looking."

John Michael thought of his brother again. He started to cry. He couldn't believe this. Philip's seventy-five dollar shoe money was exactly what he needed to get him home. Little did his baby brother know how important that money had become. He stood up, shoved everything back in his bag, and placed the watch on his wrist. He ran back to the bus station as fast as his legs would take him.

Bursting through the glass doors of the bus station, he saw that the lady behind the counter was closing out. She had shut her computer off and was picking up her purse when John Michael ran to the counter.

"Ma'am, please." He could barely talk, he was breathing so hard. "I've got the money."

"What?" she said, startled.

"Remember me? I was in earlier. You said you would cut me a deal to go to Willowbrook, Kansas, for ninety-five dollars. Is that offer still good?"

She paused for a moment. Her hand was on the light switch. "Well, I was just closing down for the evening. The last bus out tonight should have already left."

"Can you check for me? When I ran by there was still one sitting out there."

"Well, sweetheart, I don't remember if it's going in the direction that you were."

"Can you check for me?"

"Well, let me see here." She picked up a radio from her desk. "Earl, are you there? Earl, come back. Have you left the lot yet?" Nothing. She looked at John Michael. "I think you're too late, son."

John Michael's body tensed. "Try again, please. He's got to be there."

She sighed loudly. John Michael wasn't so cute anymore. "Come in, Earl. Are you there? Earl!"

There was fuzz, and then a voice. "Lou, is that you? I thought you went home."

"I thought I did, too. Listen, you aren't in the lot, are you?"

"Actually, I am. I'm having trouble with a passenger. She broke her leg so we're trying to get a comfortable seat for her."

"Yes!" exclaimed John Michael.

"Well, have you got room for another one?"

"Well, it will make this lady with the broken leg a little more uncomfortable. But, we got the room. Why? I thought you closed up."

"I know. Fit someone on for me." There was a pause and she stared straight at John Michael. "Call it a favor. I owe you one. Say, what direction are you headed?"

"Uh, Kansas. This one ends in Kansas," he cracked back.

John Michael's eyes lit up.

"Say, Lou, is this one of your family members again?"

"No, just a friend. A friend that we need to get home."

"Get him out here then. I'm already late."

"You got it, Earl. I'll send him out."

John Michael handed her the cash. Instead of turning her computer back on, she wrote him out a ticket and took his money.

"How did you find enough?" she said counting it.

John Michael paused and grabbed the key that was dangling around his neck. "Family."

"I didn't think you had any around here."

"I don't. But my little brother has always had a way of finding me."

"Well, I'll be. That's great. Here's your ticket, and I believe that bus is heading exactly in the direction you needed."

John Michael smiled. "I thought it might be. It's my father, I can feel it. He wants me home."

"Well, I hope you get there. Best of luck to you."

"And you. I'll never forget you. Thank you for all you've done." He grabbed the ticket from the counter and ran down the corridor and out the door. Lou stepped into the hall and watched him. She switched off the light inside the ticket booth, then smiled.

John Michael ran out the terminal doors and headed for the bus. He climbed in and handed his ticket to Earl.

"You're lucky, boy."

"I know. Thanks."

"Oh, don't thank me, thank her." He pointed to Lou who was walking through the parking lot. John Michael tried to wave to her, but she didn't see him.

As he walked down the aisle he noticed he had the attention of everyone on board. Their facial expressions showed their disapproval of his appearance. One older lady even shook her head at him after she rolled her eyes. John Michael tried to hide how rejected he felt. There was one seat open in the very last row next to the lady with the cast on her leg. Earl had given her the extra spot so she could stretch her leg out. Although there wasn't much room to move, John Michael didn't mind. He was going home. He didn't care how he got there, just that he got there.

Twenty-eight

Elley

The bus made its way through the corn fields of central Illinois. Everything was covered with the darkness and all John Michael could see from the window were the passing lights that flickered by. It was late. The midnight hour was at hand. After a few stops, the bus was scheduled to arrive in Willowbrook tomorrow in the late afternoon. John Michael yawned. He wished he could stretch, but the lady with the cast had him pinned next to the window while she stretched her leg out in the aisle. It didn't matter; he was going home. He closed his eyes and went to sleep. Although his body was at rest, his mind was dreaming about the future. Dreaming about meeting his father.

John Michael saw the house in the distance. It was just as he had imagined it. He took a few more steps. There were butterflies in his stomach. Leaves from the family tree blew by his feet and the smell of a nearby field being harvested came to his nostrils. He stared at the house again. Could he really do this? After all this time, would he really be brave enough to knock on the door? He wondered as he took a few steps closer. He squinted his eyes. Philip's bike was on the porch. John Michael wondered where he had been riding lately. His father's car was in the driveway. Even the porch swing was moving back and forth gently in the wind. It seemed picture perfect. John Michael was getting excited. This was going to be the homecoming he had been dreaming of! He took a few more steps. Then a few more. Inside his chest his heart was pounding. John Michael took one last look at his childhood home from a distance, then he started to run. He ran up the driveway and onto the porch, stopping abruptly at the front door. He raised his hand to knock, then stopped. He thought about turning around and running away one more time. He couldn't, not now, not after all this time. He pounded on the door. There was no answer. He pounded again. No answer.

"Dad, it's me, John Michael. Are you there? I've come home! Dad, it's Johnny!" he yelled at the top of his lungs.

There was a shuffle of feet, then the doorknob turned. This was it. Home at last! The door opened just a crack. He could see Lewis's face.

"What do you want?" asked Lewis with a cold tone.

"To see Dad. I've come home, Lewis. Can't you see me? It's John Michael."

"Yeah, I see you. That's the problem. We thought you were never coming back."

"But it's me, Lewis. It's your brother. Where's Philip? I want to see Dad!"

John Michael started to panic. The dream was now becoming a nightmare.

"Philip hates you. You really hurt him at the bus station."

John Michael started to explain himself. "I didn't mean to. I've changed. You'll see, Lewis, you'll see. Really."

"I thought you might say that. See for yourself. We don't need you anymore."

The door swung open. There stood his father, staring at him awkwardly. Beside him was Philip. His arm was around his father's side. All three of them just stared at John Michael. It took his breath away. He didn't know what to do. His father spoke in a somber tone.

"So, you decided to come home."

"Yes, Dad. I'm sorry. Really. I made a big mistake..."

His father cut him off. "Yes, you did. One that goes beyond all compassion, forgiveness, and unconditional love I had for you." There was a pause, then his father continued. "Son, I don't know if I love you anymore."

John Michael stood there shocked. It was as if he had just died. His hands felt cold. He started to shake with chills. A tear ran down his cheek. He had nowhere left to go.

"John Michael, we think you should find somewhere else to call home."

And with that, the door shut.

John Michael jumped as the bus hit a pothole. He was sweating. The coach was still headed down the dark highway. He realized he wasn't standing at his front door and breathed a sigh of relief. John Michael dozed off again.

He knocked with such intensity that his knuckles started to bleed. Still, no answer. He tried the door. It was open. The door swung open and he stepped inside. The house was empty. He darted from room to room frantically looking for any signs that his family was still there. The kitchen table was gone, along with his chair. The television, the refrigerator, all gone. Every cupboard in the kitchen had been cleaned out. He ran up the stairs and threw open the door to his room. Nothing. He sat down in the middle of the room and started to cry. How could they have moved without him?

"They are gone. All gone! I missed them! I missed them!" He dug his fingers into the carpet. This was the worst feeling he had ever had. There was no one left. No mother, no father, no one. His world had shattered. This man lay, a crumbled boy, on the floor. John Michael felt a deep sense of regret.

"No!" he screamed at the top of his lungs.

The peaceful bus was now full of onlookers as many of them turned around to see what the commotion was in the back seat. John Michael's scream had startled even himself.

"Are you all right?" asked the lady sitting next to him sensitively.

"Oh, uh, yes, I'm fine." He paused for a moment. "Did I just scream something?"

"Did you scream? You woke me up from a sound nap. Believe me, it takes a lot to wake me up, and you did."

There was an awkward silence. John Michael was embarrassed. "Uh, what did I scream?"

"I believe you said, 'No!' " she said with the same intense tone. A few people turned to look again. She smiled and waved back without being embarrassed at all.

"That's what I thought," replied John Michael. He leaned back in his chair and stared out his window. An older woman sitting in front of him turned around in her seat and glared at him for a second.

"Don't worry about it," she said. "I've done it before. Maybe not on a bus, but I'm sure I've screamed before." She stared out the window with John Michael. "That must have been some dream."

"It was more like a nightmare."

"Really? As a child I had a reoccurring nightmare that aliens were taking me away. I never understood it. I haven't thought about it in years. It was probably just too many sci-fi movies as a child. I'm sure you didn't have a nightmare about aliens."

"No, it was about my father."

"Father?"

"Yes, my dad."

"I don't think I've ever had a dream about my father. For all I know he could have been an alien."

"What?"

"I've never had a father. So I guess he was an alien to me. Not that extraterrestrial garbage—I mean, I just never knew who he was."

John Michael looked away from the window and straight into her eyes.

"You never knew who your father was?"

"No. He died in a small plane accident when I was a baby. He was the pilot."

"What happened?" asked John Michael tenderly.

"A wing fell off or something. We tried to sue for damages, but they said he had been drinking the night he was flying."

"Do you think he was?"

"What?"

"Was he drinking? Do you think it was his fault?"

She thought for a moment. "To be honest, I don't care. I never knew the man. I really don't have an opinion on him."

John Michael was puzzled. How could someone not want to know her father, even if he was dead?

"What about memories of him? Has your mom shared memories of what he was like?"

"I guess. I never really listened much. I've just always kind of done my own thing. I've survived without a dad."

The older lady in front of them turned around again. She couldn't seem to get back to sleep or mind her own business. Her eyes glared at both of them again.

"Sorry," said John Michael.

"My name is Elley. Really Ellen, but my friends call me Elley for short."

"John Michael Davis," he said in a whisper as he shook her hand.

"I like that, John Michael. What's it like having two names?"

"I guess you just get used to it."

"What do they stand for?"

"My dad's name is Jonathan, so I got my first name from him. And, my mom's dad's name is Michael, my grandfather. She wanted me to have part of his name, too."

"Really? She must have had a pretty good relationship with him to give you his name."

"She had a good friendship with her father. Our family still does."

"What do you mean, had? Did your mom and dad get divorced or something?" Elley asked.

John Michael paused. It was easier to talk about it than ever before. "My mom passed away three years ago."

Elley was quiet for a moment. She couldn't think of anything of value to say. "I guess we have more in common than we think," she fumbled. "You lost your mom, and I lost my dad."

"Yeah, I guess you're right. It's a small world, isn't it? It's amazing what people go through and you don't even know it."

"So why are you headin' home to your father? Why haven't you been there all along?"

John Michael stared out the window. It was a good question and required an honest answer. He kept focused on the lights flashing by in the distance and answered to himself almost more than to Elley, "I've been running. I've been running from what I've needed the most—my father's love." He looked back at her. "How about you?"

She glanced at her watch. "How long you got?" Then she laughed to herself. "I'm traveling home to live with my mom for awhile. She lives in Wichita, of all places. I didn't think it would ever come to this. I left home when I was 18 to start my own life. I was tired of her telling me what to do, so I got out while I could. I've always been pretty independent 'cause of not having a dad and all. I had to practically grow up by myself while Mom worked to keep me alive. I met a guy named Steve who I really thought was going to be good for me. We'd been living together for several years. Well, I had a car accident a few months ago and shattered my knee, which explains the cast." She pointed to it. "I came home from the hospital and walked in on Steve with someone else. I tried to forget about the whole thing. I really needed him in my life—I needed someone. But my insurance ran out and my hospital bills grew, so Steve left me a note last Monday saying I was costing him too much. He asked me to move out. Jerk! So I packed up my things and asked my mom if I could come home."

John Michael was overwhelmed at the complexity of her problems. He was starting to feel compassion for Elley. A hint of Jonathan was coming out in him.

"That's tough. I'm really sorry."

"Well, that's life. I figure some people got it worse."

"Yeah, but you still got it bad. You know what I think?" he said to her with a smile, "I think you're going to make it."

"I hope so."

"Let's believe it then. My dad has always taught me to listen with my heart when I make tough choices in life."

"You must sound a lot like him," she replied.

"Like who?"

"Your father. He sounds like an extraordinary man."

"Oh, he is. I'm telling you, he is."

"There's not a lot of sons trying to be like their dads these days."

"Yeah, I figured that out the hard way."

"I wish I would have had the chance to have a father."

"Maybe you will someday."

The two talked until the bus drove in to the Wichita station. John Michael helped Elley get off the bus.

"John Michael, I hope you see your dad soon. And thanks."

"For what?" he said as he carried her baggage to the station waiting area.

"For just being a friend. I don't have a lot of those in my life right now."

They could hear a voice calling out Elley's name in the distance. The faint cries became loud ones as Elley's mom reached her daughter. John Michael politely waved good-bye and Elley waved back.

John Michael climbed back on the bus for the final journey to Willowbrook. With only a few scattered passengers left on this route, the ride would be a quiet one. Time to think, time to hope and time to pray his father would still accept him. John Michael watched Elley hobble on her crutches into the parking lot as the bus drove away. He tried to wave, but Elley couldn't see him through the tinted windows.

Twenty-nine

1967 Bethel Drive

John Michael was the only passenger that needed to stop at the small Willowbrook bus station. He stepped off the bus and onto familiar soil. The small Kansas town hadn't changed much since John Michael had left. The old buildings were all in the same place, and except for a few new restaurants and an apartment building, not much had been built. The fall colors were still as beautiful as ever. Willowbrook wasn't known for its beautiful scenery, being out on the plains. But, the few trees the town had were in full bloom with color. Orange, brown, yellow, and red crumpled leaves were hanging by a thread on the trees that lined the downtown main street. John Michael's feet brushed through a few that had fallen. He'd spent the rest of the afternoon walking around the quaint village. He wondered if anyone would notice him, but no one had yet. A few people passing by stared at him strangely, but no one welcomed him home. Home. He was so close. Just a few more streets, a left turn, then a right, one stop sign, and by then he could see the house in the distance. He didn't feel as nervous as he thought he would. Maybe it was because he was passing by so many familiar places. John Michael smiled. He strolled by the elementary school he had once attended. It was still there. The silver metal slide shined brightly in the late afternoon sun. He'd been down that slide a million times. He turned to the ice cream shop he used to ride his bike to. Two scoops of mint chip, every time. He thought about getting a scoop, but focused on his journey. He kept walking, and remembering. His first bus ride. The first bike he ever owned. Every street was filled with sweet sentiments. Memories of yesterday, memories of Mom. He wished she was there. Everything would be different.

He was almost there. He walked by the last stop sign when he caught a glimpse of the rooftop of the house, his home. His heart was starting to pound. It was just a rooftop, but it was his rooftop. One last landmark before he was on Bethel Drive, the street that would lead him home. He started across an old bridge that covered a small creek flowing through the town, then into a nearby river. The creek looked low for this time of year. Oh well, it didn't matter. The bridge was still needed. John Michael crossed it, then turned around to look back one last time.

It was his last chance to turn around and run away. He knew that once he'd crossed the bridge, there was no turning back. He couldn't change the past. The pain. The anger. The bitterness that even his father may have felt towards him. There was no stopping now. Either burn the bridge or cross it. A tear ran down his cheek. He wished he would have burned the bridge a long time ago. Instead, he chose to cross it just days back in a jail cell. Never again, at least in John Michael's mind. He held onto his duffel bag tightly and turned away, headed for the final stretch home.

There it was, standing like a beacon in the darkness. 1967 Bethel Drive. Home. The porch light was shining brightly against the early evening sky. He stopped under a street light at the opposite end of the road. The view from here was awesome.

Golden light glowed from the windows. A few birds flew over the rooftop. The yard was full of freshly fallen leaves from the family tree. A few flowers had lingered through the early stages of fall. It was all more beautiful than he had remembered. And, the porch light was on and it wasn't even dark yet.

Jonathan looked out the screen door at the setting sun. A cool breeze blew through his hair and a familiar chill went down deep into his heart. Another night without his son. Jonathan stepped out onto the porch holding a cup of coffee. That was normal routine, night after night. He would step out of the house and lean up against the railing that lined and surrounded the porch. Jonathan would stare up the road for hours looking aimlessly for his lost son to come home. So, in normal routine, he leaned against the porch railing and took a sip of coffee. As it refreshed his chilled heart, he noticed something in the distance. It looked like a mirage of John Michael.

"It couldn't be," he whispered to himself, "could it?"

He blinked. Could this be real? Could this really be true?

John Michael noticed his father on the porch. It was still safe to run and hide without really being known, or seen, but this was a homecoming he needed to face. A moment in time he needed to touch. He took a deep breath and stared at his father.

Jonathan stared back. It was John Michael. He dropped the coffee cup. It landed, pouring out its warm contents on the wood floor. Without a thought, Jonathan stepped off the porch and started to run to him.

John Michael dropped his duffel bag. He, too, started to run. At first slowly, but then he started to sprint. Faster and faster. One step, then another. Both of them breathing harder. Through a few leaves. Past cars and houses. The wind blew past their faces. One of John Michael's shoes was falling apart. It finally flipped off and was left in the middle of the street. Even with one bare foot hitting the pavement, John Michael continued to run.

"Johnny!" his father cried out.

"Dad!" cried John Michael.

They ran.

"Johnny! My son!"

John Michael started to cry so hard he could barely see. It didn't matter, his father's arms embraced him even though he couldn't see them. They met, crumbling in one another's arms. A father and a son, reunited. Had there been an audience, they would have been on their feet cheering, celebrating a son who had come home.

They embraced for what seemed like hours. Although no words were spoken, the hot tears that dropped onto one another's shoulders were enough. John Michael was living out a dream in his father's arms. He was fully accepted, fully forgiven, fully loved. Nothing could ever come between them, ever again. A prodigal had come home.

John Michael fell to the ground and latched his arms around his father's knees. He rested his head on Jonathan's knees sobbing uncontrollably. Jonathan looked down at his son and placed his hands on his shoulders tenderly. John Michael resembled a prisoner who had just been released from his chains. Jonathan stared at his son's ripped shirt and nylon jacket tied around his waist. His head had been shaved. He noticed John Michael's bare foot. Up the street lay an old tennis shoe, worn out and useless from the journey his son had made to come home. All the pride John Michael had left was gone, emptied on the street. Now he rested on the cold cement ground with nothing. His money, honor, reputation, and self-respect had vanished. The only dignity John Michael had left was the key that was dangling around his neck. The key that would open the door to his home and his father's heart. John Michael had come to his senses.

Jonathan slipped down to his knees and wiped the tears from his son's eyes.

"I love you, Son," he whispered gently into John Michael's face. "I love you."

John Michael whispered back, "I love you, too."

In a split second of time the hole that had been so deep in John Michael's heart was suddenly filled. All the love he had craved for in friendships, acceptance, money, independence, and freedom was suddenly found in the eyes of one dad. His dad. He was so glad he was looking at his dad. There was nothing like staring into the eyes of his father. John Michael had found the security he needed in his father's eyes. He felt so safe.

Jonathan reached down and wiped the tears from his son's cheeks.

"Dad?" cried his son through heated sobs. "Dad?"

"Yes, Son," said Jonathan, lifting John Michael's chin.

"Will you kiss me and tell me everything's going to be all right—the way you used to do when I was a boy?"

Jonathan smiled at his son through his own tears. "Of course I will. You'll always be my boy."

As he stood, he raised John Michael up off his knees. Jonathan held him tightly and kissed John Michael's tears away.

"Don't stop holding me, Dad. Don't stop holding me. I need to know you are there. I just want everything to be all right. Hold me and make this all go away."

"I will Johnny, I won't stop holding you. I'll hold you for eternity."

"Dad! I love you. I love you!" John Michael cried out, squeezing harder.

A few neighbors glanced out their windows to see what all the commotion was. What they witnessed was a reunion. A little boy resting in the arms of his father. A father holding tightly to a long lost son.

Thirty

The Coat

John Michael had spent most of the night in his father's arms. Philip had nearly fainted when he saw his older brother. He ran onto the porch after hearing his dad's coffee cup hit the floor. When he saw his father and John Michael embrace, he ran to them, too. It was a sweet reunion. They walked back to the house embracing—a reconciliation each one of them had been dreaming of. All of them but Lewis. He was away registering for classes at college a few hours away in Wichita. He planned on coming home for the weekend to finish packing his things. After attending a year of community college, he had been reluctant to transfer to the state university, but his father had insisted. And Lewis liked using the money from his mother's insurance policy for something that was more useful than how he figured John Michael had spent his.

John Michael slept late the next morning. For the first time in months, he had slept through the whole night. The pillow was soft. Real hot water would soon be running between his fingers. The Saturday morning sun was shining brightly through the windows. John Michael had stayed in Jonathan's room; the father wanted to do everything he could to help his boy feel like he was truly home. Besides, John Michael's room was littered with Lewis's things, since he had been staying in there for some time.

The door to Jonathan's room burst open. In came Philip and their father carrying a tray of hot pancakes, scrambled eggs, and Elizabeth's homemade biscuits.

"Good morning, Son," said Jonathan in a very cheerful tone.

"We didn't know when you had a good breakfast, so we thought we would make you one." Philip was excited to have his brother home.

John Michael sat up and yawned. "You guys, you shouldn't have. For real."

"Son, for real, we should have. Besides, when was the last time you got breakfast in bed?"

"I don't think I ever have."

"That's the point. This will be a morning we will never forget."

"And that's not all, Johnny," interrupted Philip. "Dad has a feast on deck for later in the day."

"I plan to celebrate all day long," added his father.

"Why? C'mon, don't do that."

"You're home, Son. Philip and I have to finish a few things to get ready for our day. Are you gonna be okay eating alone?"

"Dad, you forget, I've been eating alone a lot lately. I'll be fine."

"All right, all right. Let's go, Philip. We've got work to do. Let the festivities begin."

With that, they were gone. John Michael couldn't remember seeing his father like this since before Elizabeth had died. He seemed so happy, so carefree, so excited about what the day was going to bring. He had never realized coming home would make his father so happy.

Downstairs, Jonathan and Philip were in a frenzy. They had slept late too, so much that they were running behind. Both of them were on chairs in the foyer of their home hanging up strands of blue and yellow crepe paper.

"Philip, can you hand me the tape?" said Jonathan to his youngest son who was trying to tape a piece to the chandelier. "It's beside your feet."

"Oh, yeah. There you go, Dad," he said, handing his father the tape.

Jonathan took a strip off and taped another end to the wall. "I don't know about you, but I can't think of a more exciting day in my whole life. You ready for the banner?"

"Just about, Dad, give me a second. There. I'm finished." Philip's palms had turned blue from holding so much crepe paper in his sweaty hands. "Ok, I'm ready."

They picked up the oblong piece of paper and unfolded it. It stretched out several feet and read, "Welcome Home, John Michael!"

"Perfect," said Jonathan stepping back up on his chair. "Let's hang it right above the door so he'll see it when he comes down the stairs."

As the sign went up, so did their excitement. They could barely believe this was all happening. They quietly hung the banner and were both thinking of the same thing. Philip spoke first.

"Dad?"

"Yes."

"How do you think Lewis is going to react when he comes home?"

Jonathan thought for a moment, then responded, taping the banner to the wall. "I don't know, Philip. After being gone all week registering for classes the last thing he'll expect when he gets home is to see his brother."

"I hope he will be excited," replied Philip. "Maybe things really will change around here." There was a long pause. "What if he doesn't, you know, act excited?"

"We need to be strong for John Michael."

"What's all of this?" said a voice from the top of the stairwell.

"SURPRISE!" yelled Jonathan and Philip, as they jumped off their chairs.

"We thought a little celebration for your homecoming was in order. When Lewis finishes registering for college classes, he'll be coming home for the weekend. The family can finally be together."

John Michael headed down the stairs. He had showered and dressed and felt the cleanest he had in months. He looked at all the decorations and blushed. "Dad, you didn't have to do all this. It's just good to be home."

Jonathan put his hands on John Michael's shoulders and looked him in the eye. "Johnny, I am going to celebrate. My son has finally come home. I only wish I could stop the whole world, just for a second, to have them celebrate with us."

He turned around, opened the front door, and walked onto the porch. Philip and John Michael looked at one another puzzled. Jonathan cupped his hands over his mouth and started to scream. His voice echoed through the neighborhood and nearby streets.

"It's my son, John Michael. He's come home! My son has come home!" He yelled at the top of his lungs! "John Michael is home!"

John Michael and Philip quickly dragged him inside. They had never seen their father this excited.

"Dad, what are you doing!?" said Philip to his father.

"I can't contain myself. John Michael is back. You're home! John Michael, you're home!" He reached out again and gave his son a big bear hug. His strong arms wrapped around his son. Jonathan couldn't let go. He had been forced to let go of Elizabeth, but he had a second chance with John Michael.

"You'll never leave us again, right?" said Philip, joining in the hug.

Huddled together in the front of the entryway, John Michael said something that brought a smile to Philip's face.

"I'm here to stay, little brother."

Jonathan broke the huddle, picked up a box, and handed it to John Michael.

"What's this?"

Jonathan smiled. "Open it."

John Michael stared at it. "Dad, I told you, I don't even deserve trash wrapped up like this."

"Open it! C'mon! It's for you."

John Michael sat down on the stairs and started to unwrap the large package. His father couldn't wait to see the expression on his face. After the wrapping was off, John Michael glanced at his father one more time. Jonathan gave him a nod to encourage him to open the box. John Michael took the lid off and stared into the box. His eyes sparkled and his mouth dropped.

"Dad, you didn't have to do this. I didn't think I would ever see it. How did you ever find this?" He lifted a leather letter jacket out of the box. It was a beautiful coat. Stitched in the worn brown leather was John Michael's football number.

His father answered. "I know you can't ever have that senior year of school back, but I wanted to get you something that represented the fact that it wasn't all in vain. I know those football dreams are still in you. You needed to be rewarded for the years you did play."

John Michael was in shock. One of the things he regretted most when he had left was not getting the letter jacket for which he had played six years of football. He had dreamed of this kind of symbol for all of his work. Jonathan knew that John Michael regretted missing his senior year of playing out on the field. The jacket would symbolize all the lessons learned while he was away from home. Philip touched the leather delicately. He didn't even know his father had been thinking of a gift like this.

"Go ahead, Son, put it on."

"Really?"

"That's what it's for. Consider it our celebration gift. Now you'll never forget the price you paid to find out how important home really is."

John Michael put the jacket on. Philip helped him. First the right arm, then the left.

It was the finest coat Jonathan could find.

John Michael zipped it up and looked at his reflection in the mirror at the bottom of the stairs. "Dad, I can't believe this. Why? Why would you spend this kind of money on me?"

"Because I love you."

Both Philip and Jonathan stared at John Michael in the jacket. They were silent for a moment or two. The silence made John Michael nervous.

"What? Doesn't it fit right?"

"Nope," replied his father. "It just couldn't fit a more perfect young man."

"...or brother," added Philip.

Jonathan spoke up again. "We've got a few more things that we collected for you while you were gone. C'mon Philip, help me get them. We are going to celebrate all day!" Philip and his father ran up the stairs. John Michael had no idea what they were up to. All the attention embarrassed him, but made him feel so good at the same time.

John Michael looked again in the mirror. He stared at the coat, changing positions to see how it fit. Side to side, head to shoulder. The leather felt good over his arms and chest. The coat made him feel warm. Home, he was finally home. This coat proved it. A few months ago John Michael never would have dreamed of wearing something like this—but here he was, in his father's house, wearing his father's gift. He looked in the mirror one last time and smiled at his reflection. Something was different this time. The face in the mirror didn't smile back. He looked in the mirror again. Were there two of himself?

Lewis? It was Lewis! His older brother stared at him in the reflection. It startled John Michael. His fuzzy memory of Lewis with his hands around his neck was a real one. He wondered if Lewis would say anything.

"Well, well, well, it looks like our lost sheep has finally found his way home," said Lewis sarcastically.

"Lewis," replied John Michael, surprised by his presence.

"When did you decide to come home, and where did you get that coat? Did you steal it?"

"No, uh, no," said John Michael, fumbling his words. "I got here last night and Dad gave me this coat today."

"Really. Isn't that nice of him? You're gone for years, then you come home to a new leather coat. Do you see me wearing one?"

John Michael was silent for a moment. He didn't know what to say. Defending himself wouldn't be the answer, not anymore, not now. "I think Dad got it because he wanted to celebrate," he replied honestly.

Lewis started to circle him, staring coldly into his eyes. "You go away for awhile and everything changes, doesn't it?"

John Michael stuttered, still not knowing what to say. "Uh, Dad just wanted us to celebrate today, that's why they put up all the stuff." Both he and Lewis looked at the large banner with John Michael's name on it.

"Celebrate? Celebrate what? My homecoming? I've been gone for the past five days. I've been away at college doing something with my life, but I guess that doesn't matter when you've been gone for..."

"Lewis, you made it," said Jonathan coming back down the stairs. "Everything ready for your first week of school?" he continued, giving Lewis a hug.

Lewis hugged his father back like a fish out of water. Cold. Lifeless. Silent. He looked over at John Michael with a glare.

"I'm glad you're home, Lewis. I see you found out who also decided to come home," replied Jonathan, wrapping his arms around John Michael from the back.

Lewis stared at them. A father reunited with his long lost son. He started feeling sick. "I was hoping it was a stray cat, then we could put it to sleep." The comment was uncalled for, and he knew it.

"Lewis," corrected his father.

"Dad," interrupted Philip as he walked in with an armful of beautifully wrapped gifts, "where do you want these?"

There was an odd tension in the room. All of them felt it, especially John Michael. Lewis broke the silence with a sarcastic comment.

"Oh, don't let me spoil your little party. I'll just go unpack my things."

Lewis started up the stairs. Jonathan reached out and gently grabbed his arm. "Lewis, we want you at this party, too. It is for all of us. Don't you see that?" he said, looking John Michael's way. "Lewis, he's finally come home."

Lewis looked into his father's eyes. "In my mind, he'll never be home," he replied, pulling away from his father and running up the stairs. "He'll never be my brother!"

"Sorry you had to hear that, Son," said Jonathan sensitively to his middle son.

"What's up with him?" asked Philip.

"More than we'll ever know. Now, I believe we have a big dinner planned, and I need a few things from the store. Philip, the list is on the refrigerator door. You and Johnny run out and pick those things up for me, all right? That will give me a few minutes with your brother. Here, this should be enough," said Jonathan as he handed Philip a twenty-dollar bill. "You can drive, John Michael."

"Are you sure you trust me, Dad?"

"Johnny, you're more important to me than the car. Yes, I trust you. As long as you still have your license, you can drive."

"I don't know if I trust you," Philip joked. They went into the kitchen, grabbed the list, and headed out the door. Jonathan headed up the stairs.

"Lewis? Lewis, where are you?"

It was quiet. There was no answer. Jonathan went to John Michael's room where Lewis had been staying. It was empty. He peeked in Philip's, once again empty. Lewis's old room? He hadn't been in there in months. Why would Lewis be in there now?

"Lewis?" said Jonathan.

Lewis was there. He was sitting by the window with his feet propped on top of the desk leaning back in a wooden chair.

"There you are. I didn't think I would find you in here."

"Yeah, well, I'm here because my former brother has taken his room back, leaving me homeless."

"Former brother? Lewis, you talk about him like he was dead."

"I wish he was."

"Lewis."

"No, Dad, I do. It would be a lot easier. I mean, I just get used to the fact that he doesn't want to be a part of our lives anymore, and now he comes back. Go figure."

"Lewis, how can you say that? What if it was you? How would you want to be treated?'

"That's the difference, Dad, this never would have happened if it had been me."

"You're not getting this, are you?"

"What's there to get? What does it matter, anyway? I'm at college during the week; I'll only have to be here on the weekends. I can deal with that. I only have to ignore him two days of the week rather than seven."

"Lewis, that doesn't solve the problem here." Jonathan gently took Lewis's feet and brushed them off the desk. Now he had

Lewis's full attention. "Lewis, there is something more here. What is it between you and John Michael? Why does there seem to be so much hatred from you?"

Lewis thought about sharing the condition he had found John Michael in that night in Chicago, but—not now, not yet.

Lewis was quiet for a few moments. He stared out the window. He was twirling a yellow pencil in his hand. The more he thought, the faster it seemed to twirl. The twirling stopped. He grabbed it and broke it in half. "I don't want to talk about it anymore," he said to his father in a firm tone.

"But Lewis..."

"There's nothing to discuss," he replied, cutting his father off. "That's it. I'm going back to school tomorrow. What does it matter?"

"When I see you like this, Lewis, it matters."

"Is that it?"

"Is what it, Son?"

"Are you done?"

Silence.

"Are you, Lewis?"

Silence again. Lewis picked up another pencil.

"Yes."

His father paused, then spoke gently, "Listen, Philip and I have worked really hard to make this a special day for John Michael. We would like to celebrate his homecoming with a special dinner tonight. We would like you to be a part of it."

Lewis thought for a moment. "Do I have a choice?"

"Yes, you do. But I would like you to come tonight. If not for John Michael, come for me. All right?"

"Fine."

"Then we'll see you at dinner tonight?"

"I guess," replied Lewis in a monotone voice. He continued to stare out the window. Jonathan wished Lewis would have looked at him, just once. Maybe then Lewis could have seen the love he had for his oldest son. Jonathan had known this would be hard on Lewis. He rested his hand on Lewis's head, tousling his hair, and then patted his shoulder. Lewis didn't flinch.

"I love you, Son."

No comment.

Jonathan left the room and stopped at the top of the stairs. He combed his hand through his hair and thought for a moment. As a father, he understood that the same love and acceptance John Michael was in need of was the same kind of love Lewis was longing for. Two different sons each looking for the same thing. Jonathan longed to give it, but it was at the mercy of the receiver. He tried so hard to understand why his sons would not accept his love. The only reason he came up with was that they somehow felt undeserving. Jonathan knew that John Michael wasn't the only one who had left home and now needed to find a place in his arms. Lewis did also.

Thirty-one

The Dinner

The day had been full of gifts and surprises. John Michael was tired. He headed to his room to take a nap, a luxury he wasn't used to. He shut the door, lay on the bed, and stared at the ceiling. It was almost too good to be true, and too much to take. He grabbed his pillow and covered his face. The last few days seemed like a dream. In the darkness, he remembered his past. He saw the streets, the faces, and remembered the painful choices that had cost him so much. The memory he had of the night he left raced through his mind. He wondered how he could have been so blind for so long? Dealing with his mother's death had taken him to destinations he never imagined. Yet the love he had received from his father was so overwhelming. John Michael let a conversation from the night of his return home run through his mind like a healing balm on a painful wound....

"But Dad, how can you not be mad at me?"

"I didn't understand at first, but after a few months went by I started to see more clearly. You see, I have three sons. Three wonderful human beings whom I love very much, but these three men are very different. Each one handles life differently. Maybe I thought you would all handle your mother's death the same. Unfortunately, it took me awhile to realize you couldn't. You're individuals.

Understanding that gave me so much more compassion for what you were going through. That's why I would not allow myself to be angry. I knew that it wouldn't be my anger that would bring you home, but my love and forgiveness."

John Michael pondered his father's kindness. His dad was slow to anger and quick to hand out mercy. His father's kind heart was what brought John Michael home. He thought about all of the secrets that still lingered inside of him. What if his father really knew about all he'd done? Would he still be so kind? John Michael couldn't trust his feelings, but knew he could trust his father.

The knock on his door startled him. He wondered how long he had been trying to sleep.

"Johnny, dinner is ready."

John Michael looked at the clock on the dresser. It was 5:32 p.m. He had been in bed for hours. He was feeling so tired.

"OK," he replied, "I'll be down in a minute." He rubbed his eyes and sat up. He looked in the mirror above the dresser before he headed downstairs. Despite how he felt about the past, there really was peace. He was showing it. He sighed and smiled. When was the last time he had had enough guts to look in a mirror and smile at himself? He was safe. He felt safe. He was safe to be John Michael, safe to be at home, and safe to truly experience his father's love.

He stepped down the stairs and into the dining room. The sights and smells reminded him of Christmas. There was joy and celebration in the air. Philip was lighting the candles on the dining room table. The table was beautifully decorated, just like Mom would have done. Dad must have taken lessons, or just tucked it away in his memory. John Michael was in awe. Jonathan had pulled out a white linen tablecloth, their finest china and crystal, and silverware that sparkled in the light. The center of the table was filled with small gifts that represented the joy Jonathan felt in having his son home.

"Wow, Dad! I can't believe you did all of this just for me."

"I wouldn't have it any other way. Dinner is almost ready. Philip?"

Philip came through the swinging kitchen door and set a dish on the table. "Yes, Dad?"

"Can you get your brother from the garage? He said he was going to be in there fixing his bike so he could take it to school tomorrow. Thanks."

Philip headed out through the kitchen and down a short hallway to the garage door. The old farmhouse creaked as he walked across the wooden floors.

Jonathan continued, "Sit down, my boy. This is your night. I talked to my friend at the butcher store downtown. I told him I wanted the best steaks in the state. He promised me these were it. So, tonight we are going to enjoy the best beef in the state of Kansas!"

"Dad, I don't know what to say. You shouldn't waste your money on me like this."

"No dime is a waste that's spent to take care of my son who has finally come home."

Jonathan went back into the kitchen. John Michael took a deep breath, smelling the steaks. He hadn't had a meal like this in ages. His reflection was beaming from the china plate that sat before him.

Philip walked back in the house with Lewis shortly behind. Soon all the preparations were complete and they sat down at the table. Jonathan had them hold hands while he said grace. Lewis was glad he was stuck in the middle of Philip and their father so he wouldn't have to hold John Michael's hand. After they had finished praying, Jonathan stood with his glass.

"I would like to make a toast to my family. It is good to have all of you home." He looked John Michael's way. "And it's good to celebrate John Michael's return to us."

He lifted his glass with Philip and John Michael. The celebrating mood at the table changed when Lewis wouldn't raise his. Jonathan toasted with the other boys and sat down to pass out the meal.

The table was silent as Jonathan passed around the food. All that could be heard was the clanging of silverware against the beautiful white china plates. John Michael finally spoke up, feeling a great deal of gratitude towards his father.

"Listen, Dad, Philip, and Lewis," he said, looking Lewis's way, "I just wanted to say how thankful I am for everything. Just a few weeks ago I was eating my dinner on the streets, not to mention behind bars. Without you guys, I wouldn't be eating at this table tonight at all."

The table was silent again. Jonathan smiled at him. Philip touched John Michael's shoulder. Lewis stared at his plate, twisting the food around with his fork. There was an angry look on his face. Moments later, he started to clap, at first quietly, then louder and louder. Before long, Lewis was cheering at the top of his lungs. The others stared at him like he was some kind of wild animal.

"Bravo! That was wonderful! In fact, this is a special night. Here," he continued handing John Michael the salt shaker. "You have just won the Davis Academy Award for best performance. The category is acting like one huge fake. Bravo! What a great job you have done fooling us all!"

"Lewis," said Jonathan setting his silverware down, "enough! No more. I've had enough from you."

Lewis wasn't about to stop. He continued on. "Enough? No, I think I'm the one who's had enough here. I have busted my butt around this place ever since this lazy thing left." He looked at John Michael, then back at his father. "Furthermore, if you haven't noticed yet, I haven't been able to eat any of the food you prepared tonight to celebrate John Michael's wonderful return. I'm afraid I might vomit it right back up in his face."

"Lewis, please stop," pleaded Jonathan.

John Michael knew it wasn't going to get any better. He offered a peace contract. "Dad, I can stay somewhere else."

"No, I can," cut in Lewis. "I'm drained, anyway. I'm tired of all the attention you've gotten for way too long now." He stood up and pounded his fists on the table.

"Lewis, I love you."

"Well, I don't know if I believe that anymore. You've proven your loyal love to the prodigal son here, but what about Philip and me? We're the ones that have been stuck watching you every day. Checking the answering machine, checking the mail, watching out the window. Do you think we didn't see it? And for what? So this piece of trash could walk in our door and be served a steak dinner? I should have gotten one a long time ago. I resent you, John Michael. No, *resent* is too nice a word in this case. I HATE YOU!"

Jonathan stood up. He was not about to let Lewis destroy his family. "That's my son you're talking to, Lewis."

"And what am I? A piece of crap? When will you start noticing how good I've been these past two years."

"I've always known it. You know that!"

"No, I don't know that. While he's been out messing around, I've been stuck here doing everything. I do dishes, wash the floor, do the laundry, and watch you cry your eyes out. One day after another."

"Your brother almost died out there. Don't you have any sense of compassion?"

Lewis looked at John Michael for a moment, then looked away. His compassion had been gone since John Michael had left.

"Ask me if I care. Go on, ask me. Really. 'CAUSE I DON'T! Maybe I should leave for awhile too! Maybe then you'll think about me every day."

Jonathan stepped out from behind his chair and moved closer to his oldest son. He was trying to be understanding, but had a sense of strength in his voice. "You don't have to leave, Lewis—you left a long time ago."

Lewis stood there for a moment, frozen in the truth his father was speaking.

"What?"

"Your heart left this home a long time ago. You're still walking through the motions, but I don't have your heart anymore." Jonathan started to cry; so did Lewis.

"What do you want from me?" he said.

Jonathan reached out to touch him. "I just want you. You! Somehow in all of this I lost you. I love you, Lewis—no more and no less than I love John Michael."

Lewis pulled away and turned towards his middle brother. "No you don't, Dad, and you won't love him after I tell you this."

John Michael stood up. He felt very uncomfortable. "What?" he asked.

"I know all about your secret, little brother."

"What secret? Go ahead. Tell me, Lewis. What haven't you said that could hurt me more? Why don't you just go for the kill!"

"Good, then I will."

Philip spoke up. "What secret?"

"Don't try to fool me. I'm the smarter one, remember? Go ahead, tell your father what he obviously doesn't know yet. Tell him, or I will!"

Lewis was yelling at the top of his lungs. John Michael yelled back.

"What? Are you going to bring up the past again?" He took control of his anger and changed his tone. "Lewis, I know I hurt you, and, Philip, I know I hurt him, too, but most of all, don't you realize how much I know I hurt Dad?"

"It's all right, Son," said Jonathan tenderly to John Michael.

"Sure it is until I tell your secret. You've embarrassed us all. Maybe Daddy will send you back to the streets!"

Jonathan spoke, "What are you getting at, Lewis?"

"Oh, I like this. I finally have you right where I want you, John Michael. For once, I do know more than you do." With that, he whispered to John Michael, "I won, little brother."

John Michael stared back.

"Dad," Lewis continued, "that night we were in Chicago, there is something I never told you—I found John Michael wasted—so drunk he could barely remember who I was."

"What?" Jonathan responded, puzzled.

John Michael wanted to quickly retaliate by revealing that Lewis' fingers had been wrapped around his neck, his older brother's kiss of death on his life. But the words wouldn't come out. He knew the bitterness would hurt how far he had come. His journey home had meant too much.

"Is this true, Johnny?" his father questioned.

John Michael remained quiet.

"Oh, and that's not the half of it. I've saved the best lies for last!"

"Lies?" Philip said defensively.

"One big secret," Lewis responded.

"What's the secret, Lewis?" begged Philip.

"What secret, Lewis?" asked John Michael.

John Michael was getting impatient. He wondered what his older brother was up to. "Lewis, just say it and get it over with. What is it you think is so bad?"

Lewis turned to their father.

"Your precious irreplaceable son is HIV positive!"

Silence. Lewis continued.

"Go ahead, spill it, brother. We got a letter a few months ago from the Illinois Health Department. They were trying to track you down to tell you that your test was positive. But, you messed up and I intercepted your message. What were you thinking when they photocopied the driver's license? Didn't you know we would eventually find out?"

John Michael sat down and rested his head on the table.

Philip sat next to his middle brother, putting his arm around him.

Jonathan stared at Lewis, then at John Michael. His eyes filled with tears. The room was silent except for the sobs of John Michael. His body heaved with every breath. He kept thinking about the clinic he had gone to while living in Chicago. It was a health clinic for people living on the streets. He hadn't been feeling well, and knew he needed to get some help. The nurse had diagnosed HIV as a possibility. She took blood from John Michael's arm, but he had never received the results. It was the night he went home only to find his apartment ransacked, and the little money he had left gone. He was feeling better lately, so the thought had slipped his mind until now. The past few days were suddenly crushed by the reality of life. Words could never express the utter sense of failure he felt, again. It wasn't Lewis who bothered him, or Philip, who sat trying to console him, but his father. He needed his father. Jonathan finally spoke, breaking the silence.

"John Michael," he said gently, "is this true?"

John Michael shook his head. He couldn't lift it. The tablecloth soaked up the tears.

"I told you, Dad. He's not worth it. All of this worry over him for so long. It was all for nothing, as far as I'm concerned."

"That's the problem, Lewis, this isn't your concern," spoke their father sternly.

"This is between me and John Michael. Just us. Not Philip, and most certainly not you."

"But, Dad, aren't you going to kick him out? I'm not going to be associated with him. He's going to ruin the family name, not to mention make us the laughingstock of this town!"

"Why don't you leave, Lewis? In fact, why don't you just stay at college?" Philip was angry.

"Both of you, you're crazy! You hear me, crazy! If you're going to allow him to stay, then I'm not. That's it. It's him or me!"

Jonathan walked over to John Michael and put his hand gently on his back. "You do what you have to do, Lewis."

Lewis stomped out the front door and onto the porch. Jonathan whispered something into John Michael's ear and followed him. Lewis was sitting on the porch swing. His breath could be seen in the cool night air.

"Lewis, we have to love him, no matter what."

"I hate him now more than ever."

"Lewis."

"I can't believe you are willing to forgive him after he's hurt our family like this. Why? Why on earth would you forgive him?"

Jonathan was quiet for a moment, then gave a gentle answer. "Because he asked for it." Simple. Unconditional. The essence of real love.

"That's it? Because he asked for it? C'mon, Dad. There has to be more. Don't you feel like he needs to pay us back in some way? Aren't you embarrassed? Dad, he's got HIV!"

Jonathan cut in. "Lewis, we must forgive."

"Forgive? I'm not even coming close to touching him. Forget it."

"Then what do you want?"

"I want him to apologize to our entire community. I mean, I want my friends to know it was totally his fault."

Jonathan shook his head.

"What, Dad, you know that's what you want, too. Think about how people will talk about you."

"That's all you care about, isn't it, Lewis?"

"What?"

"Yourself. Forget your brother's pain, you're more concerned about yours. John Michael could never do enough for you. Even if we made him wear a sign that said, 'I'm HIV positive because I messed up. I'm sorry I've embarrassed my family,' and sent him from house to house, door to door, that still wouldn't be enough. When all you think about is you, he'll never do enough."

Lewis was quiet now. He looked away. He cleared his throat but didn't speak.

"It amazes me," his father went on, "how different one's children can be. They grow up in the same house. I don't get it. For instance, I would think that through my years as a judge you boys would have seen the best example I could give of being fair. You know, that's the hardest part of my job. Fair judgment. It affects people for a lifetime, Lewis. Whether they get sentenced or not, it affects them. And, I watch you judge your brother with no compassion, no sense of understanding. As far as I know, your mother and I never taught you to judge the way you do your brother."

Lewis didn't look at his father. His eyes were fixed on a star in the sky. "Dad, it's simple. I've watched him hurt you. I've watched him hurt Philip. And yes, I've watched him hurt me. I hate him for all the pain he's brought into our house."

"How can you say that? Let's get to the bottom of your hatred for him. Where does it come from? Who ever did anything to drive such a wedge between you and your brother?"

Lewis had no response.

"Where does this bitterness come from?"

It was quiet again. Lewis was staring at his sneakers. They reminded him of the same ones he had worn the night his mother died.

"It's Mom. That's why I hate John Michael!"

"Because of your mother? What does your mother have to do with this?"

Lewis looked out beyond the front porch at the stars. "She always liked John Michael more than me."

Jonathan was quick to jump in. "You know that isn't true. She loved all of you the same, besides you were her firstborn."

"John Michael could do all the things she knew I couldn't." He went on. "Sports, school, even the computer. It all came so naturally for him. Why didn't it for me? Huh?" he asked, raising his voice. "Why?"

It was now becoming clear to Jonathan. The years melted together. Lewis had been their first. A special first. But any first child feels left behind when a second or even third comes along. They never had to share the attention of their mom or dad when they were the only one. Jonathan wondered if he could have done anything different. Jealousy and hatred caused even the greatest families to separate.

"Lewis, I know things are sometimes hard to understand, but just because you did things differently than your brothers doesn't mean they were better than you."

"That sure isn't the way it feels."

"I know, Son, but your mother loved you for who you were, not for what you could do. And I've always loved you for who you are. Nothing can change that." Jonathan gently turned Lewis's chin so they could see one another eye to eye. "I am your father, Lewis. Your father. It doesn't matter what you do to me. You could run away, steal all that I have, or ignore me every day. Nothing is going to change my love for you. I don't care if you're not good at sports or the computer. Lewis, I want you to pass all of your college classes with straight A's, but, if you don't, it's not going to change how I feel about you. I love you."

Lewis started to cry. The tears ran freely down his cheeks. He tried to wipe them away quickly, but they came faster than he could dry them. Jonathan reached out and hugged him. Lewis didn't hug back.

"I love you. Always. You were my first boy. Nothing can change that." Jonathan let go setting his hands on Lewis's shoulders.

"Lewis, do you remember that border collie we had when you and John Michael were just boys?"

Lewis nodded his head.

"Remember that really bad storm we had the first summer we had her? What was her name again?"

Lewis paused. "Mary Jane."

Jonathan grinned at the past memories of their pet. "A tornado had hit the west end of Willowbrook and was moving our way fast. Mary Jane had gotten loose that afternoon and we still hadn't found her before the bad weather had rolled in. I'll never forget searching for her. In my head I was sure she was gone. With the sirens blaring, the wind rising…I didn't expect to find her running down the middle of the street. Now, you have to admit you wanted her back, right?"

Lewis stared at his shoes again. He shook his head and agreed with his father.

"We were all so excited to see Mary Jane when I found her lying helpless on the side of the road down by the Keller's farm. Do you remember what we did for her?"

Jonathan let go of Lewis's shoulder and started to walk across the porch staring out into the darkness. He wasn't talking to Lewis anymore, he was talking to himself.

"We cleaned her up and bandaged her wounds and brought her to the best vet we could find that night. We took care of her until she was fully able to get up on her feet again. I could have gotten rid of her, you know. But, I knew how much you and John Michael loved her. Now your mother, she wasn't that fond of animals. Even so, we kept her around many more years than we had ever expected that night. And, that's what we need to do with your brother. Why? Because it's the right thing, isn't it?"

He turned around to see if his son was still listening. Lewis was gone. Jonathan noticed him walking across the yard and down the street. He wouldn't be gone for long. Jonathan knew it. He had just given Lewis an awful lot to think through. He didn't want to celebrate just one son coming home, but two. It was time. John Michael's homecoming was the perfect situation to bring Lewis to terms with who he really was. All Jonathan could do at this point was love him unconditionally. Jonathan hoped they could resolve things before he went back to college in Witchita.

Jonathan sat down on the porch steps where he had many nights before. He thought about John Michael, who was still sitting at the table. Philip was with him. He would be all right, for now. Jonathan knew he had some decisions to make. How do you handle news like he had just received? It's not every day your child walks into the room telling you he may eventually die because of wrong choices he's made. He sighed. Accepting John Michael back home would be easy; dealing with the consequences of his past wouldn't. Jonathan knew he was dedicated to his children. Through thick and thin. The good times, and the bad. In health or sickness. Jonathan reminded himself that sickness isn't always physically related. Although John Michael was physically hurting, his heart had been healed. Lewis was physically well, but his heart was very ill. Who was worse off? Jonathan wanted to see them both healed, from their hearts to their heads.

Jonathan had no idea how to handle the months ahead, but, he would take Elizabeth's advice. "Day by day," she would say when they faced obstacles.

Day by day, Jonathan thought. That's what it would take. He got up and headed back inside to pick up more pieces. At least they would face this together.

Thirty-two

Gone, Again

Jonathan opened the front door and stepped inside the house. He heard some shuffling upstairs and made his way towards the stairwell. He could hear Philip pleading with John Michael as he headed up the stairs.

"Johnny, not again. You can't go again."

"I have to, Philip. It's right this time. You'll see."

Jonathan stood in the doorway of his middle son's room. John Michael was packing his green duffel bag again.

"Son, what are you doing?" asked John Michael's father. "You're not leaving. I'm not sure how we'll make it, but I'm not scared of the truth. We've come this far, and now the next part of our journey will be just different than we had imagined, but we'll make it. We'll make it."

John Michael was listening, but continued to pack. He was a man on a mission, but this time he wasn't running.

"I'm going back, Dad."

"You're what? But, John Michael, you just came home. What do you mean, you're going back?"

"I'm going back to the streets."

"Forgive me if I sound stubborn here, but can you start thinking about us? Can you start thinking of others before yourself?"

"I am."

"You are?"

"They're out there, Dad. And they'll die a lot emptier than I ever will. I don't know how much time I have. I've got to go back, Dad. I've got to bring them home. Home to a real dad. They need a real dad."

Jonathan was confused. He wondered if John Michael had broken down amidst all the stress. Jonathan had seen it happen many times in court. But with his own son? John Michael stopped packing.

"Dad, you don't get it. I'm talking about the people that I lived with for over a year. Most of them were fatherless—that's why they were there. They were searching for someone to be there for them. To love them. To father them. I've got to bring them home."

"But, John Michael, you can't just expect to walk out on the street and think they'll all come home with you. Besides that, the most important thing we need to do at this point is get you to a doctor. I want you to get tested again. And, I want to get you the best medicine available. They are making so many advances with HIV drugs. Who knows, you may have your entire life ahead of you."

"Dad, I could care less about myself right now. All I'm thinking about is bringing my friends home. Even if *one* does, Dad, it will make a difference. When I came home, you gave me a real chance. You could have done anything to me. Anything. But you ran to me. Nobody will ever run to them. Nobody. I want to be like you, Dad. I'm willing to run to them."

Philip spoke up. "But, Johnny, where will we put them all? Won't it seem weird having people live here that we don't know?"

"Look at all the extra space we have in this place." He paused and zipped up his duffel bag. "Dad, I know you don't understand me right now, but I can't stop thinking about them. I know I can't change everyone, but I can try to change one. You understand that, don't you?"

Jonathan sat down on the bed with him. "Yes, I do."

"I'll be back. It's not like before. This time there is purpose in what I am doing and where I am going. I don't know how long I'll be gone, but you have my word I'll be back. I'll be back, Dad."

"I know you will," Jonathan said in a whisper, breaking into tears. He went to hug his son, the one he promised he would never let go of again. But letting go this time wasn't as hard. When a child grabs their own purpose in life, who can hold them back? Jonathan knew he had to let him go.

"I just want to get you to a doctor. I want to get you to the best. You deserve the best, John Michael."

"Don't do it for me. I'll be all right. Let's do it for them. I'll see one when I get back. You have my word. I want to live, too. If something happens before then, I'll call. Dad, if I die this time it will be all right. For once I am not afraid of failure. For the first time since Mom died, I believe in myself. I know what I've got to do."

Jonathan, Philip, and John Michael hugged for a long time. Jonathan wondered if it would be the last time they could. He hoped they would hug like that again—next time, with Lewis in on it. John Michael ran down the stairs and out the front door. He took a little cash, a brand new purpose, and the acceptance of a father who loved him enough to let him go, again.

Jonathan watched John Michael walk down the moonlit street, his body silhouetted in the streetlight at the end of the block. Sitting on the porch, he was reminded that parenting was all about letting go. Tonight, he let his little lamb go. Again.

Thirty-three

Reunion

The porch light was on again. Jonathan stepped out into the brisk evening air. A fresh light snow had covered the ground. The porch floor was cold under his slippers. He set his steaming cup of coffee down on the railing and stared at the wintry red setting sun. He looked at the street corner he had seen John Michael walk down just months before. He was waiting again.

Jonathan wondered if he had ever really understood how much waiting true parenting required. He'd waited for them to get on their first bus ride. He'd waited for them to return from their first day of school. He'd waited for them in the emergency room when they broke their arm. He'd waited for them to return from their first bike ride with their neighborhood friends. He'd waited for them to come home from their first sleepover. He'd waited with anticipation for them to pull up from their first drive alone with a new driver's license. He'd waited up for them on the night of their first date. He'd waited for them at the bottom of the stairs while they put the finishing touches on their graduation gown. He'd waited for them to come home from college.

He would one day wait for them to walk down the aisle with someone they wanted to love for life. Then he'd wait for the news of his first grandchild. At some point, he knew, he would wait by the phone for a simple call amidst their busy lives. He'd wait and wait and wonder if they cared as much as he did. And one day he'd stare down a long hallway with the wheelchairs and walkers, waiting for them to visit him. Waiting. His life as a parent was filled with waiting. Jonathan pondered the patience he had learned while waiting for his son. That patience had taught him to trust his instincts and not rely on his feelings. If he lived his life by his feelings, he would have never let John Michael go.

He looked at the oak tree that towered in his front yard. The tree was a reminder that they had planted it together. All the leaves hadn't dropped yet. Even the oak tree was waiting for the right time to let go. Jonathan wondered if it too struggled to allow all of its leaves to tumble to the ground and blow away in the wind. But if it wasn't willing to let its leaves go, the tree would never experience new growth. He smiled to himself. He had grown up as much as his sons had. Elizabeth would have wanted it that way. She loved growth. Even her death had pushed Jonathan, Lewis, John Michael, and Philip to grow in areas they might never have reached without her passing. Elizabeth's death had shown Jonathan that life is made up of seasons, each one a needed time for the soul. Each one a needed time for growth. But it doesn't always come overnight. The seasons of life are all about learning to quietly wait. There is a silent strength that comes when one learns to be patient. Jonathan's strength had been renewed. It was like he had mounted up on a pair of wings to fly like an eagle. He could run now, and not get weary. He was walking through these difficult days and not becoming faint. All because he had learned to wait. Not an easy thing to accomplish in a furiously fast-paced society. He hoped his life had taught his boys to wait.

The small town of Willowbrook had caught news of John Michael's homecoming, and unexpected news at that. Jonathan had been judged harshly for allowing John Michael back into his house. A close friend even told him that John Michael's mistakes were Jonathan's fault for letting him go. People glanced at him in the courtroom. A few friends separated themselves from contact with the family. Willowbrook hadn't ever exerpienced anything like this. Even so, Jonathan remained strong. He didn't waiver from his decisions, or regret his choices. Jonathan firmly believed that when you walk in what is true and right even the most tragic of circumstances can be turned around for good.

The night air was chilling him to the bone. The sun was almost gone. Another night of darkness approached. Another night of waiting. Jonathan wondered where John Michael was. Except for a few phone calls and a postcard, his son's whereabouts were unclear. All John Michael said was that he was doing whatever he could to bring them home. Jonathan knew that whoever they were, they were fortunate to have a friend like John Michael—someone who longed to give them a home.

Snow started falling—at first just a few flakes, then millions more. Jonathan squinted to look up the street one more time. He saw nothing but a few cars racing by and a man holding a shovel ready to take on the snow. There was not a trace of John Michael. Jonathan turned around and headed for the door. His feet were freezing. His coffee wasn't steaming anymore. He longed for the warmth of a cozy fire. Maybe he and Lewis could build one together this weekend. He headed inside and shut the front door. Although the streets of the small town were dark now, the house at 1967 Bethel Drive wasn't. Jonathan had just turned the porch light on. It was a beacon for all who needed to see it, a lighthouse for those wandering aimlessly through the night. But there was a light far deeper than any eye could see, shining brightly in Jonathan's heart. This father knew that his son could see it. Maybe not with his eyes, but down deep in his heart. Jonathan knew that was the light that would lead his son home.

Jonathan had just finished putting the dishes in the sink when he heard a knock at the door. Philip was in the living room trying to salvage a string of Christmas lights. Philip was determined to make them work so they could finish decorating the tree. They reached the door at the same time.

"Who do you think it is?" asked Philip.

"I have no idea," replied his father. Jonathan knew what they were both thinking. John Michael. They hoped it was him. Philip turned the door knob and cracked open the door. The hinges began to squeak.

" 'We wish you a Merry Christmas. We wish you a Merry Christmas. We wish you a Merry Christmas and a Happy New Year! Good tidings we bring, to you and your kin, good tidings for Christmas and a Happy New Year!' Merry Christmas!" yelled the group as they waved and headed to the next house.

"Merry Christmas to you, too!" yelled Jonathan.

Philip and Jonathan pushed the door shut and looked at one another.

"Well," said Jonathan, "at least someone's trying to give us some Christmas cheer."

"Listen, Dad. I'm trying to get this tree done before Lewis comes home from college tonight so we'll at least have a tree for Christmas Day."

"I know, I know, I spend more time outside than in. But I knew if John Michael came home this month he wouldn't have any trouble finding the house."

"You went all out this time."

The porch light wasn't the only bright star to lead John Michael home. Jonathan had put so many lights on his home, he was told that next year he would need a city electrical inspection. From the roof line, up the driveway and outlining the windows, the house was a beacon in the neighborhood. Passersby couldn't help but notice the lights at 1967 Bethel Drive. Jonathan didn't do it for the neighbors or the city. He didn't even do it because of the season. Jonathan did it for John Michael. The porch light wasn't enough. He wanted every light to symbolize the love he had for his son. Jonathan didn't want John Michael to sense any fear in coming home. Jonathan wasn't merely celebrating Christmas this year, as much as he was celebrating the love he had for each one of his sons.

Lewis's car rounded the top of the hill. He noticed an illuminating light at the bottom. He glanced twice, realizing it was the home he had grown up in. For the first time in a while, he smiled. What was his father up to? Lewis hadn't been home since Thanksgiving and the lights were not the normal routine. As he drove into the driveway he realized the lights were probably for John Michael. There would be a special sign to welcome his brother's weary eyes. His father didn't know it, but they were welcoming his, also. He grabbed his backpack and bag of dirty laundry as he headed into the house. More than ever before, he had been looking forward to coming home this time.

Lewis, Philip, and their dad stayed up and talked for awhile before heading to bed. Jonathan noticed something different about Lewis. Maybe it was the time away, or maybe Lewis was finally coming to terms with the condition of his heart. Whatever it was, Jonathan felt like Lewis was finally home.

Although the lights coming from inside the house had long been off, the ones on the outside would stay on until morning. Inside, the house was quiet and serene. Nothing could be heard but the occasional sound of wind blowing against the roof, and the occasional buzz from the lights outside. Suddenly, almost unexpectedly, there was a knock. No one responded. No trace of life. Another knock. Then, a set of them. Jonathan sat up. Who on earth would be at his door in the middle of the night? He didn't think the carolers would have come back. A neighbor? A coworker? John Michael? JOHN MICHAEL! He put on his housecoat and slippers and headed for the front door. By the time he got there, the knocks were louder. As he reached for the front door latch, he heard a familiar sound. A key had entered the lock and was turning. Philip was home. Lewis was home. John Michael? Was he home? Jonathan grabbed the handle and opened the door.

The hinges squeaked and the light outside illuminated a young man's face. Jonathan squinted his eyes. IT WAS JOHN MICHAEL! They reached for one another and embraced.

"John Michael," his father screamed.

"Dad!"

Jonathan hugged him so hard that he picked him up off the floor. The reunion had been a long awaited one.

Philip stood at the top of the stairs. He was rubbing his eyes. Could he be seeing things clearly? Was he dreaming? He rubbed them again and realized it was all real. He ran down the stairs faster than he ever had before and right into his brother's arms.

"Oh, Johnny, you're home. You're really home."

They gave each other unforgettably tight hugs and let go.

"Dad, the house, I couldn't believe it. Once again, you've done it. I wasn't the only one who couldn't believe it. I have some friends I want you to meet."

John Michael widened the door opening for all the onlookers peering in.

As John Michael said each of their names, they stepped inside.

"Dad, this is Mort, and Shawnee and Esmerelda. This is Garret, but we call him Bob. And Stan. Dad, this is Stan."

The view took Jonathan's breath away. Colored hair, pierced noses and lips, dark rings around their eyes, and faces to match. This little Kansas town hadn't seen anything like this before. They stared at Jonathan, wondering if he really was the kind of father John Michael had convinced them of.

"You guys, this is my dad!"

Jonathan noticed a woman who didn't fit into the group John Michael had just introduced. She was wearing tan slacks and a sweatshirt under her blue wool winter coat. "And, who is this?" he said to his son.

"Elley, Dad. She's from Wichita. She wanted to come with us and meet you."

"Well, hello, Elley. All of you, it's so good to meet you." There was a genuineness they heard in his voice. Then, Jonathan did naturally what he did best. He went to each one of them, embracing their hearts, their minds, and their weary souls.

"Welcome, all of you. Welcome to our home. Your home. Philip, heat some hot water for hot chocolate, and put a pot of coffee on. We've got to feed this group!"

Before Philip could get to the kitchen, and before Jonathan could move through the line, a silence filled the foyer area, drawing everyone's attention to John Michael. He was staring at the top the stairs. There Lewis stood staring back. Jonathan's heart jumped. He hoped he had judged his son's character change correctly.

Lewis looked around at the unfamiliar faces that had entered the room. A cold breeze blew through his hair from the open front door. From this point on, his life would be forever changed and he knew it. The question was, would he be willing to accept it? His brothers and father would be moving on; would he?

They stared at one another for what seemed like hours. John Michael looked deep into his brother's eyes. He searched for an answer, but couldn't find one. He knew he needed to make the first step, but before he could get his feet off the ground Lewis was at the bottom of the stairs and had grabbed John Michael in his arms. Philip started to cry. Jonathan began to weep. The two boys were sobbing.

"I'm sorry, John Michael. I'm so sorry."

"Me, too. I love you, Lewis. I love you."

"I love you, John Michael. I love you."

Words that hadn't been said in years were now tumbling off their tongues. Words most men rarely say. Words many men never hear. The group of onlookers stared at the reconciliation. Although they felt uncomfortable to see this kind of emotion, they longed for the kind of forgiving love Lewis and John Michael were experiencing.

Thirty-four

What Life Is All About

A tattered group of leaves rustled by Jonathan's feet as he stepped from the street pavement to the grass. He was in a field of graves and was surrounded by cement markers reminiscent of life lived and lost. A torn American flag was blowing in the distance marking the saints that had died for a cause. *Dying for a cause, isn't that what life is all about?* he thought. *No, living for a cause, that is what life is for.* Jonathan walked by a grave with the word "Mother" on it. Another with "Loving Brother." An epitaph read "Two lives that left this life together." Grandmothers. Grandfathers. And fathers. The graveyard had many markers that symbolized a loving dad. A real father. That was just what he was. Whether he had a child that was alive, or dead, no one could ever change the fact that Jonathan was a father.

A few leaves blew by his feet again. They signaled the passing of life. *How quickly it fades*, he sighed. In a strange way he loved the graveyard. The quiet he sensed there represented a peace that could be found in the midst of death. Jonathan turned a corner and up an aisle. Flower after flower. Gravestone after gravestone.

He finally reached his destination. "Wife. Mother. Friend." He hadn't noticed many graves with those words. They were chiseled into the marble face of the one he came to visit.

What a beautiful epitaph, he thought. He pondered again on what was etched on Elizabeth's marble marker. "A loving mother who cared for her sons. A wife, mother, and friend who made a home for her family." That's what Elizabeth's life had been all about. She and Jonathan spent the days they had together creating a place all three sons could always come home to. And, that is exactly what had happened with John Michael. A son had come home. A son had found life, again. Life. He was so thankful John Michael was still full of life. Although time and the disease had taken a toll on his son's body, there was till breath left in him. John Michael wasn't about to give up the battle he faced every day. Not now, after all they had been through. The love he felt from home is what helped him triumphantly see that every day he was alive counted. With medication, John Michael had been told he could live for many years. But, there were no guarantees. No promises. Life was a gift and John Michael was taking full advantage of it. Jonathan bent down and touched the grass that now grew near Elizabeth's tombstone. He ran his finger across the gravestone. *That's all you get*, he thought to himself. *A lousy piece of stone.*

Jonathan traced his fingers inside the carved word, 'family.' The individuals buried in this graveyard were worth far more than a cold piece of granite. *What they lived for, now that is what counts*, he thought. Although his middle son was living with the consequences of his choices, he wasn't dictated by them. His future was bright. John Michael's life still has destiny. His days on this planet still had meaning. Jonathan had a great deal to show for that now. His house was presently full of them. Lives that were off the streets, away from the pain, awakened to the reality of what a real father can be. Some of them stayed for a long time. Some of them stayed for a few days. Regardless of how long, they all had a chance to "come home," even if it was just to visit. Jonathan always hoped it was to stay. Fathers are called to be providers of a home in more ways than just financially. John

Michael had discovered this truth. He had left a prodigal, and had come home to his father's heart. Now he had made a life out of doing that for others. The freedom he longed for drew him to the streets, and later the love he had for the lives there brought him back. He didn't leave again to run away, but to bring hurting homeless hearts back to the only place he could find real unconditional love. John Michael was living his days becoming everything he had always seen in his father. He was bringing people home, helping them come to terms with the truth. He was providing a shelter on the stormy seas of life. Even Willowbrook had taken to it. The town now simply referred to 1967 Bethel Drive as, "John Michael's House."

Jonathan knew that someday he would be buried here, also. He had already purchased the plot next to Elizabeth's. What would people remember about him? Maybe one of them would touch the grass over his grave one day and realize life's value. Maybe they would then understand the effect love had on others.

Coming home. John Michael's long journey had brought them all home one way or another. Jonathan. Lewis. Philip. In their hearts, they were home. Life had purpose now. Life had meaning. He stood and took a deep breath. A mystery in life had been unveiled. Jonathan had loved John Michael so much that he allowed him to leave. Jonathan knew his love was there at the beginning, and would reunite them at the end. He had always been waiting with outstretched arms to receive him back again— to whisper in his ear, "I love you, Son."

Jonathan could walk through the graveyard and feel good about this life he lived. From a father's perspective, home really was where his heart was. John Michael had come home. He glanced towards the clouds and grinned. He was living a father's dream. All of his children were home. Maybe not at 1967 Bethel Drive, but the lives he cherished were home. He was living a life of no regrets. Jonathan pulled out of his pocket a piece of worn twine with a brass key tied to it. He squeezed the key in his hand and then put it over his head so it dangled around his neck. Jonathan stepped away from the grave. It was time to go home.

Additional copies of this book and other
book titles from DESTINY IMAGE are
available at your local bookstore.

For a complete list of our titles,
visit us at www.destinyimage.com
Send a request for a catalog to:

Destiny Image® Publishers, Inc.
P.O. Box 310
Shippensburg, PA 17257-0310

*"Speaking to the Purposes of God for This
Generation and for the Generations to Come"*